SPLINTERED
SILENCE

Also by Susan Furlong

Peaches and Scream
Rest in Peach
War and Peach

Written as Lucy Arlington

Played by the Book
Off the Books

SPLINTERED SILENCE

SUSAN FURLONG

KENSINGTON BOOKS
http://www.kensingtonbooks.com

KENSINGTON BOOKS are published by

Kensington Publishing Corp.
119 West 40th Street
New York, NY 10018

All Kensington titles, imprints, and distributed lines are available at special quantity discounts for bulk purchases for sales promotion, premiums, fund-raising, educational, or institutional use. Special book excerpts or customized printings can also be created to fit specific needs. For details, write or phone the office of the Kensington Special Sales Manager: Attn. Special Sales Department. Kensington Publishing Corp, 119 West 40th Street, New York, NY 10018. Phone: 1-800-221-2647.

Library of Congress Card Catalogue Number: 2017951253

ISBN-13: 978-1-4967-1166-3
ISBN-10: 1-4967-1166-1
First Kensington Hardcover Edition: January 2018

eISBN-13: 978-1-4967-1168-7
eISBN-10: 1-4967-1168-8
Kensington Electronic Edition: January 2018

10 9 8 7 6 5 4 3 2 1

Printed in the United States of America

For our son, Patrick
". . . until we meet again, may God hold you in the
hollow of his hand."

May you have the commitment to know what has hurt you, to allow it to come closer to you and, in the end, to become one with you.

—Abbot Finton of Ireland

Author's Note

In late November 2013, a tornado ripped through central Illinois, devastating hundreds of homes and leaving many residents in my rural area homeless. Contractors could not work quickly enough to repair the damage. Subcontractors were hired, and workers came from throughout the United States to ensure that families could be back in their homes by Christmas.

Our home received only minor damage, but it was during that time that I met a family of Irish Travellers. They arrived in a caravan of work trucks, pulling trailers laden with the tools of their trade. The family that came to our house travelled from Tennessee and had their young son with them. While both the mother and father worked, their son hung out in my family room, eating snacks and watching television. He was shy at first, but once he felt comfortable, he told me about his travelling adventures, how he loved to be on the road, and how he couldn't wait to be old enough to carry his own weight. I found this young boy utterly charming and his family's lifestyle fascinating.

It's estimated that over 25,000 Irish Travellers reside throughout the United States. Descendants of nomadic Irish peoples who immigrated to the United States during the Great Famine, the Travellers settled throughout the country in extended family groups or clans, with the largest concentrations living in South Carolina, Georgia, Texas, and Tennessee. As itinerant workers who speak distinct dialects of either Irish Gammon, Cant, or Shelta, they are often marginalized for their unique lifestyles and esoteric customs.

I am not an Irish Traveller. I'm a story writer, and while I have tried to portray Irish Travellers as accurately as possible, they are a secret, closed sect of our American culture. Endogamous, they prefer to live quietly, frequently going to great extents to protect their privacy. Travellers are often stereotyped as immoral and lawless, yet these characterizations overshadow what I have come to know as a culture filled with decency and built on strong family bonds and unbreakable fortitude. Through my writing, I hope readers will come to have a greater understanding and appreciation for the Irish Travellers' unique way of life.

CHAPTER 1

The sound of gunshots cut through my nightmare and jarred me from my sleep. I jerked up, drenched in sweat, anxiety tight in my throat. On the pillow next to me, Wilco stirred but didn't wake. I nudged him, then rolled off the bed and crawled across the floor, taking shelter behind the corner dresser.

I huddled there, crouched low, my breath heavy as I assessed the distance to my service weapon, infiltration sights, escape routes . . . but something wasn't right. I saw pink walls, lacy curtains, and a pretty flowered bedspread. Where was my cot, my tactical pack?

The shots sounded again: a sharp, pounding rhythm that came from just outside. *Bam . . . bam . . . bam.* Not gunshots, I realized, but the sound of a hammer. *Stupid, stupid, Brynn!* The all-too-familiar taunts of embarrassment and self-disgust came rushing back.

My body was safe from war; my mind wasn't.

And neither was Wilco's. Sensing my fear, my dog had jumped off the bed and now stood in the middle of the room, trembling and staring at me with wide eyes. I crawled from behind the child-sized bureau and wrapped my arms around him. "It's okay, boy." I clutched my quivering, sixty-pound, combat-trained best friend. Weeks of intensive drills, hours upon hours of discipline, airlifts and drops from parachutes in howling desert storms, scouring rubble for the dead and the injured—all that and my fearless companion had been reduced to a quaking mass of fur. Deaf and missing a hind leg from our IED "incident," as the military so euphemistically called being nearly blown to bits, Wilco relied on his sight—and on me. I choked at the thought. As if I could even care for myself, let alone for my dog. A damned hammer noise and I'm a blithering imbecile.

Breathe!

I placed my face alongside his. *In, hold, exhale.* I could still hear the doctor's voice leading me through exercises designed to control the surge of emotions that came with my flashbacks.

I continued inhaling and exhaling, until both of us stopped trembling. "Okay. We're okay," I stupidly whispered against his muzzle. My dog was deaf, for God's sake, and I was not okay. This was only too obvious by the fact that I was cowering in a pink bedroom in my grandparent's mobile home.

I held on tight and took another minute or two of comfort before reluctantly unwinding from Wilco and hurrying to find my duffel bag. After cramming my legs into rumpled jeans, pulling on last night's sweatshirt, and tying on one of my many wool scarves, I squinted at my reflection in my dresser mirror. The lines around my eyes were more pronounced than before. The hot desert sun had baked my skin, and sleepless nights since had deepened the crevices. War had aged my features beyond my twenty-eight years. And aged my spirit beyond recognition.

Wilco pranced by the bedroom door, so I motioned for him to stay while I quickly ducked into the hallway bathroom to do my own business. Afterward, as we made our way through the trailer home, I glimpsed into the spare room, where Gramps was still sleeping. His oxygen tank hissed a rhythmic sound, like a whispered *death, death* with each puff. I should've felt sad about his failing health, but I didn't. Instead, I felt guilty. Guilty because, in some small way, his death would bring respite from the years of tension and resentment that had built up between us. And relief from the daily burden Gran endured taking care of him.

Wilco, anxious to go out, nudged me out of my thoughts, so I led him to the front door, where he fumbled his three legs down the steps to the grass to relieve himself. Out on the stoop, Gran was hunched over, working on something.

She looked up, tossed aside the hammer, and held out her arms. I stepped down to her embrace. Her dark gray curls, still damp from her morning shower, were wet against my cheek, and she smelled of soap and rosewater, a scent I remembered well from my youth. She was the only mother I'd ever known, the only anchor in my life. I clung to her just a little longer, reluctant to let go.

She pulled back a little, her blue eyes sparkling with joy. "*Me Lackeen.*" Our Shelta language for "my girl." She gestured toward her work tools. "I'm making a ramp, so that dog of yours can get up these steps easier."

I pressed my palms to her cheeks and leaned in until our foreheads touched. "Thank you."

She gave me another squeeze, then let her arms drop. "Sorry I wasn't here when Meg brought you home last night. I'd run to the market for a few things. You were already asleep when I got back." *Or passed out drunk*, I knew she was thinking but didn't say. I'd stopped off for a little liquid encouragement before coming home to face Gramps. As it turned out, I'd taken in more than I could handle. My cousin, Meg, drove me home.

"I was tired. I said a quick hello to Gramps, then went to bed." That wasn't *exactly* true either. I'd come in last night and had gotten barely a nod from the old man before I went to my room. No hello, no nothing. 'Course, I hadn't said anything either.

She touched my cheek. "You're wearing your hair longer."

I cringed, brushed away her hand, and adjusted my scarf.

She bit her lip. "I know you don't really want to be back here. But I hope you'll stay a while."

I looked around: mobile homes, trailers, and RVs; jacked-up trucks emblazoned with chrome accents, ATVs, and sleek motorcycles as far as the eye could see. The wheels of the Bone Gap Travellers. Gypsies, as most called us. Pavees, as we called ourselves. A culture built on wheels, and meant to move, but that had somehow settled in this Tennessee backwoods. She was right. I didn't want to come back. I'd worked hard to escape this place. And paid the price. But Gran was the one person I loved most in this world, and she needed me.

"I'll stay as long as you want me." Relief washed over her face, and I felt a pang of guilt because there was a good chance this was another half-truth between us. Could I keep such a promise? I'd been restless since returning stateside, blowing through several jobs and relocating every couple of months.

I avoided her gaze and instead let my eyes wander to where Wilco pawed at a patch of weeds. He was still distressed: his ears flicking, flinching at a trembling leaf, his nostrils constantly working. I kept a close eye on him. The explosion had forever changed Wilco too. And not just the obvious physical wounds. Once a war dog at the top of his game, who anticipated my orders and showed excitement for his work, Wilco had become unpredictable. A challenge. We were alike in that way.

"How's he doing?" Gran asked.

"He has his days."

"And how are you gettin' along? With the injury, I mean." Her eyes were drawn back to the area covered by my scarf. No longer blazing red, my scar had morphed into a deep crimson color with white edges raised and puckered like a crumpled napkin. Everyone told me that I was lucky; it could have been worse, it could have been my face. They were right, I supposed.

"Are you still in pain?"

"No." *Thanks to a steady supply of Vicodin.* "I'm fine, Gran. Really. The VA doctors fixed me right up. I'm almost as good as new."

"I was worried about you, Brynn." Her eyes darted away, then back again. "We both were."

A sour taste entered my mouth. "Somehow I doubt that."

"Give him a chance. It's been a long time since you've been home. He's changed. He's not the same man."

And I wasn't the same woman. Never would be again.

The squeal of a screen door drew my attention across our yard to a brown and yellow corrugated metal trailer with rust lines dribbling from its fastenings. A half-dressed man stepped out and took note of Wilco pawing around in his yard. "Get out of here, dog!"

Wilco, deaf to the man's command, continued happily clawing at a garbage can next to the trailer. Then he turned, lifted his stubby nub of a leg, and gave it a good dousing.

"You damn dog!" The guy headed toward Wilco, the muscles in his lean torso rippling with anger.

I sprinted across the yard, my hands in the air—less to protect Wilco, who could handle himself, than to protect the man. With the guy coming up unexpectedly behind him, it was hard telling how Wilco might react. "He's deaf! I'll get him. I'm sorry."

The man studied me for a second. His long, dark hair partially covered his angular face; still, I sensed something in his eyes—the insolent stare of a man who thought very little of excuses and had no use for others. I held his gaze long enough to show I wasn't intimidated, then rubbed the prickles down on my arms and turned back to Wilco.

Only Wilco wasn't there.

"He's gone 'round the other side of the tra-ailer," the man said, his "trailer" elongated in a light Irish accent with hints of the Pavees' Shelta dialect. I'd heard that brogue from the old-timers in our clan, but not men in their thirties, as he seemed to be. He must be new to Bone Gap or at least from a different clan.

I scanned the area as Gran made her way to the far side of the trailer, calling out Wilco's name. She'd forgotten that he was deaf.

I caught up to her. She pointed toward the tree line. "There he is! Go after him. I'll get his leash."

My gaze caught on a familiar flash of tan fur. I went after him, cursing myself for not clipping on his lead in the first place. I knew better. How many times had he run off lately?

I was closing in on him when he flattened his tail and wildly pawed at the ground. He'd sensed something, caught a smell of who knew what. I picked up my pace as he sniffed his way into the woods that surrounded the trailer park. For only having three legs, he was amazingly quick. A few minutes into the chase, I lost him.

I used to love the woods. As a young child, I'd happily lose myself for hours under its green canopy, playing out the stories in my head: Davy Crocket, Robin Hood, and Pocahontas. A thick tangle of tree trunks would serve as my hideout, the colorful underbrush my magic carpet; a stick could easily become a rifle or a bow, whatever I needed to defend my territory against marauding pirates or masked robbers. But that was back when the world still seemed innocent, before I knew and had experienced real evil. Now the forest surrounded me with a menacing tangle of unknowns, and every unknown spelled danger.

Tree trunks formed a dense black crop of shadows, their bare branches knotted against the sky like snarly witches' hands. My eyes darted about, drawn by every new scuffle of sound in the thick underbrush of decaying leaves. From somewhere in the woods, I heard the sound of voices, low and masculine, the words indistinguishable. Probably hunters. The forest was full of them this time of year, and not all of them sharp enough to know a deer from a dog—or woman in dark denim jeans and a shadow-gray hoody, for that matter. I carefully treaded through the patch of trees, one eye peeled for any more activity ahead of me.

Behind me, the neighbor man called out. "Hey, lady! Lady!" He'd put on a shirt and carried Wilco's leash in his hand. Gran must have given it to him. "Wait up. You shouldn't be out here alone. These woods are no place for a woman."

No place for a woman. How many times had I heard that? It seemed the world was full of places where men thought women didn't belong. "And why's that?"

"Because you never know who you might run into." His eyes nervously scanned the woods. We both wheeled around at the sound of rustling leaves behind us.

It was Gran.

"Have you lost him?" she asked, then flinched as a sharp howl ripped through the air.

Shivers ran through me. *Wilco!*

Another doleful canine cry reached my ears, and I turned and bolted toward the sound. I plunged through the under-brush, swiping tree branches aside, my temples pounding. I skidded my way down a rocky ravine, my dog's distress pulling me forward despite stone outcroppings that poked out at an-gles nearly impossible to navigate. Several times I lost my foot-ing on the boulders and pitched forward, gashing my skin.

"Wait!" the man called from behind.

I ignored him and kept moving forward. A couple of times, I stopped and listened in order to regain my bearings. I located Wilco's baleful howl in a spot known by locals simply as The

Rocks—an area where the dense cove forest gave way to mounds of sharp, jutting boulders with deep crevices that made natural traps for animals. It was common to find intact skeletal remains of whole animals inside many of the rock-like pits, which is why the indigenous people aptly named the area Bone Gap.

Now I spied Wilco trapped at the bottom of one of these fissures—seven, maybe eight feet deep—and he was unable to paw his way out. He was whining, barking, and frantically scratching at the side of the pit. Then he'd drop down and race back and forth, like he did when he wanted me to follow him.

I pressed my belly flat against a boulder and reached toward him. "I'm trying to get to you, buddy." But it was no use. He was too far down.

"Is he okay?" I heard Gran ask. I stood and saw the neighbor man helping her the rest of the way down the rocky hillside. They reached the edge of the crevice and peered down.

"He's okay," I reassured her. "Just stuck. And freaked out."

The man stepped forward. "I could help. If you want." *This from a guy who'd just cursed my dog a few minutes ago?* I took a good look at him. There was something unnerving about him. Anger and tension hummed around him like dark waves, yet there was an undercurrent of something else. Sadness? Vulnerability?

Gran had moved closer to the side of the pit. "This is Kevin Doogan, our new neighbor. And you'd better let him help you, hon. That dog of yours is working himself into a frenzy."

I weighed my options: I could get in and out of that crevasse by myself, but there was no way I could lift Wilco all the way up. I looked over at Doogan. "I'll go down there and lift my dog up to you, okay?"

"Fine by me."

I flipped around and lowered myself into the opening. Instead of rushing toward me, Wilco sat down, faced away from me, and stared deeper into the shadows, his ears pricked forward, his focus concentrated, on duty and on alert—the way

I'd trained him, the way I'd seen him too often in our past. A chill shot up my spine and down my arms. I knew why he was so keyed up.

He'd found something.

I clamped my eyes shut. *This isn't a war zone.*

"You okay down there?" Gran called out.

No, I wasn't okay. But I opened my eyes again to see what Wilco had found. He'd done his job—alerted me. I needed to do mine and show that I'd taken his cue.

Probably a dead raccoon or squirrel. I was just kidding myself. Wilco was trained to detect and alert for only one scent:

Human scent. And he was good at it.

Tentatively, I peered closer. My fear was confirmed: Against the back wall of the pit, the rocks narrowed to a thin crevice where leaves, twigs, and brush had collected. Sticking out from under the debris, blending in with the bright russets and orange colors of fall foliage, was a mass of tangled red hair. A sick feeling chewed at my gut, the scent of decayed flesh pricked my nostrils, and bile threatened in the back of my throat. I'd seen enough death to last a lifetime, handled it time and again without any reaction. But I'd left all that behind . . . and now Wilco had found a body.

I snapped back to my military training, crouched low, and maneuvered into the crevice the best I could without disturbing anything. The scene was unnerving, even to me, someone who'd witnessed torsos with tattered shreds for arms and bloodied scraps of blown-up flesh scattered and seeping into desert sands. But this was different. This woman wasn't a casualty of war. She had a round, dark-red bullet wound in her left temple, indicating that her death had been either suicide or murder. She'd been there for a while. Putrefaction had set in, and bugs and rodents had gotten to her face. Probably other parts of her body too, but I couldn't tell without further penetrating the scene. I stepped back, pulled out my cell, and snapped a few pictures, something I'd been trained to do at wartime crime scenes where evidence was often quickly disturbed by the harsh desert elements.

I looked upward. This part of the pit wasn't visible from above. Kevin and Gran couldn't see what I was doing and were calling out for me. I walked back to Wilco, who was still sitting on alert, confident and proud, and praised him with long strokes down his back until he flipped over for his ultimate reward—a generous belly rub. "Good boy. Good boy!"

"What are you doing?" Doogan asked. He and Gran were peering down at me.

I stood and dialed 911, but there was no reception. "Could one of you try calling the cops?"

"The police?" Gran asked.

Doogan chuckled. "No need for the cops. We can get your dog out of there."

I pocketed my phone. "No. It's not that." I ran sweaty palms down the side of my pants. "There's a . . . someone was . . . hurt here." I looked up, silently meeting their stares. I'd said "hurt" but asked for the cops, not an ambulance—and the meaning was all too clear to them both.

There was a period of stunned silence; then before I knew what was happening, Doogan maneuvered over the edge and dropped down next to me. I held out my hands, but he pushed past me, then stopped cold.

"Oh God, please no . . ." He rushed forward. I tried to pull him back as he dropped to his knees and brushed at the debris that covered her body. "Sheila, Sheila." Then he stopped blathering, his shoulders collapsing inward as he turned his tormented face my way, away from the gnawed features of the woman. "I think it's her. I can't tell for sure. But the hair. It's the same color as hers."

"Who?" I gently tugged him away from the body. "Who do you think this is?"

"My sister."

CHAPTER 2

I plunked down on a rock next to Wilco and sank my fingertips into his fur. After witnessing the cold cruelty of death, the warmth of my dog felt comforting. It'd hit us both—what we'd found—and we needed our time together. A unit, we were capable of doing a job few could stomach. A job that had to be done. And one I'd thought we'd left thousands of miles away.

A little ways off, Gran stood with her hand on Doogan's slumped shoulders and spoke in consoling tones. I should've joined them and tried to offer some support of my own, but I couldn't muster any words of comfort. Instead, I kept my distance, turning inward, trying to think of anything except the sight of the decaying body in the crevasse below us.

My eyes wandered over the rugged terrain. I'd come here often as a kid to be alone, to daydream, to be myself—or, more accurately, forget myself. Out here, I wasn't a weirdo or gyspy whore. Yes, I'd been called those things by my non-Pavee, or what we called "settled," peers. Settled kids teased me, bullied me, shunned me, as they did all us Pavees. Only I got the additional taunt of "even gypsy parents didn't want you." Of course, later, when I was older, I found out my mother had died, and that she'd never be coming back. I didn't know which hurt more, knowing she didn't want to come back, or knowing that she could never come back. My grandparents were my saving grace through it all—well, Gran anyway—but that blight of never knowing my parents, and having it thrown at me, cut the deepest. The very subject of my parents had been forbidden under Gramps' roof. Gran had privately confided only a little: that my mother had gotten pregnant by a settled boy and then left town. Without me. I was the product of a double shame: I was an illegitimate baby and only half Pavee. I supposed later that these duel curses were what caused Gramps to be so strict as I grew up. He didn't want the same thing for his granddaughter and could only trust half my genes anyway. If it weren't for this place, my happy place, as my shrinks later identified it, I may have never survived my teen years.

My eyes slid back to the edge of the pit. *Guess I need to find a new happy place.*

I dwelled in my miseries, regrets, and uncertain future for another twenty minutes before the first officer arrived on the scene.

Seeing the officer, Gran crossed herself. "*Solk us away from the taddy.*" It was our Shelta language for "Deliver us from evil." Did she mean the monster who killed the poor girl or the lawman coming our way? Travellers, my grandparents included, often distrusted police officers or any form of settled or non-Pavee authority.

I stood and straightened my shoulders. The cop was young, with a military haircut and a boyish face that showed very little emotion. He identified himself as Deputy Harris and proceeded to radio in our location. "We're approximately one mile north of the AT. After you've passed over Settlers' Creek, you'll see a cairn marked with two white blazes; take that side trail out toward the rocks."

He disconnected and focused on Wilco. "Whose shepherd?"

"Mine." Most people mistook Wilco for a German shepherd, but he was a five-year-old Belgian shepherd, or Malinois. I saw no reason to correct the man now.

He squinted at Doogan. "Do I know you?"

"I was just in the sheriff's office the other day," Doogan said. "I filled out a missing person's form for my sister, Sheila. Sheila Costello."

Costello? Had Sheila been married to Dublin Costello? I looked at Gran. Her expression confirmed my suspicion. Was that even possible? As a young girl, I'd been matched to Dub—as was Traveller tradition—but as the time to wed grew closer, I'd rebelled and refused. My grandparents didn't understand, nor could I tell them that I secretly had been seeing someone else, a settled boy, an outsider name Colm Whelan. Traveller girls weren't allowed to date outside the clan. It was taboo, against Pavee tradition. Refusing to marry the family's chosen groom wasn't just taboo, it was blasphemy. Something punishable, as I'd soon found out in spades.

Harris rocked back on his heels. "That's right. I remember now. I went out to that place where you people live and followed up with the husband." Instantly Doogan stiffened, Gran swallowed, and I gritted my teeth as his "you people" soured the air. "Mr. Costello claimed your sister took off with another man." He walked over to the edge of the pit. "So you think that might be her down there?"

Not only did this jerk have zero sensitivity, but a zero in the intelligence category as well. It was likely the man's dead sister lay only a few yards from us and this officer was kissing off Doogan's report of her missing. Or perhaps Deputy Harris was a homegrown McCreary boy and, like most settled locals, held a deep-seated prejudice against the Bone Gap Travellers. What's a dead gypsy to him? Just another one of "those people" getting themselves killed. He probably thought she deserved it.

Doogan swiped at his brow. "I don't know. The woman down there is . . ." He was unable to find the words to describe the grotesqueness of what might be his sister's remains.

The deputy exhaled, pocketed his notepad, and slid off his tactical pack. "Well, then, guess I'll have a look for myself."

After some maneuvering, he dropped into the hole. He was down there less than a minute before we heard a retching heave. At about that time, another officer worked his way down the rock formations. He was older and about twenty pounds overweight. Pockmarks etched a mottled landscape on his face. A toothpick dangled between his lips. He didn't say much, except to identify himself as Sheriff Frank Pusser. He gave us each a long look, and when his eyes connected to mine with piercing authority—like the commanders I'd served and sometimes suffered under—I felt the urge to look away.

But I didn't.

He pointed out a spot where he wanted us to wait until he was ready to question us, then moved toward the edge of the pit. Gran and Kevin moved on, but I hovered a bit, pretending to fuss with Wilco's leash.

"What are you doing down there, Harris?" He leaned over the side. "I told you to wait until I got here." He got a whiff of vomit and stepped back, gagging. "What a dumbass."

At least he's a good judge of character.

The sheriff lowered himself into the pit, a move that probably would have looked more graceful twenty years and that many pounds ago. I shuffled closer to the edge and watched as he approached his deputy, who leaned against the rocky wall, pale and ashen.

The deputy's voice broke. "It's bad. Her face . . . something's been eating on it."

Pusser cursed as he sidestepped the puddle of vomit and moved toward the body. He was out of my view, but I heard him bellow, "Get over here, Harris! Did you do this? Someone's disturbed the body."

"No, sir. I think they moved her. The man was upset. Thinks it might be his sister."

"Looks like the body's been here a while. See the blisters? That's from gasses gathering under the skin. And animals have been gnawing on her. Coons probably. See the way her left eye's gouged out. I swear, a hungry coon will eat 'bout anything."

I glanced over my shoulder, glad to see Gran and Doogan were out of earshot.

"You okay, boy?" I heard Pusser ask. "You're looking a little green around the gills."

"Yes, sir. Just fine."

"Good. See if you can bag a few of those maggots from the face. Doc will need 'em to help formulate a timeline."

Harris ran back to my side of the pit and hurled some more. I stepped back, shielding my nose. Behind me, Wilco whimpered.

Pusser blew out a disgusted sigh. "Hell, never mind. I'll get it."

A second later, Pusser reappeared, bag in hand. "Death's never pretty, kid. You might as well get used to that now."

Harris straightened up and swiped his sleeve over his mouth. "Yes, sir."

"There's no evidence of brain matter. She was probably killed somewhere else and dumped here. Start securing a perimeter. Can you handle *that*?"

Harris stared at the ground.

"And call the county crime scene unit and see if you can get ahold of Doc Patterson. He'll need to look at the body before it's moved. Tell them to bring lanterns and a ladder. We're going to be at it for a while."

Pusser looked up and glared at me. "Stay right there. I want to talk to you." He clamored out of the pit and approached.

Despite the chill in the autumn air, his shirt stuck to his back like plastic wrap on a hot dish. He glanced over at Kevin and Gran before scowling back my way. "Who discovered the body?"

I clenched Wilco's leash. "My dog. His name's Wilco."

He looked at Wilco then back at me. "What's your name?"

"Brynn Callahan."

"Callahan." He squinted. "You from over in Bone Gap?"

"I was raised there. Been away for a while. I'm back visiting my grandparents."

"Which Callahan are you?" There was only a handful of surnames in Bone Gap, the Callahans being one of the five original families to settle the area.

"Fergus's granddaughter."

Pusser's expression tightened. "I see. Tell me what happened here."

I told him about Wilco running off and then me finding him in the pit, the discovery of the body and Kevin's reaction. "He thinks it might be his sister." Out of the corner of my eye, I saw Harris walking about, sticking wire flags into the ground, sectioning off a perimeter. Would Pusser scout the area outside the rocks for tire tracks too? If the woman wasn't shot here, then she was transported and dumped. Nobody could carry a body this far up the trail.

"You know the guy well?"

"Never met him before today. That's my grandmother over there with him. He's her neighbor."

"And what's your story? You said you've been away."

I told him my story, bits and pieces of it anyway: left Bone Gap at eighteen, joined the Marines, did three tours of duty in the Middle East with my cadaver dog. Both of us discharged on a medical after an IED a year ago. Back to Bone Gap. All he needed to know. All anyone needed to know.

He took down my information, Gran's address and phone number, and told me to wait around until someone came who could take me and Gran back home. I waited and watched while he briefly talked to Gran and then moved on to Doogan. I could tell by their rigid expressions and short answers that both viewed the sheriff as all Travellers view settled law—with a distrust and contempt that clamped jaws and tightened fists.

Eventually, other officials arrived over the ridge like ants descending on a piece of discarded food: a few guys with coveralls stretched over their street clothing and carrying equipment bags; a lady deputy—a matching khaki brown bookend to Harris; and a stern-looking black male with short cropped hair and scowl lines that ran marionette-like from the corners of his mouth. Doc Patterson, I guessed, judging from COUNTY CORONER printed in bold white on the back of his windbreaker. The lady deputy, who introduced herself as Deputy Nan Parks, came to take Gran and me back to the trailer. She was short for a deputy, maybe five foot four, but built like a bulldog. With her round face and the pudgy hands on her wide belt, she would have given most suspects a second thought about messing with her. But her brown eyes and soft voice held nothing but comfort as she spoke to Gran.

Doogan refused to leave, unwilling to vacate the site until he had gotten some answers. Gran was hesitant to leave him alone, but she needed to get back to Gramps. Parks picked up on that and encouraged her, saying that going home was the best idea. We turned down the trail to where the deputy had parked her cruiser, and Wilco began limping. I stooped down, running my hand along his right front leg. He flinched as I reached his swollen shoulder joint. "Wilco's been hurt."

Gran leaned over and gingerly touched Wilco's back.

Deputy Parks stopped and turned back. "Something wrong?"

"It's my dog. He's limping."

"My cruiser's not far down the main trail on a lumber access road. Maybe a quarter mile up this path. Think he can make it okay?"

"Yeah, he'll make it." *He's made it through much worse.* I

rubbed along either side of Wilco's head, touching my forehead to his muzzle—a gesture used to show approval to my deaf dog. I stood and gave his leash a tug, and he obediently continued along the path. He'd been off his game since the explosion, but Wilco would still do what I asked, even if he was in pain.

"There's a good animal doctor in town, been here a long time," Gran said. "We'll call him when we get back to the house. See if he can look at your dog." I didn't say anything, but Gran must have read my mind. "Don't worry, hon. Doc Styles treats Travellers fair. Your cousin Meg's new boyfriend works for him part-time, and she's met the doc. Says he's real nice."

A lot had happened since I'd been gone. Meg, who'd lost her husband in a tragic car accident a year ago, had moved on to having a boyfriend, which was a good sign. And now there was a settled professional that Travellers, or at least Gran, trusted to treat us fairly. Just maybe my generation had broken down some of the barriers between settled people and Travellers, and rightly so. Still it seemed many of the older folks, like Gramps, weren't too happy about it. They worried about the watering down of our rooted culture and traditions. "Pavees stick to their own," he'd always said. Yet another rule I'd broken. Again, I thought about Colm and wondered if he was still in the area.

Deputy Parks stopped and held up her hand. We froze in place. She looked to the woods. "Who's there?"

Silence.

"Deputy Parks, McCreary County Sheriff's Department. Show yourself." She dropped her hand to her holster.

I ran my tongue along my suddenly dry lips and strained to see what had alerted her. Other officers coming to the scene would have responded instantly. Hunters too, unless they were poachers. Travellers would be hesitant when they heard her say she was a deputy.

All around us there was nothing but trees—dense, dark, and eerily silent. My once beloved woods now loomed like a dream turned into a hellish nightmare, shadows hovering, moist air thick with threats. I tightened my hold on Wilco's leash and stepped in front of Gran. Then I saw it, or rather heard it first: a sudden crackle of dry leaves, breaking twigs, followed by pounding footsteps. In the distance, I caught a glimpse of color darting between the trees—dark blue or maybe black—moving away from us and fading quickly into the woodland shadows. Deputy Parks drew her gun and yelled "Stop!" and took off in pursuit. The dense tree trunks swallowed her from sight, and her running footfalls faded, leaving Gran and me bewildered and alone.

A few seconds later, gunshots punctuated the air: *pop, pop, pop.*

I unclipped Wilco's leash, grabbed Gran, and headed down the trail toward the deputy's car. "Come on!" Behind us, Wilco struggled to keep up, but I didn't slow my pace. I couldn't take a chance with Gran.

My brain scrabbled for a quick plan of action: get to the vehicle, take cover, break the window if necessary . . .

"Just a little farther, Gran." Small and frail though she looked, a combination of inherent stamina, and now fear, propelled her alongside me, not missing a step. A couple hundred yards ahead, the trail intercepted a dirt road. I caught a glimpse of sunlight gleaming off a chrome bumper. I looked behind me. Wilco was a ways back, his eyes glued to me as he labored along, his ears high, whether alerted to danger by my reactions or by his own senses, I couldn't tell.

We reached the car, and I pushed Gran below the fender, opposite where the shots had rung out. I crouched next to her, pulled out my cell, and fired off a 911 call. Service was spotty, my voice ragged, but I relayed the situation and our approximate location. Gran leaned against the vehicle, her face flushed.

A harsh growl ripped the air. I disconnected and wheeled toward the sound. Wilco stood about fifty yards away with his snout raised. He wasn't in his alert stance but was bobbing his head, sniffing first the air, then the ground. He was onto something. Unlike many military dogs, Wilco was trained as a single-purpose dog. He detected the scent of human decay. That was it. Not explosives, not drugs, not fresh human blood. He wasn't trained for patrol, crowd control, or live search and rescue. He was single-minded, but the best at what he did. No other cadaver dog had revealed as many bodies in a single tour. But he was also something else: loyal. I'd trained with some fine dogs at Lackland AFB—where I learned to be a handler—and balked when they assigned Wilco to me on my first tour. He was green in the field. Straight out of DTS (dog training school), wily and unpredictable even then. But we quickly bonded. More than bonded. I was his world, his pack, and he was my constant companion, my friend. And despite his sometimes unpredictable behavior since the explosion, his loyalty had never wavered. Wilco would do anything to protect me. And right now, he sensed something: body odor, blood, sweat . . . a smell that didn't belong: danger.

I looked toward Gran. "Stay down! Crawl underneath the car if you have to. But don't show yourself for any reason. Do you understand?"

Her blue eyes grew wide and terrified against her pale face. Wilco's growl deepened. He now bared his teeth, his fangs flashing under curled lips. He stood rigid, tail high and bristled, with his eyes boring into the woods. I scrambled toward him, picking up a piece of fallen timber on the way. The branch felt solid in my hand, heavy enough to crack a skull. I crouched low, not far from my dog at the edge of the woods, ready to spring up and take on whoever approached. I guess I was part pack dog too. I'd do anything, sacrifice anything, to protect Gran.

A rustling noise drew my attention to the trail. I clutched my impromptu weapon.

"Miss Callahan?"

Tension drained from my muscles. "Yes, we're over here." It was Deputy Parks making her way through the underbrush. I stood from my position and relaxed. I held up my hand and signaled for Wilco to stay put.

"I went back to the trail but didn't see you. Where's your grandmother?"

"Over there. Behind your vehicle."

Parks glanced to the side. "Come on. Get her, and let's get out of here."

She already had her keys out. The radio on her shoulder emitted a series of unintelligible blips: "10-22," she responded. "I'm at my vehicle. Subjects are present. I'll meet you on the main road." Then, breaking code protocol, she snapped, "No, dammit. I lost him. He's heading north by northwest, blue sweatshirt, knit hat . . . no, that's all I saw."

I helped Gran into the back seat. She was badly shaken, but okay. Wilco climbed in with her. He sat with his tongue out, panting in her ear. I'd barely made it into the passenger side before Parks cranked the wheel of the SUV—a Tahoe, a specially equipped Police Pursuit Vehicle. "Can't believe the SOB took a shot at me," she said. "And that I lost him."

"Any idea who it was?"

"No idea. Maybe they'll intercept him." She glanced my way. "Sheriff said you're a cop."

"Ex-military cop. There's no sign of a car. Wonder if he was just a hunter and mistook you for deer."

She reached into her front breast pocket and pulled out a bag with a spent casing. "Right. A deer that talks and tells the SOB to identify himself. I found this."

"Looks like a .223 Remington. Probably from a semi-auto rifle." I'd carried an M4 in the military. With its collapsible stock, it fit my smaller frame and was more portable than the M16 or an AR-15, but I'd trained on a variety of weapons and easily recognized that caliber of ammo.

"Yeah. Guys use SARs for hunting all the time, or"—she dropped the casing back into her front pocket—"he could have been our killer. Otherwise why shoot and run?" She slammed her palm against the steering wheel. "Damn! Can't believe I lost him."

I sank back into the seat. The road was rough. We hit a bump that knocked me against the passenger door. I glanced over my shoulder into the back seat to check on Gran. Wilco swiped his tongue alongside her face. She leaned into him. I hadn't had the chance to officially introduce Gran to Wilco yet, but it looked like a run for their lives in the woods had bonded them. I turned back around and eased against the seat.

I kept my mouth shut, but this guy in the woods wasn't the killer. There was no way he'd go to all the trouble to dispose of a body in such a remote location, just to hang around and get caught. Dump and get out. That's what he'd do.

The car veered off the access road, with a final bump onto the smooth main road, and came to a stop near another police car. Deputy Parks got out to talk to the other cop waiting there, and I looked behind us. Who would shoot at an officer and why? The deep shadows of the woods held secrets, that much I knew. Doogan's words came back to me. "No place for a woman," he'd said. I'd have to find out what he meant by that.

CHAPTER 3

By the time Gran and I made it back home, she was worried sick over being away from Gramps for too long. She rushed to his bedside, checked his oxygen, and straightened the medicine bottles that lined his dresser. "How are you feeling this morning?"

"Half-starved, that's how I am. Where the hell have you been? Been waitin' on my breakfast." A wheezing noise escaped between every other gravely word.

She patted his shoulder. "I'm sorry to have worried you, Fergus. But the most terrible thing happened—"

"Tell me about it after you get my food, will ya?"

Gran looked my way. "Can you help him while I fetch some breakfast?"

She scurried off to the kitchen, leaving me alone with Gramps. Wilco hobbled over to give him a friendly introductory sniff, but Gramps pushed him away, tossed aside the covers, and swung his spindly legs over the bedside.

I rushed to his side. "Let me help you."

He batted my arm away. "Just hand me my wheels. I need to get to the pisser."

I gritted my teeth. I'm not sure what I'd expected. He'd ignored me when I came home the night before. Did I think the light of day would bring a new attitude—an embrace, some small talk, a nice word or two?

Biting back a retort, I retrieved a walker parked against the far wall and handed him his portable oxygen pack. Gramps used to be a hulking figure, tall and broad with muscles well-honed from years of manual labor, anything from construction jobs to farm work, whatever came his way. But a forty-year pack-a-day habit caught up to him. The cancer had eaten most of his lungs, reducing him to a shriveling mass of bone and thinly stretched skin. His eyes had a sickly yellow tinge, and his nearly white hair was wiry and sparse from a couple of failed chemo attempts.

I hovered nearby, biting my lip as he pulled himself upright. He grunted and murmured a curse or two. Wilco stayed close. He seemed intrigued by Gramps. Why? Did he smell death on him, the type of decay that starts deep inside the body even before the last heartbeat?

Gramps was fully standing now. I backed off as he picked up the walker and plopped it back down again. A small bell tied to the handle made a ringing sound. It must've been something Gran rigged to keep track of him when he was on the move. She was always worried he might fall. *Ring, ring, thud. Ring, ring, thud.* Gramps paused and squinted down at Wilco, who was limping next to him. "What's wrong with that stupid dog now?"

Instantly, my inner monster writhed, and I swallowed back the words I wanted to say: *You mean a stupid dog who is loyal to his kin, demands nothing but love, and doesn't smoke himself to death?* I bit it back, spit out, "He hurt his leg this morning. I'm taking him to the vet. Gran asked me to take care of you first."

"I don't need your help. She takes care of me just fine."

"She's upset. There was a dead woman up in the rocks. Wilco

found her. That's where we were this morning. The police detained us for questions."

He stopped and leaned heavily against the handles of his walker.

I continued, "They think it's Sheila Costello. Her brother was there with us. He's pretty upset."

Gramps narrowed his eyes. "Dub's wife?"

"Guess so."

"Dub made a mistake when he married that woman. Nothing but trouble, she was."

My jaw muscles clenched. "Well, she won't be trouble anymore. Someone shot her in the head."

"Jeezus." It came out as one long wheeze followed by a coughing spell.

I snatched a couple of tissues from the box on the dresser and took them to him. "Was she not getting along with Dub?"

"Hell if I know. It ain't none of my business."

Meaning they weren't getting along. Otherwise he'd have said so.

Gramps lifted his shoulders and sucked in air. "I know she wasn't much on this place. We weren't good enough for her." He didn't look at me, but we both knew he'd shot the accusation my way. "'Spose she, at least, came by that naturally. She was from that clan down in the Carolinas. They live different from us. Big mansions and money like it's growin' on trees." He pressed his lips together and inhaled through his nosepiece, sliding his eyes my way. "He should've stuck to his own, married a girl from here."

"Maybe no girl from here would have him."

He opened his mouth to snap back, but a sharp inhale sent him into another coughing spasm. I watched without a pang of regret. Sure, I knew it was the wrong thing to say. Yeah, okay, he's dying. *Give the old man a break, Brynn.* Yet for all my inner tongue-lashing, still I hated the old man for what he'd done, and I couldn't let it loose.

"Fergus!" Gran shot back into the room and inserted her small frame between us. Either she'd been listening in on our conversation, which isn't difficult to do in a compact mobile home, or she'd sensed an impending fight. She'd always played the peacekeeper, running constant interference between Gramps and me. It was her role in the family. She played it well.

With a simple look and light touch, she redirected the situation. "Come on now, Fergus. Let's get you situated so you can eat your breakfast." She shuffled him off to the bathroom. Glancing back my way, she said, "Meg left a message. Said she had to leave, but could give you a lift tomorrow before her shift."

Crap! I'd forgotten about my car. Meg had driven me home from Mack's Pub the night before. Good thing. I was drunk off my ass, and the road between McCreary and the tiny municipality of Bone Gap, where my grandparents lived, where I used to live, where I guess I lived again now, was a viciously curving tract of highway infamous for its treacherous switchbacks. It was also a great deterrent for visitors. Which is why my Irish ancestors had chosen to locate in the area generations ago.

Gran continued, "And I called Dr. Styles for you. He said he'd be happy to take a look at Wilco. I left the address on the counter. Why don't you head on over there now? You can take our car. I can handle things here."

I thanked her and headed for the kitchen to gather my stuff. Just before walking out the door, I turned back to see her help Gramps settle into his favorite recliner. As she tucked a blanket around him, their eyes met. Then Gran leaned forward and rested her cheek against his. For a second, a tender gesture, so full of love, fluttered between them like an autumn leaf on the first snow of the season—a glint of vibrant red and gold, too fragile to endure the cold end to come.

*   *   *

I parked Gran's Buick and glanced hesitantly toward the wood-frame barn that served as Doctor Styles's clinic. The building might have originally housed only eight to ten stalls, but it had been restructured into a clinic and painted in the typical barn red. I steeled myself. Our last stint with a veterinarian ended with Wilco practically tearing the arm off the poor doctor. Hopefully, this time would go better.

Or maybe not. Wilco balked when I opened the car door, his nose furiously twitching as he hunkered down with his black head between his front paws. Even from here, his powerhouse of a sniffer picked up familiar and terrifying scents: antiseptics, other animals, disease . . . Who knew what that nose could detect? I clipped him to the coil leash on my belt and gave a gentle tug, but he dug in deeper. I leaned into the car and hefted him out as gently as I could, holding him like a baby, placing him on the ground. This was the same dog that earlier, out in the woods, had stood on alert, prepared to pounce and rip the flesh off anyone who threatened me; now he stood quivering, with his tail tucked nervously around his hind leg. PTSD sucked.

The front door of the clinic opened and a middle-aged man in khakis walked out to greet us. "Brynn Callahan?" He approached with a smile. I stood and gripped his hand. He was clean-shaven, with salt-and-pepper hair, a strong jaw, and a ready smile. "And this must be Wilco." He bent down a little closer, made eye contact, but didn't reach out to pet him. Smart man. Dogs, like humans, have a sense of personal boundaries. They don't want their space invaded by strangers, any more than you or I'd want someone to reach out and tousle our hair upon first meeting. I felt a little more at ease.

He invited us to follow him inside and patiently trudged along as I half walked/half dragged Wilco through the door. "A reluctant patient, huh?"

"Clinics set him off. He's not had the best experiences with vets. Nor they with him," I added as a not-too-subtle warning.

"I understand. Why don't we pass the normal check-in then and get right to it. I hate to prolong his agony." He chuckled. "Or mine."

We were in a sparse waiting area, separated from the rest of the building by a paneled wall. A beat-up leather sofa was parked against one side; a desk, a copy machine, and two tall file cabinets lined the other wall. Dr. Styles walked over to the desk and snatched up a pair of reading glasses and a clipboard, then motioned for us to follow him through a door and out into an open area. We made our way toward a row of doors that lined the back of the barn.

"I just have a small operation here," Styles explained. "I'm a country doctor. I used to specialize in bovines, but now I care for horses, pigs, sheep . . . and dogs, of course." He peered down at Wilco, who limped along, his head swaying as he incessantly whined. "Mostly I travel to see my patients. But I do treat a handful of animals here. I handle most everything myself, but I have a part-time assistant to help with office work and such." He opened the door to one of the rooms and motioned for us to enter. The well-lit white examination room had a counter at one end with cabinets above it and little else. No exam table, like a typical vet office. From the sounds of it, most of his patients were a bit too big for a table anyway.

"I brought his records with me, if you want to have a look." I never travelled anywhere without Wilco's medical history. I handed the records over, then gave Wilco a reassuring pat and a quick hug. "His shots are up-to-date. No allergies that I know about."

"Excellent. If you don't mind, I'll make a copy of these before you leave. Just in case Wilco needs to stop by again. Your grandmother mentioned on the phone that you might be staying a while."

"Yeah. For a while, I guess."

He leaned against one of the cabinets, glasses perched on his nose as he scanned over Wilco's records. After a while, he set the records aside and approached Wilco, holding out his hand and letting my dog take a good whiff. "He's deaf."

"Yes."

"He's got quite the story. I'm sure you both do." He opened a nearby cabinet and pulled out a muzzle. "Just a precaution."

"A two-hundred-pound bite force isn't something to mess around with."

He smirked. "Agreed." I clamped my hands on Wilco's neck, holding his head in place while Styles secured the muzzle. "Okay. Let's see what we got," he said.

I watched as he gently prodded along Wilco's front right leg, mumbling to himself as he worked. "Pad's okay, metacarpus and carpus seem fine, elbow joints okay, aw . . . see how he reacted here? I'm willing to bet he's pulled a tricep muscle. I'd like to take an X-ray, just to make certain, though."

"Sure." I gulped back my reservations. I had about three hundred dollars left to my name. A vet bill could easily be more than that. I should've been out looking for a job today.

We moved to another room, where the doc tried to gently lift Wilco onto the X-ray table. Wilco stiffened, widened his stance and put his head nearly on the floor. He let out a few whimpers at first, which quickly turned to a deep growl, and then his muscles rippled with tension. His pupils enlarged, his tail stiffened and bristled. He lunged and snarled through the muzzle.

"Whoa, boy." Doc Styles took a few steps back.

I tightened my grip on the leash, grabbed him for an instant by the scruff, followed by long strokes down his back. Instantly, he settled. Then his taut muscles quivered and turned to full-blown shakes. Trembling, he hung his head, his eyes unfocused as he let out a series of high-pitched whines. "He's terrified." I looked around, wondering what had set him off. My

eyes settled on the large X-ray machine that hung over the examination table. Wilco had had dozens of X-rays after the explosion. I'd been recovering from my own injuries at the time.
We were apart for the first time since we'd been matched together. I have no idea what happened to my dog during those
weeks. I looked at Styles. "I think maybe he's having a flashback."

Doc seemed to understand. "Do you want to continue? I can
give him something to calm him. Just a light tranquilizer. It'll
wear off quickly."

He opened a small fridge and took out a vial and syringe. He
filled it, pinched at the meaty part of Wilco's haunch, and inserted the needle.

The shakes softened, then ceased. Wilco lowered himself to
the floor. I ran my hand along his side and stared directly into
his eyes, now dulled, as the nightmares that haunted his days
chased through the trails of his mind. Flashbacks. Anything
could trigger them. I knew how real and horrifying they could
be. I felt his pain, the injustice of it all. Wilco had only ever
done what was commanded of him. He was trained to serve, to
please. He didn't deserve this. Neither of us did.

Later that evening, I remained in Gran's car, staring at the
trailer, my hand stroking Wilco, who lay half asleep on the passenger seat, still exhausted after his ordeal. The diagnosis was a
muscle pull, just as the doctor had initially thought. The treat-
ment was an anti-inflammatory drug and rest. But no fracture
was good news. So was the invoice. It was a third of what I had
expected to pay. Doc Styles must have given me a break.

It was half past five now, and the sun was already setting,
making it easy to see inside the lit front room. Gramps was in
the recliner, with the television going. I didn't see Gran but
imagined she was in the kitchen getting supper ready. I dreaded
going inside.

After the visit with Dr. Styles, I'd been in no shape to do anything productive, so I went through a drive-in outside of town, got a plain burger—no bun—for Wilco and a burger with everything for myself and then drove the two of us to a ridge that overlooked the valley. We spent the afternoon relishing our burgers (well, Wilco inhaled his) and enjoying the landscape between naps. Once the sun edged toward the horizon, we reluctantly headed back. Now I sat in front of Gran's place, not wanting to get out of the car.

Movement from inside the trailer next door caught my eye. Doogan's trailer. Or at least the trailer he was renting from our old neighbor, who, according to Gran, had come into a little money and upgraded to a double-wide a couple lanes over. I thought back to earlier, and how upset Doogan had been about his sister. I hadn't offered much in the way of condolences. I imagined him inside, alone, heartbroken. I roused Wilco, and we ventured over to his front door.

"What?" He stared at us through a crooked storm door. His stringy dark hair was tied back off his face. His sleeveless T-shirt clung to him in patches of sweat.

"Thought I'd stop by and see how you're doing."

He pushed open the door. "My sister's dead. Murdered. How do ya think I'm doin'?"

I hesitated, confused by the invitation of an open door and the unwelcoming tone of his now heavily brogued words.

"Well, are ya comin' in, or what?"

I stepped inside. Wilco, still groggy from his shot, ambled to the corner and plunked down. Kevin's front room looked like a gym: a weight bench, racks of dumbbells, and a punching bag on a stand in the corner. "You training for something?"

"Just working off some steam." He grabbed a towel off the bench and wiped down his face and arms.

I swallowed hard and shifted. "I didn't say too much out there today, the shock of it, I guess, but I *am* sorry about your sister. I just came over to offer my condolences. And to see if there's anything you need."

His words lost a bit of accent and aggression as he answered quietly, "I'm fine. Thanks."

"Did the sheriff have anything else to say?"

Doogan didn't look my way. Instead, he walked over to the front window and gazed out into the darkness. "Not much. Just asked a bunch of stupid-ass questions. I went with him to break the news to Costello."

"How'd that go?"

"He put on a good act, but I could tell he didn't give a crap. Not really."

"You don't think he loved your sister?"

He continued silently staring outside. I moved closer and followed his line of vision. A row over, between two other trailers and beyond a vegetable garden gone to weed, was Dublin Costello's place. "Do you think Dub killed her?"

He wheeled around, his tone louder again. "Why do you ask that?"

I took a step back. "You don't seem to care for the guy."

He hesitated before answering, "My sister . . . she'd changed."

"Changed?"

He frowned slightly. "We're from the Murphy clan in South Carolina. Our parents met the Costellos, I don't know, years ago at some gathering or other."

That made sense. Different clans often met up for celebrations or holidays, providing some of the camaraderie we Travellers can never feel with settled people.

He shifted and went on. "Sheila used to call Ma at least once a week. Just to check up on things with the family. We're close, ya know?"

The ties that bind, as Gran always says.

He continued. "At first everything seemed fine. She and Dublin were getting to know each other and all that." He glanced at the floor. "It was an arranged marriage."

Yeah. I knew only too well how that went. "How old was she?"

"Nineteen, almost twenty. The baby of the family."

My stomach turned. Dublin was a few years older than me, so he was nearly fifteen years older than Sheila. Endogamy was a way of life for most Travellers, and our clan was no exception. Couples were often matched at birth. Or at least as young children, as I was to Dublin Costello all those years ago. I rubbed down the sudden prickles on my arms. Thankfully, I'd taken a different route. Not that military tours weren't dangerous, but the service family around you supported you, and you were not only given the means of defending yourself, you were expected to. What I did might have disgraced my grandparents, but if I had married Dublin, that might have been my body out there today. I'd experienced Dub's temper before. I had no doubt he was capable of such a heinous crime.

Doogan went on. "Something must have changed between them, though. About a month ago, Sheila asked if she could come home. She wouldn't say why, but Ma said she seemed upset. We all figured she was just homesick. But then her calls stopped, and no one could reach her."

"That's why you came up here?"

"Yeah. I came as soon as travel season was done. Finished a roofing job down in Alabama and came straight here. But by the time I got here, she'd gone missing." He shoved his hands in his pockets and lowered his gaze. "I called home this afternoon. The news about killed Ma."

I reached out to touch his shoulder but pulled back and folded my arms across my chest instead. What could I say? *Sorry about that? Things will work out? It'll be okay?* Hollow words or outright lies. Nothing would ever be right about this, and I knew it. He knew it. "Did she say things were bad between them?"

"It wasn't like Sheila to complain. She was a good girl."

A good girl. A Pavee's way of saying she was obedient. Like most Traveller women, Sheila was probably groomed from a young age to accept her role in the clan, which would mean by-passing any education beyond state-dictated schooling and set-tling into the role of wife and mother at a young age. In our culture, the woman was the heart of the family, the man the head, and what he said was the law. I'd been brought up the same way, taught to respect the traditions of our clan. As a youngster, I hadn't thought it was such a bad thing; guess I as-sumed it worked. Yeah, it worked alright—if the man your family matched you to wasn't a violent-tempered drunk. For me, it didn't work. Guess I've never been the obedient type. Wasn't a *good girl*.

I pointed to a pair of military-grade binoculars on the window-sill. "You've been watching his place."

A shadow crossed his face. "I don't trust the guy. He's claim-ing that Sheila had a boyfriend."

"Who?"

"Says he doesn't know. He just thinks she was cheating, but I know better. She wasn't like that."

"Even if she was lonely?"

He faced me with an incredulous look. "Not a chance."

I recognized where he was coming from and believed him. After all, she was a *good girl*. If she was obedient enough to marry as she was told, she sure wouldn't be the type to sleep around. "Did she ever mention any friends?"

"No. Not that she ever talked about. Don't think she made many friends here." He folded his arms and steeled his eyes on Dub's place. "I'll wait until the body's released, then I'll take her home for burial. Coming home was her last wish, and I in-tend to make it happen."

A set of headlights sliced through the darkness that now buried the neighborhood. The sheriff's car pulled in front of the trailer. Doogan quickly pushed past me and headed outside. I motioned to Wilco and followed.

Pusser stepped out of his SUV and crossed the yard. The

light from Doogan's open door spotlighted the sheriff's stoic features. He was wearing a navy blue wool watchman's cap and a poorly fitting overcoat. He worked a toothpick between his lips as his gaze swept from Kevin to me. "Ms. Callahan. Mr. Doogan."

"What is it, Sheriff?" Doogan wanted to know.

"The medical examiner's come up with something. I wanted to discuss it with you." Pusser frowned my way, then glanced toward the open door behind us.

Doogan didn't invite him inside, and he didn't tell me to leave, so I stayed put. So did Pusser.

"Just tell me what you've found," Doogan said.

Pusser shifted his feet, then pulled out his cell phone. He scrolled for a second, then tapped on the screen. "This is a photo of a tattoo. The coroner found it during the initial examination. It looks like a round cart or a wagon of some sort. Do you recognize it?"

Doogan's brows furrowed. "No."

"May I?" I moved in closer to look at the screen. The tattoo was distorted, but there was no mistaking the symbol. "It's a gypsy caravan. It's a common Traveller symbol."

"This was on the body?" Doogan asked.

"On the small of her back. It's a little over an inch wide."

Doogan frowned. "I've never seen it before."

"There was something else." Pusser shoved his cell back into his coat pocket. "Did your sister ever have abdominal surgery?"

"Abdominal surgery? No. Why?"

"Because the medical examiner found a scar from an abdominal incision. He guesses it was from some time ago."

"A cesarean birth?" I asked.

"Doc thinks so," Pusser said.

"That's impossible. Sheila's never been pregnant. We would have . . ." Doogan's words trailed off. His eyes lit up with hope. "You mean . . . ?"

"We're still working on identification," Pusser said. "Much of the body was pretty far gone, and since you said she'd never had any dental work done, we're having to run testing on the tooth enamel, which is time-consuming. It should help us pinpoint an age. But the coroner suspects the victim was older than your sister. Confirmation's gonna take some time, though."

Doogan's head bobbed up and down. "I understand, Sheriff. But I know for a fact that my sister's never been pregnant."

"When was the last time you saw her?"

"Seven months ago. At the wedding in South Carolina. There's no way. It *can't* be her." He swiped at his face, his skin flushed, sweat beading along his hairline.

Pusser held up his hand. "Let's just wait until we have more information. I haven't talked to the husband since our initial findings. Maybe he'll have more information."

"I'm tellin' ya, Sheriff. My sister didn't have no baby! There's no way she was pregnant before she got married."

"Okay, okay. I believe you."

Doogan's eyes zeroed in on the sheriff. "So . . . my sister's still alive!"

Pusser looked down and shuffled his feet. "I've got all my resources out there looking for her," he said.

"She's alive, I know it!" Doogan turned back to the door. "I'm goin' to call my mother. Let her know the good news."

Pusser watched him go inside, then turned to me. His face was grim. "Got any opinions?"

"What do you mean?"

"You're a cop."

"Ex-cop. Marine."

He spat out his chewed toothpick and pulled a plastic cylinder from his coat pocket and extracted a fresh one. A whiff of cinnamon stung my nostrils. "If you say so, Ms. Callahan. But being that you're an *ex-cop*, *Marine*, you know damn well that it doesn't look good for his sister. If she didn't leave Bone Gap on her own, then she's probably already dead."

My chest tightened. The sheriff was right. But I wasn't in some damned combat zone where dead, decaying bodies covered the ground like litter. I was home, where things should make sense. I refused to give up on Doogan or Sheila yet. "There might still be hope."

His mouth twitched at the corners. "Y'all seem pretty chummy. Thought you'd never met Mr. Doogan before today."

"I haven't." Then I realized what he was thinking. "I live right there." I pointed to our trailer. "I'd just come home and thought I'd see how he was doing."

"Just being neighborly, huh?"

"Yeah. Just like, you know, neighbors." What'd he think? That we all lived like heathens out here, hopping from one trailer to another, boozing it up and having wild sex parties? McCreary people always thought the same thing about the Bone Gap Travellers. Why did I expect Pusser to be any different? No wonder I'd escaped this mountain years ago. I had to take crap from both sides: the settled residents' prejudice, thinking we were all immoral, and the Pavee stigma of me being born from my mother's sin against the clan's creed.

I crossed my arms, and he lowered his gaze, bent down, and ran his hand between Wilco's ears. I half hoped my dog would take a chunk out of his arm. "If you really want to do something to help the guy," he said, "then you'll get this dog of yours back out there and see if he can sniff up another body."

My arms dropped. My heart did the same. *Another body?* Visions of torn flesh and eyes glazed with death strobed across my brain. He had no idea what he was asking. I forced my eyes to take in the evening's litter of lights in the trailers around us, inhale the smells of propane and diesel oil, rotting leaves and peat. My inner monster sneered, "Sounds like you're pretty eager to assume Sheila's dead. Anxious to clear your docket, Sheriff? Or maybe a *gypsy* girl just doesn't warrant the time."

Pusser jerked upright, his pockmarked face exaggerated in Doogan's porch light. "Don't get me wrong, Callahan. I hope to hell we're not too late. Then again, if she's out there, buried in those woods somewhere, Doogan deserves to know. Otherwise, he's going to spend the rest of his life looking for her. And that's no way for a man to live." He took a step closer, his nostrils flaring. "Believe me, I know."

Gran was at the kitchen sink, finishing the supper dishes, when I came inside. "Let me do those. You've got to be exhausted after everything today."

"I am tired. But keeping busy helps keep my mind off things." She held up a wet plate. "Want to dry?"

I snatched up a towel and joined her at the sink just as she finished scouring a pan. Her washing. Me drying. Just like old times. It felt as if nothing had changed. Yet so much had. Still, I felt happy standing next to this woman with wrinkled laugh lines and piercing blue eyes, skin fragile as tissue paper, and a mind as tough as oak.

Wilco had found a warm spot near the stove and curled into a ball. He slept quietly, motionless, his chest slowly rising and falling. He seldom slept so peacefully anymore, and at first I thought it was his meds, but then I realized why he slept well now: He'd fulfilled his task today. Now he was at peace with himself, maybe for the first time in a year or more. How ironic that the only way he'd been trained to feel good about himself was to successfully find a dead body.

Gran prodded me from my thoughts. "How'd it go with Doc Styles?"

"Oh, good. Seems it's just a sprain. He gave Wilco some pills."

"I'm glad it's not more than that. That dog's been through quite enough already."

The smell of tangy beef and fresh bread hung in the air. My stomach growled.

Gran heard it. "You missed supper."

"Sorry. I wanted to stop in next door and pay my respects to Doogan."

"Of course you did. How's he doing? Poor man. I feel for him, I do. Losing his sister that way. I can't think of anything more terrible."

"Actually, the sheriff stopped by with some promising news." I took another wet plate from her hands. "They don't think it was Sheila."

She looked up from the sudsy water, her eyes wide with question. "Not Sheila? But I thought Kevin was sure."

"No, not completely sure. It was hard to tell much of anything . . . the body was . . ." I busied myself drying the plate. I'd spared Gran the gruesome details earlier. Not telling her about how deteriorated the body was, how animals and insects had gnawed it beyond recognition. "They couldn't tell much about her except the color of her hair." I pushed away the image of the woman's hair, red and tinged redder by the blood it'd soaked up from her fatal wound.

"The color of her hair? Sheila was a redhead."

"Yeah, and so was the woman we found. But that's irrelevant now. The coroner found a couple of other identification marks."

"Marks?" She picked up another plate to wash.

"A tattoo of a gypsy wagon on the small of her back. And something else. An old scar on the body. Apparently, the victim had delivered a baby by C-section. Doogan swears his sister never—"

Gran turned to me and dropped the plate. It hit the floor and shattered into pieces.

"Gran, what is it?" I tossed aside the towel. "What's wrong?"

She brought trembling fingers to her face. Her features crumbled. "I didn't . . . I really didn't think she'd come."

I grabbed her hands and held them in mine. They were ice-cold. "Who? Who are you talking about, Gran?"

She looked toward me, but her gaze settled somewhere beyond me, the crystal blue of her eyes glistening as she spoke. "When I wrote to her that he was failing, I thought . . . well, I knew better than to even hope she'd come." A shudder quivered down from her shoulders to her fingertips. Then she moaned as she repeated, "What have I done? What have I done?"

I gave her a little shake. "You're scaring me, Gran. Tell me what you're talking about."

She focused on me. "That dead woman . . ."

"What about her?"

Her hand flew to her mouth. "Oh, God forgive me . . . my baby . . ."

"Gran? What are you saying?"

"The dead woman . . . I think she's your mother."

CHAPTER 4

I called Sheriff Pusser right away. He drove back out to the trailer with the medical examiner's report and pictures of the tattoo and scar.

The instant she saw the tattoo, Gran collapsed to her knees and wept; my grandfather also cried out, but with his weakened lungs, his grief instead escaped in an eerie, high-pitched wheeze. He turned a hateful face toward Pusser. "Get the hell out of my home." He pushed up from his chair and pointed to the door. "You're not welcome here, you damn copper."

"Gramps!"

Gramps collapsed back into the chair and erupted into a coughing spasm, his chest heaving and the color draining from his face. I ran to him, but he brushed me aside, still glaring at the sheriff.

Gran rose quickly, crossed the room, and held the door open for Pusser. He glanced my way. I motioned for him to leave, and with a begrudging nod, he excused himself.

"Gramps, let me help you." I knelt down to pull the lever and raise the legs on his recliner.

"Don't touch me!" He batted at me, his fingertips connecting with my nose. Waves of pain shot upward to my eyes. I took a step back, squeezed the bridge of my nose, and blinked.

Gran rushed over, inserting herself between us as she adjusted his oxygen. She kept her back toward me, ignoring me and the unspoken questions that hung between us: *How can this be? My mother? You'd told me she was dead?*

The sound of the door opening drew my attention away. I expected to see Pusser returning, but instead my cousin, Meg, rushed inside, still wearing her work apron. "I was on my way home and saw the sheriff's car. What's happened?" She stepped forward and helped untangle a section of tubing. "Everything okay with Gramps?"

Gran looked her way, her face relieved at seeing Meg. "The sheriff brought bad news."

"Bad news?"

I stepped aside while Meg snatched the afghan off the back of the sofa and unfolded it over Gramps' legs. He gazed up at her. Lovingly.

My shoulders tensed. "Gran and Gramps think that the body they found in the woods was my mother."

Meg's eyes grew wide. She looked from me to Gran. "Your mother? I thought . . ."

Gran shot me a warning look, before turning back to Meg. "I'm glad you're here to help. Fergus needs his meds. They're on the nightstand in the bedroom."

"Of course. I'll get them."

Meg headed off to get the meds, and I looked to Gran, hoping for some sort of explanation, but she'd busied herself again, adjusting this and that and doing nearly nothing. Both she and Gramps acted as if I wasn't in the room. I was left in the dust, useless to help, dazed. Their ambivalence toward me stung.

I turned away, snatched up my bag, the keys, and Wilco's lead. On the way to the door, I tapped him between the ears.

"Come on, buddy. We're out of here." Enough of this crap. I could find something better to do for the evening. Besides, more tests needed to be done before an official ID could be made. And I was unwilling to think about the situation until we knew for sure if . . . what? That my long-dead mother had not been long-dead at all? But was now?

"Wait up!" It was Meg. She'd caught me in the driveway.

"Tell Gran I'm borrowing the Buick again."

"Where are you going?"

"Out."

"Back to Mack's?"

"Maybe. Yeah. So? You got a problem with me going there?"

She quirked a brow and tucked a piece of unruly coppery hair behind her ear. I'd always been a bit envious of my cousin's hair. It flowed in crimson waves down her back, while mine hung in stringy black curls against my pale skin. "I'm sorry, Brynn. Could it really be your mother? I thought she had died a long time ago."

"That's what we all thought." Bitterness edged my tone. My eyes slid to the trailer. "Well, not all of us, apparently."

"What do you mean?"

"Never mind." I opened the car door and motioned Wilco inside. I needed to get out of here.

Meg stepped closer. "You should stay. Your grandparents need you."

I turned, my jaw tight as I bit out my words. "They don't need me. *You're* here."

"Stop it, Brynn. You know they want you here. It's all Gran's talked about for the past few weeks. She's upset. Gramps is upset."

"He keeps pushing me out. Always has. He doesn't want me here."

"He's sick. And he's not used to you being here, that's all. You've been gone a long time. Things have changed."

I adjusted my scarf and peered inside the car at my maimed dog. "Don't we know it."

Meg touched my arm. "I'm worried about you, Brynn."

"Don't be. I'm fine. Really."

"Yeah, right. You mean like last night when you were too piss-faced to find your car, let alone drive home."

Why am I taking my anger out on her? Meg was the one who'd been on my side since I'd come home. Besides, she didn't understand half of what was going on—hell, neither did I. "Thanks for last night, cuz. But it'll be okay. I'm just going to have a couple of drinks. Blow off some steam. That's all. I've got an early morning. I'm looking for a job. I need to help out around here."

"Where are you looking?"

"Thought I'd try that motel off the highway."

"The Sleep Sleazy?" The real name was Sleep Easy, but no one except out of towners called it that. "Why there? There are other places. Better jobs."

"It's just temporary, until something better comes along." Another half-truth. Temporary as in an easy job to quit if I ended up leaving town. Because I'd tried *better* jobs since returning stateside. Couldn't handle them. Blame it on the horrendous flashbacks, or the plaguing nightmares, or whatever. For a gal maimed by an IED, the monotony of changing bed linens and scrubbing toilets sounded blissful.

I shuffled my feet, looked around a little. "So, can you put in a good word for me with your boss?" Meg's boss, Johnny Drake, owned the diner where she worked as well as the motel and a few other businesses in town.

"Sure. A job's a job, I guess." She smiled tightly, then shot me a way too sympathetic look. I hated that look.

"What? What's that look for?"

She didn't answer. But I knew what she was thinking. *Poor Brynn, can't even get a decent job.* She had no idea. No one did. Official reports lumped me into the eloquently phrased "wounded in action" and listed me as a "combat medical casualty." Terms that civilians understand. What they couldn't handle was the horror, the heat, the brain-splitting sound, the smell of burning flesh . . . I tugged at the scarf that covered my scar, my constant reminder, and rolled the tension out of my shoulders, only to feel the pull of skin melted into marbled scar tissue along the left side of my neck, over my shoulder, down my side . . .

Truth was, the realities of war were too much for most people. Meg included. I glanced back at my dog, and our eyes met in a knowing stare. That's why Wilco was so important to me and why I'd fought through mountains of paperwork and months of government bureaucracy to bring him home. He was the only one who truly understood me.

As I drove off, shadows settled over me, just as they did over the wheeled trailers and slightly less mobile of homes of our clan. Travellers lived in the shadows of society, always had. By morning's light we could abandon whatever security Bone Gap had offered us for over two generations and disappear like the proverbial gypsies in the night. It was in our nature, maybe in our need, to retain the wandering essence of ourselves; maybe it was our only grasp on security. For me, the idea of leaving now, just driving off, appealed more than ever—getting away from the lies and hurt and confusion of family and clan. There was only one problem: I had nowhere to go.

So I went back to Mack's Pub.

"This one's on me." A thin man with a Fu Manchu the color of an old penny slid onto the stool next to me and placed a couple of bills on the bar. "You don't mind if I buy you a drink, do ya, darlin'?"

Why not? Better his dime than mine. I tipped back my whiskey, letting the heat slide down my throat, then turned and thanked him, trying to speculate on what he thought he'd be getting for payback. *No way, buddy.*

He leaned over and gazed at the floor. "And who do we have down here?"

"That's my dog. Wilco."

"Wilco?" His lips stretched into a smile that revealed a couple of chipped teeth and a discolored crown. "What type of name's that?"

"It means 'will comply.'" I turned back to my drink, hoping that would be the end of our conversation.

But the guy persisted. "Poor fellow. He's missing a back leg. Hit by a car?"

"Nope. His leg was blown off by an IED."

The slack-jawed look on his face gave me an instant of gratification. Good. Maybe that would shut him up.

It didn't. "Sorry to hear it." His eyes roamed over my petite frame and settled on the thighs of my jeans, etched white with time and neglect. "Your legs are lookin' fine, though. Real fine."

The bartender spoke up. "I think you've had one too many, Al." He was running a yellowed rag over the countertop in front of us. "You're drunk. And making a fool of yourself."

"Drunk? I ain't drunk." He leaned in closer. I recoiled at the reek of his stale beer breath. "Do I look drunk to you, darlin'?"

I turned back to my own drink. Maybe he didn't want to be drunk, but I did. Despite what I'd told Meg. For the past year or so, the addictions had seized me like a jealous lover, unwilling to relent even a small fraction of my old sanity. I shoved my hands deep into my sweatshirt pocket, felt the pills there, and pulled out one. I popped it and threw back the rest of my whiskey. Out of the corner of my eye, I saw Al nod. The bartender poured me another. Two sips in, Al shifted closer and slid his hand onto my thigh.

An instant later the scrawny bastard lay sprawled on the floor.

I looked down. *Oops.* Guys like Al learned quickly that the touchy-feely stuff didn't go over well with me. My ugly past with men coupled with a Marine's training usually triggered an explosive reaction.

I threw back the last of the drink this joker had paid for and slid off my stool. Time to go home.

But Al had a different idea. He jumped up, his nostrils flaring. "What the hell—"

Wilco also jumped up and stood at full alert, waiting my command, his growl echoing through the now-silent pub.

Al took one look at Wilco's curled lips and white canines and backed against the bar. He raised his hands. "Hey. Call your frickin' mutt off, lady."

I motioned for Wilco to stand down. He obeyed, but his eyes glistened with a willingness, no, an eagerness, to attack on command. My fingers twitched in response. Yeah, part of me wanted to take this drunken jerk head-on too. Wilco and I fed off each other's emotions, and we both harbored inner monsters. Mine had reared its angry head several times over the past year, causing me to alienate almost everyone in my life and to get canned from my last three jobs. I'd vowed that I wouldn't bring that monster back home with me. I couldn't bear for Gran to see that side of me.

But damn, it'd feel good to put this guy out of my misery.

"On the house." The bartender pushed a glass to me and motioned toward a table away from the bar. I unclenched my fist, ready to grab the glass, then thought better of it. I thanked him and headed for the door. I'd had enough.

Out in the lot, my step faltered. The pill had kicked in. Or maybe the booze. But I hadn't had that much, had I? I sucked in the brisk night air, hoping it'd settle my spinning head. It didn't. I focused my blurred vision on my car. Or Gran's car. My car was still parked down a ways, left over from last night's bender. I jingled the keys in my hand and made my way to the Buick.

One foot in front of the other, Brynn. Nice and easy. I should have stopped at the booze. I could handle my booze. It was the Vicodin that'd be the death of me.

Death? Now there was something I knew about. Death. It followed me everywhere. From the desert sands to the—

"You don't look like you're in any shape to drive, Callahan." I did a double take. Pusser was walking my way.

"You following me?"

"No. I was driving by and spotted your vehicle in the lot. I've still got questions. Thought you might answer a few."

I looked down at Gran's Buick. "You recognized this car?"

Pusser squinted over at a dented, rusty station wagon, circa 1990-something, with *Semper Fi* and *Caution, K9 on Board* decals that practically glowed neon under the street lamp's glare. "Isn't that your car?"

My cheeks burned hot. "Yeah. That's my car."

He looked back at the Buick I was getting ready to key into. "You're drunk, Callahan. Try driving out of here and I'll ticket you for a DUI."

I stood, suspended in confusion. What to do? I couldn't call Meg. And there was no one else to call. "I'm fine." I explained about the car situation.

"Like hell you're fine. That's all your family needs, one more tragedy. Come on, I'm taking you in. You can dry up in a holding cell."

"What about my dog?"

Pusser looked down at Wilco. "Bring the dog. At least there'll be one sober ex-Marine in holding."

*   *   *

I woke up Thursday morning on a built-in concrete bunk, Deputy Parks peering down at me. Thank God, she had a cup of hot coffee in her hand. "Bet you feel like crap," she said.

Crap was an understatement. I sat up, took the coffee, and thanked her. It was tepid and overly bitter, but I took a couple quick gulps, hoping to wash away the dull ache lingering at the base of my skull. My back was killing me. I reached into my pocket for another pain pill, then realized I wasn't wearing my sweatshirt. A quick pat on the side of my cargo pants told me my knife was gone too. *Funny, I don't remember being searched.*

Parks must've read my mind. "You were pretty wasted when Pusser brought you in. We locked up your personals. It's just procedure."

I glanced at Wilco, who sat nearby, his nose twitching at the grease-stained bag in Parks's hand. "Is it customary procedure to have a dog in the cell?"

Parks chuckled, her brown eyes twinkling. "Pusser broke protocol on that. Usually we call the doggie warden, but Pusser insisted that the dog stay with you. He cited some ADA service-dog rule, but I think he's just got a soft spot for the mutt."

I went back to my coffee. This wasn't the first time Wilco and I had spent the night in a holding cell—me sobering up, Wilco charming the local PD.

Parks remained standing, hovered over me, clenching the bag and shifting from foot to foot.

She seemed on edge. "Everything okay, Deputy?"

"We've got a positive ID." She sat down on the far end of my cot. Her voice had softened to that comforting tone, the one she'd used for Gran yesterday.

I lowered the coffee and sat up straighter. She continued. "Seems your mother was in a bicycle accident when she was fourteen. She suffered a severe concussion. Broke a couple teeth. Sheriff was able to obtain X-rays earlier this morning from the hospital. We compared root curvatures and tooth positions. He's still at the morgue, but he asked me to let you know the results." She briefly looked away. "They were a perfect match."

It was official: Mary Anne Callahan, age forty-six, was killed by a single gunshot to the head.

I should have felt impacted by the news. My mother was dead, and I felt nothing. Then again, I hadn't known she was alive in the first place. I felt the same insulating cloak surround me that I'd used in the Marines.

I was told to remove my emotions from the job. We were there for a single task: honor the dead and bring the family closure. *Closure.* I quickly came to realize there was no such thing.

Wilco and I would find a body, a young soldier, nothing more than a boy or girl really, and I'd see the marriage that would never be, the kids and grandkids that would never happen, a family tree altered forever. I grew to understand that there was no closure for the heart-wrenching grief felt by those who have loved and lost. They'd hold their sorrow for a lifetime of milestones that would never be. And that realization slowly ate away at me.

I'd had to grow stronger, tougher, resilient . . . cold. I had to learn to view the corpses we recovered as just the end product of our job, not as the people they had been. "Found another brown bread," a British recovery team leader once told me in his Cockney slang for the dead. That was another insulating cloak—they were retrievals or brown breads or anything other than a person's name.

No problem with that in this case. My mother's name had already been taboo in our household. No pictures of her on the walls, not even a whisper of her name over the years. As a young child, all I'd known of her was that she left or, as I often expected, was kicked out because of her rebellious nature, or because of me. A fatherless child. A bastard . . .

"Ms. Callahan?"

My head snapped up. "Yeah."

"I'm sorry about your mother."

"It's fine. She was a stranger to me."

"You never knew her?"

"She left when I was a baby."

Her brows shot up. "Your father?"

My shoulders tensed. "He wasn't in the picture."

"I'm sorry. That must've been a rough way to grow up. Especially without a mother."

"My grandparents raised me."

Her mouth drooped. "Still . . ."

An awkward silence ensued. I'd said too much. I shut my mouth and turned my full focus to my coffee.

Parks pulled a piece of bacon out of the bag and dipped her chin toward Wilco. "Can he have some?"

"Sure."

She tossed it his way. Wilco snatched it mid-air, his ferocious jaws clamping down with a snap. Parks flinched. "Glad I'm not a piece of bacon!"

"Two hundred pounds of bite force."

"Ouch." She quickly tossed another piece and tipped the bag my way. "I have doughnuts too."

Chocolate glazed. My favorite. I eyed them warily. Parks looked like she'd had her fair share of doughnuts during her career, but I doubted this was just something she happened to have on hand today. Bacon for my dog, doughnuts for me. She was being just a little *too* nice. "No thanks."

She shrugged and took one for herself. "I've got a couple kids. A boy and a girl. Boy's a sweetie, girl's a handful, though." She chuckled. "She's going to give me hell when she's a teenager. I can already tell. Know what I mean?" She shot me a wink.

That's right. A wink. Parks and me, we were just two girls chatting it up over doughnuts. *Yeah, right.* My eyes slid toward the closed cell door. Pusser had put her up to this. A woman cop, he thought, one of my own, certainly I'd open up, bear my soul, spill the beans . . .

My grandparents were right: There's no trusting the settled law. At least not in these parts.

I sipped my coffee and took a good look at Deputy Parks: middle-aged, dark hair pulled back tidy and tight, no makeup, broad shoulders, short clipped nails over gray-stained fingertips. Gunpowder stains. She'd been out on the range already this morning. That told me two things: One, she'd been too busy to clean her gun; and, two, she worked hard to keep up with her male counterparts. I liked this gal. Liked, not trusted.

"You have kids, Brynn?"

"Nope."

"Husband? Boyfriend?"

"No on both accounts."

"Footloose and fancy-free, huh?"

"Guess so."

"I remember those days." Her eyes took on a dreamy look. Parks was a good actress. "Still, I wouldn't trade my kids for anything. My husband maybe, but not my kids." She giggled. I didn't.

Enough with the games, lady.

She cut the giggles short. "So . . . all these years you never saw or talked to your mother?"

I shook my head.

"Never talked to her on the phone. No birthday cards, nothing?"

I shook my head again. Slower this time.

"And you had no idea she was coming back to Bone Gap?"

"No."

She leaned forward. "Someone in your group up there must've known she was coming back."

Group? There it was: another term that belied a blanket stereotype. "We're a clan of families. Travellers. Pavees. Not a group."

She ignored me and continued. "Didn't your grandparents know? One of your cousins? Maybe one of your mother's old boyfriends?"

Okay, enough. I knew exactly where Parks was coming from. These local cops were so predictable. Another crime? *Must be one of them crazy, immoral, backwoods gypsies. Who else could it be?*

"Am I being officially held for questioning?"

Parks looked hurt. "No. Why?"

I stood and handed her my empty cup. "Because I need to get back to my 'group.'"

She stood and met my gaze. "The sheriff's going to want to talk to you."

I tilted my head toward the closed cell door. "He knows where to find me."

She removed Wilco's lead from her pocket and handed it to me. I secured Wilco and followed her down a short hall that held a half-dozen more cells. All were empty except the last. I stole a glimpse inside as we passed by. A guy hovered in the corner, visibly trembling, and practically scratching the skin off his arms. There was a puddle of vomit on the floor next to him.

Terror flashed over his face at the sight of Wilco. He screamed, "Wolf! Wolf! Someone help me!"

"Damn addicts," Parks mumbled.

I looked away.

His terrified screams followed us through a series of doors until we ended up in a central lobby of sorts. A couple of heavy security doors lined one wall; one had a sign that said CENTRAL BOOKING, the other was unmarked. Across the way, on the far side, two uniformed females hunched over computers at a counter fronted by bulletproof glass. One was older, with a gray bob and reading glasses perched on her nose. The other was much younger and heavyset, with frizzy yellow hair and a dark brown stripe running along her part. They both looked up as we approached.

The older one stood and spoke through a metal insert in the glass. "This the Bone Gap woman?"

Parks nodded.

The fake blonde leaned back and gave me a hard stare, her eyes lingering on my neck scar.

Parks looked at her with raised brows. "She's checking out. I need her stuff."

Blondie let out a huff and rose from her chair, her fat behind sashaying across the room to a small bank of lockers. She keyed into one of them and removed a plastic tub. Walking back over, she plunked it down on the counter and shot me a nasty look.

"Gray sweatshirt, wool scarf . . ." The gray-haired woman was checking my items against her paperwork. "Black tactical knife, and . . ." She looked quizzically at Deputy Parks and held up a small plastic baggy. "And seven white tablets?"

Parks squinted at the pills. "Looks right. Thanks, Barb. Pass the paperwork through."

Barb slid a small stack of papers and a pen under the glass. "Sign here and here, please."

I did. The papers went back under, and my stuff came sliding out. I put on my sweatshirt and adjusted my scarf. I'd just pocketed my meds and knife when a door behind the desk popped open. Deputy Harris strolled in with a stack of papers and crossed over to the blonde. "Hey, darlin', would you mind—"

He looked up from the papers, saw me, and stopped short. His expression hardened, his eyes darting back to the blonde. A telltale blush crept over her face.

Aha. So this was Harris's girlfriend? Guess that explained her attitude toward me. Their recent pillow talk probably included a mention or two about us criminal gypsy types.

The room seemed to shrink in on me. I turned to Parks. "My car's at Mack's Pub."

Harris snorted. "Yeah, we figured."

The other two women laughed as Parks and I pushed through the door.

On my drive back to Bone Gap, my irritation at the settled law's attitude morphed into an even deeper anger at my own kind. The bitter taste of betrayal gnawed at my gut, and by the time I'd pulled up in front of Gran's trailer, all I could think of was all the time that'd been wasted. Had I known my mother was still alive, things might have been different.

I thought back to my teen years. I was obsessed with my mother back then. What was she like? Her wants, her dreams? What was her favorite color? Her first kiss? I was relentless in my pursuit to know more about her. I spent hours on the local library's computer, searching the Internet for her name. Then I questioned others, intent on asking everyone in the clan if I had to. That's when Gran and Gramps broke the news to me. They said they'd been hesitant to tell me, wanted to spare me the grief, the embarrassment of knowing that my mother had committed what we Pavees consider the ultimate sin: suicide. A condemnable act, strictly forbidden and rarely discussed in our deeply religious culture. The clan didn't know, and they wanted it kept that way. For my sake. I'd accepted this news. I'd even grieved my loss, in my own way—privately and alone. Maybe that's why I felt nothing but numbness now. I'd already grieved for my mother. Thanks to my grandparents, I'd lost her years ago.

Lies. How many had my grandparents told me over the years?

And had my grandparents told this same lie to others? I had no idea. Probably no one had asked about my mother's absence. That's the way things operated within the clan. People minded their own business. Unless there was an occasion to celebrate; then everyone became involved. Births, First Communions, engagements, weddings, and, yes, deaths—the exception being suicides—brought about raucous parties. Especially death. Settled folks never fully understood the rituals that surround a true Irish wake: after a brief period of intense mourning and keening for the deceased, usually a couple of days, and after the funeral, we'd set aside our grief and begin celebrating our loved one's rebirth into eternal life with lively music, dancing, and an abundance of booze. People come from near and far—family first, then other folks. A Pavee never mourns alone. Or parties alone.

And by the looks of it, Gran didn't need the official report to start the wake process. The bereaved had already begun to arrive. The front yard was cluttered with vehicles; some of them I recognized, some I didn't.

Inside, I found mourners crowded by the dozens in the small front room of our trailer. For the rest of the day, cigarette smoke, grief-filled murmurings, and tidbits of comfort in both English and Shelta dialect drifted back and forth. My mind found it cloying and insincere. Had any of these people ever even *asked* about her in years?

Then I heard one of the clan's elders say to Gran, "*Swart a manyath.*" She's in heaven now.

"Took her long enough," I quipped. The elder glared at me, and Gran quickly turned her back on me. *Me and my too-quick mouth.* It was yet another of those insulators: the gallows humor soldiers fell back on. Yet part of me didn't care anymore what I said, not now and not in front of my grandparents either. After all these years of thinking my long-dead mother was burning in hell for committing the ultimate sin, was I supposed to find some comfort in his thought that she was in heaven now—finally—because someone shot her brains out and dumped her in the rocks?

I'd once heard someone say that one man's sin was another man's virtue. Had my grandparents considered it virtuous to let a little girl think her mother had done such a horrible thing?

And all that time, I'd believed them. "When I wrote to her about his failing." That's what Gran had said the night before. Those words, unmasked and spoken in grief, cut worse than the truth of knowing that I'd discovered, and not recognized, my own mother's dead body. I might have expected a lie of that magnitude from Gramps. But *Gran*? How could she? I didn't know what was real or what was a lie. All I knew was that I couldn't stand to face Gran or these grievers any more. I wanted to leave, but I was trapped. So I retreated back to the kitchen, wordlessly dishing out more food and drink to accommodate our visitors, all the while slipping into a deeper, darker mood. Wilco, who sensed my decline, hovered close by my side.

I was at the sink washing some dishes when one of our neighbors, Mrs. Black, stepped up beside me. "Coppers came by first thing asking your grandparents all sorts of questions."

"They did?" Funny, Deputy Parks hadn't mentioned that my grandparents were questioned this morning. Just one more reason the deputy was so chatty: buying time so the police could come back here and harass my grandparents.

"Yes. But don't you worry none, dear. Your Gran didn't tell them nothing about us. Real strong, she was."

I pressed my lips together, my eyes sliding to the bread she was holding: a round loaf, the top scored in a cross, its thick crust curled open at the marks to reveal its dark and heavy texture. Its fresh-baked, sweetish scent rose to my nostrils. Wilco's nose lifted and flared as well.

Mrs. Black cocked her head. "Should I slice some up now, dear? Or do you want to save it for later?"

"Now." My comment came quickly as I dried my hands on my jeans and opened a drawer for the bread knife. I hadn't felt hungry for any of the offerings brought earlier by clan members, but this smelled delicious. We sat at the small kitchen table, and I realized I hadn't eaten anything this morning. As she sliced the bread and I opened the butter dish, she babbled on about her recipe, as if I cared . . . or cooked.

"It isn't soda bread. Not really anyway. I mean, I do use buttermilk and soda instead of yeast. But this has blackstrap molasses and uses only whole-grain, not white flour."

"Uh-ha." I took the first slice and spread the softened butter over the dense treat. I raised it to my mouth for the first warm bite.

"So you can't call it Irish soda bread, although some mistakenly do call it that. It's actually a very proper Irish brown bread."

I choked, spewing brown globules of dough across the table.

"Oh, honey, are you alright?"

"Brown bread?" I glared at her—*desert corpses: brown breads*—and grabbed a napkin to wipe off the remnants still clinging to my mouth. "How appropriate of you."

"I just knew your family would like it." She beamed, ignorant of my tone. "But brown bread can be a bit heavy to swallow in one big bite. Here, let me get you some tea." She hustled to the simmering kettle on the stove, still going on about her family recipe, oblivious to my sarcasm. I pushed the loaf to the side. She had no idea how heavy a "brown bread" could weigh on a family.

She handed me a cup of tea, then busied herself making another in one of Gran's heavy ceramic mugs. "A spot of tea should warm your grandmother too, I think." She poured in a nip of whiskey, a gift from a well-meaning friend.

I raised a brow. "Gran doesn't much care for whiskey."

The woman tipped the bottle again. "Nonsense. It's just what she needs at a time like this."

A whiff of the amber liquid floated to my nostrils. My mouth watered. *It's just what I need too.*

I should have stayed inside, played the part of dutiful granddaughter, offered to be of more help, but all I wanted was to numb the strange mix of ambivalence and anger that was quickly consuming me. As soon as Mrs. Black left the kitchen to deliver Gran's tea, I snatched the bottle from the counter, grabbed my coat from the peg by the back door and motioned to Wilco to follow me outside.

I sat at the bottom of the back steps with Wilco curled around my feet and brought the bottle to my lips. The warm liquid enveloped me like a hug from a dear friend. One I'd just visited the day before, one that I'd spent too much time with already, but nonetheless welcomed. My shoulder muscles loosened. The grinding feeling in my stomach eased as I sucked in the chilled air. Tennessee's autumns are a brew of aromas that reek of summer's decline and winter's threats: sodden soil molds, pungent burnt leaves, all trapped in mountain air. I slumped back and continued drinking until a few minutes later when I heard the back door creak open behind me. I turned to see a face from the past.

"Colm?" His name came out as a whisper at first. I stood and blinked, the whiskey bottle still clutched in my hand. How could it be possible that he was here? "Colm Whelan? I didn't know you were back in the area."

"I've been back for a while. I came as soon as I heard." He tugged at his soiled jacket. "Excuse the way I'm dressed. I was doing some yard work when I heard the news about your mother."

"You look great." I cringed at the eagerness that rang through my voice. For all I knew, he was married now. Maybe he even had kids. A lot of time had passed. Even so, he hadn't changed much over the years. Tall, with a strong build and a vulnerable bend to his posture, he was never really handsome. His nose was too big, his jaw too strongly set. But time had been good to him, softened his features a little. And his dark eyes still held that mischievous gleam that always sent a zing of attraction through me. Still did.

My cheeks stung with heat as I noticed him eyeing the whiskey bottle in my hand. I giggled and raised the bottle. "Remember that time you lifted a bottle from your father's stash and we went up to the rocks?"

His smile stiffened. "I remember. We got plastered and . . . well, we were just kids. It seems like so long ago now."

A flood of memories rushed back: the warmth of the sun-drenched rocks that day, the heat of the whiskey, the even hotter rush of excitement as we explored each other's bodies. Instantly my body responded, ready and all too willing. My eyes wandered to his chest, down to his belt, and down to . . . *Don't go there, girl!* I turned away and sat back down.

He stepped down to my level and joined me on the steps. I offered him a drink, but he waved it off. Embarrassed, I capped the bottle and tossed it aside on the ground, as if it meant little to me, and then ran a finger between my scarf and now sweaty neck as I struggled for something to break the awkwardness. "I'm surprised you've kept up with the people in Bone Gap. How did you know to come here? Do you know my grandparents?"

"I've just gotten to know them since I returned. Mostly your grandmother. I've been helping her and your granddad."

"I don't understand. Helping them?"

"Since your granddad's illness." He shifted and rubbed his palms over the knees of his jeans. "Your grandmother told me you were coming back. I'm glad you're here. She needs you. Especially now. I'm sorry about your mother, Brynn."

He sounded . . . so businesslike, so professional. I still didn't understand the connection between him and my grandparents. Helping my grandfather? Was Colm a doctor now? Now that would be interesting. Doctors should know all kinds of things about a female body, how to . . . I pressed my lips together, thwarting the stupid grin threatening to break out.

He looked over, searching my face, avoiding my neck. "She told me about what happened to you over there. I can't help but feel responsible. If I hadn't left the way I did, I can't help but think you never would have joined the Marines and—."

"You think too highly of yourself," I shot back, any potential grin smacked away by his words. "Life goes on, you know. Well, except when it doesn't." I cocked a thumb back toward the house.

He looked surprised, then sickeningly sympathetic.

My gallows humor really doesn't fit in here.

But no way was I letting him take credit for what happened in my life. Even if it was true. I'd given my heart and so much more to him. Then he left for college, without looking back, it seemed. I'd assumed he'd come back for me. He had *said* he would! But he never did. No phone calls. Nothing. So I joined the Marines. Like I'd said—life goes on. Obviously he'd gone on too. "So did you marry?" I tried to sound pleasantly interested.

He shrunk back against the step, his brow wrinkled in disbelief. "You haven't heard?"

How would I have heard about anyone in McCreary? Then it hit me: She was probably a celebrity of some sort. Beautiful and refined. Smart and classy. It made sense, since Colm's prominent McCreary family ran in the circles of the well-bred and well-heeled. No matter who she was, she certainly wasn't a Pavee or damaged goods, like me. "No, I haven't heard. Is it someone I know or should know?"

"No. It's not that. I'm not married." He hesitated and cleared his throat.

I groaned. Audibly. He was gay! His first, and maybe only, roll in the hay was with me, and that was enough for him to beg off women for good. Like I needed this news right now.

"Brynn, I'm a priest now. At St. Brigid's in McCreary. I was appointed there to help Father Donavan run the parish."

"You're a damned priest?" I slapped a hand over my mouth but way too late.

62 *Susan Furlong*

Colm blinked, then his face crinkled. "Well, the point is not to be *damned*. But yeah, I'm a priest." He bit his lip to avoid laughing in my face, but ended up choking in the process.

"Here," I swept up the bottle and offered it to him. He waved it off. Yet again.

"What? Priests don't drink anymore either?"

Which only made him laugh louder. I found myself feeling stupid, not only about my sexual reactions when he first appeared but the fact that his warm and hearty laugh now still warmed my nether parts. But I also felt dirty for sitting with a priest after all I'd been through in the past ten years. You can't be in a war without chalking up a bunch of sins. And now all of mine came crashing in on me. I set the bottle aside, wanting, more than anything, another slug of it.

Colm quit laughing and sobered himself. Which I realized wasn't about to happen to me anytime soon. "I thought you knew. Didn't your grandmother mention me?"

"No. Why would she? She doesn't know about us. I never told anyone." At the time, I was promised to Dub, the wedding date set, the dowry money all but handed over. No, my time spent with a settled boy was my secret. I'd never told a soul.

"Father Colm?" Meg was standing in the doorway looking down at us. "My grandmother is asking for you."

"I'll be right there." He looked at me, seemed about to say something, then quickly stood and walked up the steps. He turned back to me as he reached the door. "We'll talk some more later, okay?" He disappeared inside the house.

I watched him leave, wondering how much worse the day could get.

Meg stepped down to join me. A whiff of her lavender soap joined me as well, pulling my attention from my moroseness to my attractive cousin. She wore a cable-knit sweater over a long skirt, her red curls held back with a jeweled clip. I ran my hand through my own hair. It felt greasy and flat. With all that had happened, I hadn't had time to shower that morning. *Great job,*

Brynn. I could only imagine what *Father* Colm saw in me: a greasy, dirty-mouthed drunk.

"Brynn?"

I refocused. "Yeah?"

"I was saying that we brought your car back from the pub. Gran gave me the keys, and Eamon took me into town. I parked it around front for you."

"Thanks."

"He's inside. Would you like to meet him?"

"Eamon?" I remembered her mentioning him earlier. He must be someone special. "I want to meet him, Meg. Of course I do. It's just that . . ."

"I understand if now's not a good time."

Well, now there's an understatement. "I just need a little time alone."

She pulled me into a tight embrace. "Oh, Brynn. I'm so sorry. I really am. This must be so difficult for you." She gave me another squeeze and pulled back until we were face-to-face. She lowered her chin, her green eyes large and round. "I'm here for you. Whatever you need."

I considered what I needed: something to eat? That hadn't worked out so well. A talk with a priest? Not so much. Another drink didn't sound so bad, but . . . "I know you are."

As soon as I spoke, she flinched and stepped back. "Brynn, you've been drinking."

Ah, well, hello? Yeah. For about two days straight now. And I intended to make it three. I dipped my chin toward the trailer. "Hasn't everyone in there been hitting the bottle?" Well, maybe not everyone, but most.

She looked about, her eyes landing on the whiskey bottle.

The look of concern—or was it disappointment?—on her face was too much to take. I turned away and tugged at Wilco's collar. "I need to take him for a walk. Let him do his business. Tell Gran I'll be right back."

Meg gave me another look, this one less concerning and

more judgmental, but she didn't object to me leaving. As soon as she shut the door, I tucked the bottle into my sweatshirt pocket and stormed down the road. *To hell with them all!* Meg with her self-righteous attitude, Colm the priest, Gran and her lies.

I kept walking. Not that I knew where I was going. Anywhere away from the trailer would do. I ended up at the small park at the end of the road. I'd come here often as a kid. It was a magical place, where I met up with my cousins and played for hours: swinging and taking turns going down the skin-burning, monstrous metal slide. The area had been neglected since then, weeds and rust overtaking everything. Cigarette butts and candy wrappers littered the ground around a nearby splintered wood bench. I used the toe of my boot to scuff off the bird splatter and settled in to continue my drunken quest.

I didn't get far before I noticed Kevin Doogan traipsing toward me through the weeds. He had a determined look on his face. *Ah, crap, like why can't a gal drink in peace in this place anyway?*

"I saw you coming this way. I need to talk to you." He glanced over at Wilco, who was napping in a sunny spot nearby. "How's the dog doing?"

"Better. It must have been pretty minor. He's not limping at all, but the meds the vet gave him make him sleepy."

There was an awkward silence. Doogan shuffled his feet and stared at the ground. "I heard about your mother. I'm sorry."

"Thank you." I blinked a few times and took another drink.

He sat next to me and, after a beat or two, turned out his palm. I reluctantly handed over the bottle. He tipped his head back, his Adam's apple sliding up and down as he took a couple swigs. I was torn between relief that here was someone who didn't judge my drinking and concern that he'd swallowed down part of the only balm I had right now. I used my sleeve to wipe the rim before taking another quick sip of my own; then I capped the bottle and set it aside. I wanted to save the rest for later, and Doogan seemed like a guy who could make quick work of a bottle.

"Are your kin planning the funeral?" His face was shrouded with concern.

"Not much can be decided until we know when Sheriff Pusser will release her body. It could be a week or more." I should've told him about the man who shot at us, ask him what he meant when he said the woods was no place for a woman, but now wasn't the time for that discussion. I could barely think straight as it was.

"I'm sorry." His gaze slid to the capped bottle, then back to me. "I hate bringing it up now, but after you left last night, I got to thinking." He tipped his chin toward Wilco. "That dog of yours. He's good at sniffing out people, right?"

My muscles tightened. I knew where this was headed. I didn't want any part of it. "Only dead people."

It was a lousy thing to say, insensitive and uncaring, and he recoiled a bit. Pain flashed through his eyes. "I know there's a good chance Sheila's dead. She's been missing for so long. I'm . . ." His voice caught. "I'm just hoping she's not."

Last night, Doogan was sure his sister was still alive. Now he seemed full of doubt. I knew from experience that families often vacillated between hope and dismay when a loved one was missing. The same hope that Doogan held last night had been in the hearts of soldiers and locals every time we'd returned with recovered bodies. Every dead body that wasn't a comrade or friend dangled the hope that someone they cared for still lived. Dangled it on a string that burned like cordite, changing from hope to despair an hour, a day, or a week later when that loved one still didn't return.

Bone Patrol, as my fellow marines called it, initially seemed like an honorable specialty. It was, but it also took a toll on me. I rubbed down the chill that crept up my arms. *Don't think about all that now, Brynn.* I'd left all that back in the desert, along with my sanity. Part of the reason I came back was to heal and to let my dog heal. I didn't need this. "We can't help you. I'm sorry."

I followed his gaze as he scanned the woods. "You don't understand."

"Yes, I do. It's just that I can't help now."

He focused back on me. "I gotta know for sure. If she's out there, somewhere in those woods like your mother was, I need to find her. I can't bear the thought of her body . . ."

Rotting? Being eaten by bugs and scavenged by wild animals like my mother's body? I glared at him. How dare he ask this of me!

His eyes widened. "I'm sorry. Very sorry about your mother. But try to understand. I have to know."

"I'm sorry, Doogan." I stood and walked over to nudge Wilco awake. "Now isn't a good time. My grandparents need me. My mother's death, my grandfather's illness. I need to help out around the place. Get a job. The medical expenses have been overwhelming, and now the cost of the funeral . . ."

"I feel lousy for asking. It's just that I don't know where else to turn. You're trained for this sort of thing. I'm desperate."

I felt my resolve crumbling. Here was a man who only wanted to find the truth, while I'd found more truth than I wanted. And I still had so many questions of my own: *Why did my mother come back after all these years? If she'd gotten Gran's letter, wouldn't she have contacted her, let her know she was coming? Why did she leave Bone Gap in the first place? Who shot her and why?* The only problem was that I was too weak to face these questions, let alone seek the answers. I wasn't sure I even cared to know the answers. I took my bottle and walked away. All I really wanted was to drink. Drink. Sleep. Forget. Repeat.

Doogan called after me. "Brynn?"

My grip tightened on the bottle.

"Please just think about it."

Next to me, Wilco stopped and turned back. I bumped him forward with my knee, but he didn't budge. What was wrong with my dog? I reached down and yanked his collar. *Come on, Wilco!* He held his ground.

Anger rose in me. Then self-disgust. I forced my gaze upward, back to Doogan, and saw what Wilco saw, what Wilco felt—anguish and despair. Doogan had folded in on himself, his hand shielding his face. His chest was heaving.

I looked away from Doogan to my dog, the bottle in my hand, then back to Doogan. *What type of person have I become? Even my dog has more compassion than me.*

"Tomorrow," I said. Quietly at first, then I yelled it out. "Tomorrow. We'll start looking tomorrow."

CHAPTER 5

A knock on my car window woke me early the next morning. I pushed Wilco off my chest and rolled my throbbing head toward the annoying *tap, tap, tapping*. It was Deputy Harris. "Ms. Callahan! I need to speak to you."

My driver's-side window hadn't actually worked since Bill Clinton was president, so I pushed open the door and rolled out. Wilco hobbled out behind me. "What is it?"

"Sheriff wants to see you."

"Now?" I ran my gritty tongue over my even grittier teeth and smacked my lips.

"Yup. Now. There's been a new development."

"Like what?" I tried to clear my throat. It was as dry as dust.

"I'm not at liberty to discuss it."

At liberty! Smug little jerk probably didn't know why. I glanced from his puffed-up chest back toward my station wagon. I'd left a little whiskey in the bottle the night before. It was right there, on the passenger seat. I smacked my dry lips and discovered a glob of dog fur clinging to the crusty corner of my mouth. I picked at the fur and ogled the bottle. An old phrase popped to mind: *the hair of the dog that bit you.* I chuckled . . . then stopped, because chuckling hurt my head.

"Is something amusing, Ms. Callahan?"

I rubbed my temples. "No. Not at all. It's just that—"

"Good." He stared down his high-bridged nose at me, his pouty little mouth curving upward in a sneer. Harris had a baby face, complete with pudgy cheeks that might inspire a pinch or two from a woman three times my age. All I wanted to do was slap them silly. "I gave you my contact information. Why didn't you just call?"

"Tried to. Couldn't get through."

I pulled my cell phone from the side cargo pocket of my pants and checked the display. The charge was dead.

Harris jingled his car keys. "I'll take you in. The dog will have to stay, though."

"No thanks. I'll drive myself. And my dog."

"Sheriff's expecting you now. It's urgent."

"If it was all that urgent, he would have come out here himself."

Out of the corner of my eye, I saw Doogan step out of his trailer and light a cigarette. He took a long drag, flicked the ash off to the side, and shot me a little wave. I waved back.

Harris kept after me. "You better not keep the sheriff waiting."

I was about to fire back with something witty when the sound of running water drew my attention to the side of the deputy's parked cruiser. Only it wasn't water, but Wilco. He was relieving himself on the deputy's tire. This time, despite the pounding between my ears, I tilted my head back and let the laughs roll. And roll. Not that it was all that funny. It just felt good to cut loose.

Harris didn't laugh. Instead, he did the ultimate in stupid. He swung his foot at my dog, trying to kick him. "Get the hell away from my car, you friggin' mutt."

I stopped laughing.

Thankfully, Wilco dodged the kick, but Harris raised his leg like he was going to try again. "Hey!" I rushed forward and grabbed his shoulder. I yanked him back, trying to get him away from my dog, but the sudden move threw him off balance. He fell backward, and we both ended up in a pile on the ground, Harris landing hard on top of me.

Wilco thought Harris was hurting me. He growled and barked. Before I could get out from under Harris and motion for him to stand down, Wilco went crazy, whipping his head back and forth, his mouth frothing with slobber.

Harris rolled off me, stood, and backed up. "Call your dog off!"

I popped up and signaled for Wilco to back down, but he was hyper-focused on protecting me, not seeing my signals. He growled, snapping and biting at the air in front of Harris.

Harris was panicking. "Call him off!"

"I'm trying. He thinks you were hurting me." I moved around Harris, so Wilco could see me, but Harris snatched my arm and yanked me back.

"Stay back!"

Not a smart move on Harris's part. Wilco lunged at Harris, catching part of the deputy's sleeve and ripping it away like wet newspaper. Harris stopped cold. His face clouded over with an emotional mix of fear and fury as he gaped at his arm. In a flash, his gun was out, pointed directly at Wilco's head.

"No!" I jumped between Harris and my dog.

Doogan was suddenly there, standing by me, facing down Harris and the gun. "Hey, man. Calm down. You don't want to shoot nobody's dog."

Harris lowered his gun. "Stay out of this, Doogan. The dog tried to attack me."

I turned to Wilco. He was no longer snapping, but his lips were curled back, showing the sharpness of his teeth. I knelt down and calmed him. "It's okay, boy. It's okay." I repeated the words over and over. Not so much for Wilco, he couldn't hear them, but for me and to get this jerk to back off. I leaned in, covering Wilco's body with my own, and we melted together, one unit. A team. If I lost this dog, I'd never recover.

Harris holstered his gun, and moved his hand to his radio. "I'm calling animal control. The dog's viscous. It needs to be put down."

"Oh, come on, Harris," I heard Doogan saying behind me. "No need to get animal control out here. The dog's completely calm now. It was all just a misunderstanding."

"Shut up, you stupid pikey. I'm making the call."

Pikey was derogatory term outsiders used for us. I glanced back and saw Doogan's jaw tightening. His fists did the same. The name didn't sit well with him. Somehow, though, he didn't throw a punch. Instead, he kept his cool and tried reasoning with the idiot. "Suit yourself, Harris. But you might want to think about it. The government's put a boatload of money into training this dog. Probably more than you make in five years' time. He's probably more valuable than you. You think they're going to put a dog like that down?"

Harris hesitated. Doogan continued, "Your boss has been eying this dog, believe me. He's already thought about how he can use his skills. He'll be pissed when he hears what went down here. First you rough up a lady, a cop even, then you threaten to shoot her three-legged police dog just because he tried to defend his master. How's that going to look?"

Harris waved his fist at him. "You better watch your mouth, boy. I know things about you."

Doogan tensed. His eyes darted my way before refocusing on Harris.

Harris lifted his chin. "Yeah, that's right, I know all about you. Bet folks around here would be interested to know you've got a record."

"That's all in my past," Doogan said. "I did my time."

Doogan was in prison?

Harris cocked a thumb my way. "She looks surprised. Didn't bother telling her about McCormick, huh?"

I had no idea what or who McCormick was, but Doogan noticeably flinched and crossed his arms. Just a few seconds ago, he was bigger than life, willing to take a bullet for my dog; now he was anxious about Harris's accusations? Stupid thing was, I could care less what Doogan had done in the past. It was none of my business. God knew, I had enough of my own past demons to contend with; no need to get mixed up in someone else's.

I shot Harris a dirty look and rubbed my wrists. "Enough of this crap, Harris. If you weren't such a jackass, I'd be showered and at the sheriff's office by now. Tell your boss that I'll be there in an hour." I touched Wilco on the head and turned toward the trailer, shooting one last look Doogan's way. "Thank you," I said.

I planned to spend the next hour with a hot cup of coffee and an even hotter shower. Maybe I'd even have a chance to talk to my grandmother alone. I'd tried the night before. After leaving Doogan in the park, I'd headed back to the trailer, hoping to get some answers. But when Gran wasn't surrounded by well-wishers, she was busy with Gramps or finding endless other things that needed tending, none of which included her own granddaughter. I gave up on her, wandered out to my car and drank the night away.

It didn't look like I'd get a chance to talk to Gran this morning either. When I walked in, the trailer was dead quiet. I tiptoed past the relatives camped out in the front room: Aunt Tinnie, Gran's oldest sister and a spinster, was curled under a hand-crocheted afghan. A couple of Gramps' distant cousins, hardworking boisterous fellows, were sprawled on the floor. Tea cups, beer bottles, and an empty whiskey bottle lay strewn about the coffee table, along with the family Bible and colorful strands of rosary beads. Father Colm had probably led a rosary, after which family stories would have been passed around with the libations. I'd missed all that, choosing instead to mourn in my own way, apart and alone. Now, as I listened to the slumbering breath of family fill the room, rising and falling almost in unison, I wondered if I could ever be a part of all this again. Could I get past my wounds, past and present, and feel once again like I belonged with these people? My own family. Good people who'd dropped everything, their work and responsibilities, to travel here and support my grandparents during their time of grief, just because that's what Traveller families did.

Keep your mind on the task at hand, Brynn. That's how you get through. Focus on the task. And right now, I needed to deal with Sheriff Pusser. So I moved about the trailer as quietly as I could. A cup of instant coffee for me, a can of Alpo for Wilco, and a hot shower. A half hour later, I was picking my way back through the trailer when a small noise drew my attention back toward the kitchen. Gran was standing there, the marks of sleep still evident on her face. Her blue eyes met mine and widened with question. She clutched the frilly neckline of her nightgown and scooted across the room to me. "*Me Lackeen.*"

"Gran." In that instant, I forgave everything and folded into her. We stayed like that for a while, holding each other, absorbing one another's pain, until I muttered the one word that I knew would push us apart. "Why?"

She pulled back, her blues eyes moist with, what? Sadness? Regret? "Because there were things you were better off not knowing."

"Things? *Things!* Like the fact that my mother was alive all these years?" I heard one of the relatives stirring. I lowered my voice. "How could you have lied to me? You. Of all people."

She slumped forward, her eyes searching the floor for answers. I waited. When she raised back up, her gaze landed on the keys dangling from my hand. Wilco's leash was clenched in my other fist. "Where are you going?"

"The sheriff's called me in for more questions."

She frowned. "Don't go."

"I have to go. I don't have a choice. Murder isn't something you can just ignore and hope it goes away. There's going to be an investigation. A lot of questions will be asked. You need to be ready for that."

"I won't answer their questions. I don't trust the police. You shouldn't either."

"The police aren't our enemy."

"You've been away for too long. You've forgotten how it is for us. How they've treated us."

It was true. Whenever a crime occurred in nearby McCreary, the cops came looking our way first, whether it was warranted or not. Sure, there are wayward among us. *Yonks*, we called them. Those of our clan who steal and scam. They've earned the title. But outsiders have judged us all by the actions of a few.

Gran's expression darkened. "But I've forgotten. You are one of them. You *are* the police."

"Not anymore."

"Maybe you're on their side now."

I placed my hands Gran's shoulders. They felt small and bony. "There aren't any sides, Gran." Her jaw was set, her lips pressed into a thin slash. I could tell I wasn't getting through to her. "The police are only trying to find the truth," I said. "Don't you want to know who killed her? She was your own daughter."

"Let it be, Brynn. Vengeance is God's right, not ours."

What type of crap is this? Something Father Colm told her last night?

She was on a roll: "*The righteous will rejoice when he sees the vengeance. He will bathe his feet in the blood of the wicked . . .*"

"Stop! Stop with the religious stuff. I don't want to hear it."

I raked shaky fingers through my wet hair. "I'm not seeking vengeance, just answers. What is it that you're keeping from me, Gran?"

The tightness in her features crumbled. She jammed her hands into her armpits, almost as if she was hugging herself. I noticed a small tremble. Was she afraid? I reached out. She backed up, dropped her arms and threw back her shoulders. A different emotion crept into her features. Anger? Hate? Toward whom? Me?

"Why would I tell you?" she spat. "So you can run to the police with it?"

The words felt like a slap in the face. "Gran!"

She shooed me away. "Just go. Go and see your police friends. Tell them all about us. Us *gypsies*."

"It's not like that . . . ," I began, but she'd already turned away.

Back in my car, I was still seething with anger and hurt. What was going on with Gran? We'd always been so close, but now . . . I felt a wet swipe on my cheek. Wilco had taken his normal position as copilot and had given me an Alpo-infused lick on the face. "Thanks, boy. I needed that." He licked me some more, and I slowly felt my anger melting away. That's why I needed Wilco. No one could calm me, tame my inner monster, like my dog. Dog breath and all.

"I love you, boy," I said out loud. He actually looked happy to hear it, although I knew better. I laughed as I turned the key in the ignition. "You know how to read lips, don't ya, boy? You're so smart." Nothing made me happy like my dog. I let the car idle, heat blasting from the dash, and took a little time to love on my dog. As I leaned in to kiss the soft spot between his ears, something caught my eye. Or someone, that is. Down the road, I saw a couple of unfamiliar vans parked by the trailer park's entrance. Outside, several people stood huddled together. One of them pointed my way. I rubbed a clear spot in my foggy window and squinted through for a better look. One of the men had a large camera balanced on his shoulder. The man next to him looked in my direction, pointed his microphone, and the cameraman swung his lens my way. Then they headed at a sprint in my direction.

The press.

Young Pavees were warned about the press—an evil tool of the settled man, we were always told. That was probably the one thing the elders had actually gotten right. Whenever the press showed up, it meant bad news for the clan. I recalled an incident from my childhood when a camera caught a young Traveller mother disciplining her child. The press ran with it. By the time the national stations aired it, Travellers, or gypsies as they called us, were all painted as child abusers. Outsiders didn't understand us, so it was all too easy for the press to peddle whatever stereotypical hogwash they wanted. What would it be this time? A crazed gypsy war vet and her body-sniffing dog?

I crammed the car into gear and headed for the back way out.

Sheriff Pusser stood and motioned for me to take the chair across from his desk. He wore a pair of half-rimmed reading glasses. His usual toothpick dangled between his lips. "How's your family doing?"

"They'd like to know when my mother's body will be released. They need to plan the funeral."

"I'll see if the coroner's got a timeline. A lot of the tests have to be sent out. We're small-time here."

I probably should have wondered what tests the county doc was running, but I wasn't used to civilian police work. In war, death was always straightforward and easily classified: small-arms fire, IED attack, suicide bomber, helicopter crash, RPG attack, and, my least favorite, non-hostile, which usually meant the soldier had taken his own life. Point being, there was rarely reason to question the cause of death. I didn't think there was in this case either. My mother had been shot in the head. I'd seen the wound firsthand. So I didn't even think to ask. Later, I'd regret not asking more questions.

While Pusser shuffled through a manila file, I checked out his office. Framed certificates lined the paneled wall behind his desk. A dirty window looked out over the parking lot. Underneath it, the shelves of a pre-fab, particleboard bookcase bowed under the strain of a couple dozen operation manuals. I stared at it for a minute, thinking that one more book and the whole thing would come tumbling down. Sort of like the block towers we built as kids. I wondered if Pusser ever played with blocks. What I really wondered was who the pretty girl was in the frame on the corner of his desk. A picture of his wife as a young girl? A daughter perhaps? Pusser didn't strike me as the family type.

I glanced at him. He was still shuffling papers. Stalling, or trying to make me nervous? I cleared my throat. "Your deputy said this visit was urgent. He said there was a new development."

Pusser tossed aside the file and leaned forward. "Harris tends to exaggerate. I called you in this morning as a courtesy."

"Oh?"

"One cop to another."

"Maybe you ought to just tell me what's on your mind, Sheriff."

"It's concerning your grandparents. We've been asking around about your mother. Most of your tribe members—"

"Clan, not tribe."

He shifted. "Clan. Sorry. Some of them seemed to think she'd died years ago."

I shrugged.

"But no one could remember going to her funeral, or when exactly she'd died."

I already knew that, of course. I thought back to that period of time when I was hell-bent on finding my mother. I was a good girl back then. Not only did I accept their explanation of her suicide, I obeyed their request and never asked about my mother again. Now, of course, I knew they'd been covering up for something else. It sounded as if Pusser knew that too.

He shifted tactics. "Parks said that you didn't know your mother."

"That's right. She disappeared when I was a few weeks old."

"Disappeared?"

"Ran off, I mean. I always thought she'd met someone. Or maybe she just wanted out."

He raised a brow. "Out?"

"Out of the clan. It can be . . . stifling."

"I understand."

No, he didn't. But I let it go.

He repositioned his glasses and made a couple of notes. "You never heard from her again?"

I dropped my hand over the side of the chair and reached for the top of Wilco's head. His fur felt warm, soft, comforting. "No."

"Had your grandparents heard from her? Maybe your grandmother?"

Mrs. Black told me that he'd questioned both Gran and Gramps already. Given their mistrust of the settled law, I wasn't surprised that Gran hadn't mentioned the letter. She wouldn't think twice about lying to Pusser and withholding crucial evidence. Clan loyalty. Of course, she'd lied to me too. Her own family. Some things you were better off not knowing, she'd said. I didn't understand what she meant, but now I needed to decide what I was going to do: tell the police what I knew, or stay loyal to Gran. *Think, Brynn . . . think . . .*

"Ms. Callahan? Had your grandmother been in contact with your mother? Did she know she was alive?"

"Not that she had said. Not that I was aware of, anyway." Over-explaining. A sure sign that someone's lying. "I mean, she'd never mentioned it to me." *Shut up, Brynn.*

He leaned back in his chair and inhaled. I kept my eye on his toothpick, half expecting, half hoping that he'd suck it down his throat. Anything to distract him from this line of questioning. "I'm afraid I'm having trouble putting this all together."

You and me both, buddy.

"A lot of people thought your mother was dead."

"Yes."

"Is that what you thought too?"

"Not at first. I just thought she'd left."

"But then you learned that she'd died?"

"Yes."

"How old were you at that time?"

"Around fifteen."

"Who broke the news to you?"

"Gran."

"When you were fifteen?"

"Uh-huh. Around then."

He squinted. "But there wasn't a funeral?"

"No. That would have been against the rules."

"The rules? What do you mean?"

"God's rules. Or maybe just clan rules. I'm not sure."

He stared at me a bit harder. I squirmed a little. "She committed suicide," I explained. "She wouldn't get a Christian burial. Not back then anyway. Now things are different." With the church. Not the clan. Suicide still signified an eternity in hell. At least in the mind of the elders. Never mind that someone might be suffering from mental illness . . . or PTSD, for that matter.

He pulled out his toothpick and started to say something, then decided against it. Instead, he stared at me for a beat or two, then tossed the toothpick into the garbage can. It missed. A collection of toothpicks stuck out from the carpet pile like tiny spears.

"Suicide," he repeated. "So she left when you were young. No one really knew why or where she'd gone. And nobody

heard from her in all those years, not even your grandmother."
He leaned back and extracted a new toothpick from the plastic
cylinder he kept in his pocket. He inserted the fresh one between his lips, chomping down hard. "Tell me, Ms. Callahan. If
no one had talked to your mother since she left the clan, then
how'd they learn that she'd committed suicide? Who told
them?"

And there it was. He knew someone was lying. He probably
thought it was me. I hoped he thought it was me. The last thing
I wanted was for him to go after Gran.

He locked stares with me. Gran was right. I shouldn't trust
the police. At least not these police. I kept my mouth shut and
held firm.

"I was hoping we could help each other," he said. "You and
me. Work together on this. It's your mother. You must want to
know who murdered her."

He was looking for information. And I had some. Not what
he was hoping for, I knew, but a small bone I could throw him.
Something to buy a little time, keep him off my back, or more
precisely, Gran's back. At least until I could figure things out.
"There *is* something I didn't tell you."

He smiled. A crazed jack-o-lantern type of grin with a
toothpick shooting out between a gap in his teeth. I stood and
pulled my cell from my side pocket. "I forgot about these earlier.
They're photos that I took at the crime scene. Before Doogan
went crazy thinking it was his sister and screwed things up."

He snatched the phone from my hand. "What the hell?"

"It's something we did as MPs. Part of the task. We photo-
graphed bodies as soon as we discovered them just in case we
were mortared and had to evacuate before we could do a full recovery. Stuff like that happened a lot. The photos were sometimes all we had to make an ID later."

Pusser was shaking his head. "And you're just now telling
me this?"

I didn't have an answer. I wasn't keeping it from him, I'd forgotten about it. Finding the body set in motion a whole lot of mental crap. I wasn't myself these days. All the more reason why I couldn't return to police work. I needed time, time to get my head screwed on straight.

"I'm sending these to my number. Is there anything else I should know about?"

Yeah. Tons. Unfortunately, it all led back to my grandparents. "Nope. But I'd like to see the case file you have on my mother."

He bristled. "I'm not going to share that with you."

Probably because it named several Pavees as suspects. "Not even as a courtesy? You know, one cop to another."

He grunted.

"What about the gun?"

"The gun?"

"The murder weapon. Make? Caliber?"

"It was a .380. That's all I know so far."

All he knew, or all he wanted to tell me?

He finished sending the photos and handed back my phone. "We're supposed to be on the same side, you know."

There it was again: sides. Why did everyone want to make this about sides? "I'm not really on any side. I'm not a cop anymore. I'm looking for a different line of work now." I bent down and picked up Wilco's leash and gave it a tug. I'd had enough of this courtesy call. What I really needed to do was find Johnny Drake and talk to him about getting a job. At the trailer yesterday, I saw one of the neighbors slipping Gran some money. Things were tight, I knew that. But I didn't want Gran feeling like she had to accept charity. Besides, a job would give me a good excuse to stay clear of the trailer for a while.

"Your dog's standing pretty good now."

I tightened my grip on Wilco's leash. "Yeah. Doc Styles has him on some meds." That's another thing I needed to do. Stop by and pick up some more pills for Wilco. Doc had given me just a few day's supply, to see if it helped. It had.

"You should put him to work out in the woods. Looking for Doogan's sister."

"We've already had this talk, remember?"

"You'll eventually look for her. I know your type, Callahan."

"Oh yeah? What type's that?"

"The cop type."

I smirked.

"Look, Callahan. I don't know why you signed on to be an MP in the first place. But it took some balls to do what you did over there—locating dead soldiers. Most men I know couldn't do that. But you did it. And you were successful. Why do you think that is?"

I just loved being analyzed. First the VA shrinks, now Pusser. "You're the armchair psychiatrist. Enlighten me."

"Because you couldn't stand the thought of the family not knowing. Bet you didn't give up until the job was done, every severed body part, every piece of flesh, every bone was found and put in a box marked for home. That's because you understand the need for closure. It was something you never had growing up. Something you were denied. It's cruel, actually. No matter the reason, it's cruel to deny someone the closure they need to move on from the trauma of loss. I get that. Believe me."

Sweat broke out on my upper lip. I struggled not to swipe at it.

"See, I think you always had your questions about your mother. Why she left in the first place and then later why she supposedly killed herself. So you buried it deep inside you. That's what people do when there's something so painful they can't bear to face it. They bury it."

I nudged Wilco toward the door. Pusser followed. "All I'm saying is that you're not going to let Doogan suffer like that. You can't help it. It's not part of your makeup to let people suffer." We reached the door at the same time. He extended his arm, blocking my way.

I didn't tell him that I'd already committed to helping Doogan. I wouldn't give him the satisfaction.

"The only real question," he continued, "is are you strong enough to help yourself? To face the questions that have haunted you your whole life."

I turned my head and looked him directly in the face. My heart felt like a jackhammer in my chest. *Strong enough?* He had no idea what I'd faced in the past. But now . . . my mind flashed back to a halfway house in Memphis. I'd landed there after getting fired from my third job stateside, an assembly-line position at General Motors in Spring Hill, where I worked with the stamping machinery. The whirring noise of the machines sounded just like chopper blades—the one memory I'd carried from the day I'd been caught by the IED, the sound of the evac chopper.

I'd thought I could handle it. I couldn't. My nightmares increased, I couldn't sleep, I couldn't function. Until one morning I sat on the edge of my mattress, a handful of pills in my palm, a bottle of whiskey on my lap, ready to swallow away my life . . . I just wanted to forget it all. Not just war, I realized, but my whole life. But I lost my nerve that day. Wilco had rubbed up against my leg, his brown eyes questioning, his ears cocked in deaf uncertainty. He'd sensed my pain, he understood as no one else could, and I couldn't do it. Who would take care of Wilco? And now . . . Who would take care of Gran?

Don't trust the police, she'd said.

Pusser was still talking. "All these years I bet you've imagined all sorts of reasons your mother left you. Maybe thought it was your fault? An unplanned pregnancy, a young mother burdened with a baby . . . Then she came back and you almost got your answers. Only someone killed her before you had a chance. Who? And why? Help me, Callahan, and I'll help you get the answers you need."

"Help you how?"

"Just keep your eyes and ears open. Keep me informed."

Gran was right. He was asking me to snitch on my own peo-ple. Nothing had changed. It was still them against us. "You think a Pavee did this. That's why you need me. Because I'm one of *them*." I brushed his arm aside and yanked on Wilco's leash. "Go to hell, Pusser."

CHAPTER 6

The instant our palms touched, I wanted to pull mine away. Maybe it was the strange up-and-down he was giving me, or the fact that he held my hand just a beat too long, I'm not sure. Whatever the reason, my potential new boss, Johnny Drake, gave me the creeps. Weird. Meg had said he was such a great guy.

"So you're Brynn Callahan," Drake said. He was a fit fifty-ish, with a gray buzz cut and heavy, black rimmed glasses that kept sliding down his nose. We were in the parking lot of the Sleep Easy Motel, a 20-room motor inn off Route 2, an old highway road that ran between McCreary and Bone Gap. "Your cousin, Meg, told me you're looking for a job. You're a war vet?"

"Marines. Three tours."

He thumped his chest, where a cross hung from a heavy gold chain around his neck. "Navy man myself. Machinist mate. Persian Gulf. We kicked some ass back in the day." He fixed on my dog. "Your partner?"

"This is Wilco."

"Good name. What type of work are you looking for, Brynn?"

"Meg said you're in need of housekeepers."

"That's right. One of my girls quit last weekend. We're running shorthanded."

"I'd like to apply."

He pushed his glasses up his nose and peered into the back of my car. "You living out of your car?"

"Huh? No, why . . ." Then I realized why he asked. All my belongings were still crammed into the back of my station wagon. I kept telling myself that I hadn't bothered unpacking yet because there wasn't much room in the trailer, but the truth was, unpacking meant a staying in Bone Gap. I wasn't quite ready to make that commitment yet. "I'm living with my grandparents in their trailer. It's cramped."

"I see." He gave me another long look. "Fergus and Anne are your grandparents?"

"You know them?"

"No. Not personally. But I heard about your mother. I'm sorry."

I didn't say anything.

"You sure you're ready to take on a job so soon after . . ."

"Yes. I'm fine. I'm ready."

"What about the dog?"

We both looked down at Wilco. He gazed back at us, then yawned and licked his muzzle with one long sweep of his tongue.

"He goes where I go."

"I understand. Thing is, I have a no-pet policy in the rooms. People have allergies."

I pointed to the side of the building where a group of trees provided a shady spot. "I could tether him to one of those trees while I'm working. I'll water and walk him during my breaks."

Drake hesitated. Whether he was trying to decide on me, or my dog, or both of us, I couldn't be sure. I shifted and fidgeted with my scarf. "I could really use a job, Mr. Drake."

"Call me Johnny."

"Johnny," I choked out. Again, he gave me a peculiar look. I couldn't decide if he was a pervert or simply not running on all four cylinders. Heard that happened to a lot of squids—Marine vernacular for Navy guys—especially the sub crews. Too much time underwater. Turned them into bubbleheads. Poor guy.

"I'd need you five days a week, Wednesday through Sunday. We're usually booked through the weekend. You'd start at noon and work until the rooms are done. If you want, you can start training today."

"Suits me fine."

He held out his hand again. "Welcome aboard, Brynn."

After stopping in at the main office, where I filled out the obligatory paperwork, Drake introduced me to my counterpart, a mid-forties, wiry gal by the name of Zinnia Crow. Her high cheekbones, straight nose, and long black hair reminded me of an exotic Native American princess. Her heavily tattooed body reminded me of some of my fellow Marines.

"Just call me Zee," she said. "Be glad to show ya the ropes, sweetie."

But as soon as Drake disappeared back inside his office, she changed her tune. "You're one of them gyspies that live up the mountain, ain't ya?"

I wondered how she'd figured that I lived in Bone Gap. Had she heard about me already? Or did we all have a certain look? "That's where I grew up. But we're called Travellers, not gypsies." I gave her my best smile.

She frowned. "Whatever. We have rules 'round here. No smoking, no drinking, and no touching the guests' belongings. If you find something left behind in a room, it goes straight to the office to the lost and found. If it's not claimed after a week, it's there for the pickin', but I get first dibs. I've got seniority."

"Oookay."

She squinted at me, obviously not pleased at my reaction. "Shit."

She stared, waiting for something from me. *But for what?* "Pardon?"

"Shit. Be ready for it."

Yeah, like what she was already giving me?

She continued, "And piss and sticky rubbers. Might as well know right now this ain't no pretty job. We pick up the messes left behind." She cocked her head at me. "Think you can handle it?"

I pursed my lips, gave a little thoughtful nod. "I think so." I bit back what I wanted to say: *You've got no idea how much shit comes out of a dead carcass or how much piss from a dying man. Yeah, I think I can handle that from the live ones.*

She looked at me a few more seconds, seemed to appreciate that I'd thought it over, then handed me a work shirt, a blue polo with white trim. On the back, scripted in loopy white cursive letters, was the name SLEEP EASY. *Classy.*

I got Wilco situated, changed into my uniform top—which I had to admit, looked a little weird with a scarf tucked into the collar—and met Zee at room number 20. Zee had a system. She liked to work from the highest-numbered room to the lowest. Easier that way, she'd told me. "It won't seem like you're always climbing uphill." She was also a bit superstitious, having told me that she had never so much as touched the doorknob to room 13, a room that was no longer used for guests but served as Mr. Drake's, "Johnny's," private office. In fact, when we passed by, pushing the supply cart along the walk between room 14 and room 12, she rubbed at a blue stone she wore around her neck and muttered something. Warding off evil spirits, maybe. Or casting some sort of curse on me. I couldn't be sure. She was short on patience, and I was long on inexperience. But by the time we reached number 9, I'd gained enough proficiency to handle a few rooms on my own. We split the work the rest of the way and finished early for the day.

Overall, my first day on the job went well. I ended up taking a liking to Zee. She joined me on break and even shared part of her packed lunch, some chips and an apple for me and some of the turkey off her sandwich for Wilco. I learned she'd grown up in the area, married and divorced young, and had one teenage daughter—Wenona, Winnie for short—who wanted to attend TSU after high school.

I was telling all this to Meg that evening, at the diner, over a burger and fries. It was a little after six. I was starving after work but couldn't quite muster the enthusiasm for going home yet. Meg had just finished her shift and joined me in the back booth. I'd attached Wilco's service dog vest, allowing him full access to the dining portion of the restaurant. He lay under the table, curled at my feet. "She's different," I continued, describing Zee. "She claims to be a direct descendent of some Cherokee Indian chief and believes in all sort of superstitions and mystical stuff." I told her about the rock necklace and room number 13.

Meg laughed. "And people think we're weird."

I swallowed a bite of my burger and snuck a piece to Wilco under the table. He snatched it up and licked my fingers. I noticed a few people staring my way. "Are you sure it's okay to bring my dog inside?"

"Yeah. Johnny's cool with it. As long as you have the vest and leash on him."

Talk about weird. I thought back to my encounter with Johnny Drake earlier: the way he looked at me, like he was studying me for some strange experiment. I didn't mention any of that to Meg, though. She thought the world of her boss. And I was grateful to have a job. I gave Wilco another quick bite and wiped my fingers on a napkin. A man a couple tables over shot a look of disgust my way. "Are you sure? People are definitely staring. I hope we don't scare away the other customers."

"It's not your dog, Brynn. It's you."

"Me?"

She cocked her head to me, "You didn't know?" She swiped

up some ketchup with the tip of her fry. "Yup. Well, both of us, to some degree. But more you, sorry to say." She sprinkled extra salt over her fries. "Did you happen to notice any cameras around today?"

"Cameras?" I winced. "Yeah. This morning."

"You were on the local news. Channel 4. You looked good, wheeling away in your car."

No wonder Zee knew who I was. "What'd they say?"

"Not much. The news doesn't seem to have the whole story. Not yet anyway." She leaned in and lowered her voice. "Speakin' of which, you left the trailer before all the excitement today."

"What do you mean?" I tensed. "Is Gran okay?"

"She's fine. She can handle herself. But I know where you get your temper." She took a couple of bites before continuing. "Like I said, the press is hot on the story. They showed up at the trailer, asking all sorts of questions. Just the *McCreary Sun.* You know, that blond dummy reporter who pretends he's a young Wolf Blitzer reporting in our third world. But I'm sure the other newspapers will pick it up soon. You know how they are. They're hungry for whatever they can find on us."

"What's all this have to do with Gran's temper?"

"The reporter was relentless. He wouldn't ease up. Came right up to the front door and yelled out his insulting questions. Took pictures of her trailer too. A lot of them. I'm sure none of them are flattering."

I thought about the half-finished ramp Gran was building for Wilco. Piles of wood and tools were strewn about. The scrub grass and weeds that could hardly be viewed as lawn. "What type of questions?"

"All the usual crap. Everything from do we have child brides to wanting to know where we're storing our weapons."

"Weapons?"

She lowered her voice again. "Didn't you know? We gypsies are planning to overthrow the government."

"Wow. No one told me."

She rolled her eyes.

"What did Gran do?" Not that I *really* wanted to know.

"Showed him the one weapon she does have."

"Oh no. I forgot about her pistol." Gramps had insisted years ago that Gran always carry a gun with her, after a Traveller woman had been beaten by a pack of bigots in Augusta.

We sat upright as a couple of guys passed by on their way to the door. "Frickin' knackers," one of them mumbled.

Yet another derogatory term used against us. My shoulders tightened. "Assholes," I shot back.

Meg cringed. The guys stopped and walked back to the table, one of them leaning in real close. "What'd you say, pikey?"

"I called you an asshole."

"Stop it, Brynn." Meg was mortified.

The other guy looked at his friend and laughed. "She packs quite a wallop for such a little package."

I turned my focus his way, letting my eyes land below his belt. I smirked. "Looks like you probably know *a little something* about small packages."

His nostrils flared. He leaned over and slammed his fist on our table. "You little bitch!"

Wilco popped out from under the table and let out a long, wicked-sounding growl. The guys slowly backed up and headed for the door.

I turned back to Meg. She glared across the table at me. "Was that really necessary?"

"You wanted to let them get by with calling us that? Besides, I've handled guys like them before. What was it you were saying?"

"Uh . . . Gran's pistol."

"I don't think Gran even has ammo for that old pistol."

"Probably not. Doesn't matter. The reporter didn't budge. Not until Paddy and Jarvis got involved."

I groaned. Gramps' younger brothers had been at the place.

They'd slept over in the front room with some other kin. They were both over six feet, packed an easy extra hundred pounds each, and looked like street thugs. Harmless if you didn't rustle them. Or if they weren't drunk. Or hung over. I could just imagine the photo op they gave that cameraman if they thought the reporter was threatening Gran.

"Yup. And Dub was there too. You know how they all get. Especially when they've been drinking. And they had been. A lot." She looked around and frowned. "Anyway, it got ugly fast. And there's been a lot of talk around town today. With your mom's death . . . ,"—she lowered her eyes—"and Sheila missing, people are worried that there's a killer on the loose."

"And they're thinking that killer must be one of us." I held up my hand. I didn't want to know any more about the press. "You said Dub was at the trailer?"

"He came by to pay his respects. That's what he said anyway. I think he was really there to see you."

A chill clutched me. I handed the rest of my burger under the table to Wilco. I'd lost my appetite. "Why do you say that?"

"He was asking about you. Old flames die hard and all that." She winked. I shivered.

"Seems he should be worried about his wife. Not me." I'd never told Meg what Dub had done to me. But I didn't want to think about that now. I tossed my crumpled napkin on the table and grabbed the end of Wilco's leash. "I'd better get back home." I'd told Doogan that I'd start the search today. Guilt shot through me. I hadn't planned on starting a new job the same day I applied, and now it was almost dark.

I reached into my pocket for some money. Meg stopped me. "It's on me, cuz. Wait up, I'm going to grab my jacket from the back office, and then I'll walk out with you."

I stood by the cash register, absently studying the pies rotating in a nearby display case. A couple of ladies came up to pay their bill. "Wish their type would stay up on the mountain," I heard one of them whisper to the other. I tugged at Wilco's leash and headed outside.

As soon as I reached my car, I noticed the scratch. A deep groove ran from the driver's-side door all the way to the back bumper. Someone had keyed me. No doubt one of the guys from earlier. I felt my fist clench.

Meg caught up with me. "You didn't wait . . . what is it?"

I opened my hand and slammed it down on the roof of my car. Wilco saw my anger and flattened his ears. "This." I pointed down at the scratch.

Meg ran her hand along the side of my car. "Who would . . . ?"

I clenched my teeth and glanced around the lot. Meg's mouth turned downward. We both knew. The two guys from the diner. I rolled my neck, calming the anger boiling inside me. Meg was looking off in the distance now. Once again, the tide of hatred against us had swelled, frothing beyond suspicion into self-righteous acts of violence. A keyed car one day. But what next?

CHAPTER 7

It was late by the time Wilco and I made it back home. Gran and Gramps must have turned in early; the place was completely dark. I hesitated on the way to the front door, glancing over at Doogan's place. He wasn't home. *Good.* I knew he'd be ticked that I was a no-show earlier, and I dreaded trying to explain it to him.

"You said we'd start searching today." I half jumped out of my skin. Doogan emerged from the shadows next to our front steps, the hood of his sweatshirt pulled low over his face. Wilco's tail wagged with excitement. I grabbed his collar and held him by my side.

Doogan's voice was tight with anger. "I waited half the day. You never showed."

"We'll head out at daybreak. I promise. I have a new job and—"

He cut me off. "Forget it. I can't count on you." He shoved his hands into his pockets and lumbered toward his own trailer.

"What do you mean?" I hustled and caught up with him. "I told you, I got a job today."

He stopped and turned my way, his posture stiff and his jaw set hard. "It's fine. I did some of my own searching."

"You searched the woods today? Did you find anything?"

"Not the woods. Costello's place."

"*What?*" I lowered my voice. "You broke into his mobile home?" I already knew that Doogan had done time, God knew what for. I wondered about the status of his parole. "That's a felony, Doogan. You shouldn't—"

"I'm sick of waiting around for people to help me find my sister." He leaned in, and even in the dim light from his porch, I could see his eyes flashing. His voice was thick with brogue. "Get out of here, Brynn. Go home and let me be."

He was close enough that I had to crane my neck upward to see his face. Against the chill of the night air, I felt the heat of his anger radiate from his torso, invading my space. And another emotion too. Something urgent and visceral and distinctively unnerving. Protective, or maybe it was possessive, I couldn't be sure. I'd sensed it earlier that day when he stepped in to disperse the situation between Deputy Harris and Wilco. His demeanor toward me had shifted from insolence to something else. Something I'd ignored then. I was trying to ignore it now. I wouldn't let myself go there. Not with this man. Not with any Pavee man. Ever.

I took a step backward, but there was no need. He had already turned and now hurried off. Again, I took off after him, this time not so much to apologize but because there was no way I was going to let him get away without hearing what he'd found. "We can go out first thing in the morning. I don't have to be in at work until noon." He ignored me, but I persisted. "Did you find anything?"

Doogan hesitated only a second, then stormed into his trailer, leaving his door open. Wilco and I followed him inside and to his kitchen, where he pulled a long-neck beer from the fridge. He didn't bother to offer me one.

"What'd you find, Doogan?" I asked again.

He took a crumpled photograph out of his pocket. "This."

I smoothed it over the kitchen counter. In it a red-headed girl's face had been gouged out with some sort of sharp tool. I glanced up at Doogan, saw his eyes fixed on the refrigerator door, where a photo of his sister hung by a magnet. Her wedding photo. She looked like a princess: veil flowing in the breeze, her wedding ring sparkling as she clutched her bouquet. It was the same red hair as the one in the crumpled photo under my hand. I squinted. "Is this Sheila?" I handed back the damaged photo.

"Yeah. That's her."

"Looks like she's leaving a room at the Sleep Easy. Who's that?" I indicated a masculine figure obscured by the shadows of the partially open doorway.

He didn't answer. He was tracing his finger over the gouged-out face of his sister, his muscles trembling with anger. "Costello has this room . . ."

"A room? At the Sleep Easy?"

"No. At his place. There's a stash of DVDs . . . and other things."

"DVDs? You mean—"

"Porn flicks." He was still looking at the photo. "*Pumpkin Pounder, Ginger and the—*"

"He has a redhead fetish." A sourness roiled in my stomach. Both Sheila and my mother had red hair. "You said there were other things. What type of things?"

He kept his gaze focused on the photo. "Sex things. Sick stuff." His jaw hardened. "Why would Sheila marry a guy like that?"

I half choked, half laughed and his head snapped up, eyes flashing. "Don't you remember, Doogan? Sheila was a *good girl*. She married whoever her family told her to. She was *obligated* to marry that sick bastard." I met his pointed stare with my own until he blinked, his lips tight against the truth of my words. My shoulders fell. He didn't deserve my anger now—he had enough of his own. "Just tell me what else you found."

He pulled something else from his pocket and threw it up on the counter. "This."

I leaned in and peered at a clump of curly threads.

Doogan jabbed at the counter. "I cut this out of his carpet. It looks like blood."

I looked closer. "It could be, I guess."

"What if it *is* blood?" His body tensed. "Sheila's blood."

I backtracked and softened my words. "It could be anything. And even if it is Sheila's blood, she could have had a bloody nose. Or cut herself."

"Or been cut. Stabbed. Killed. Right there in that room." He stepped back from the counter, folded his arms across his chest, and set his jaw firmly. He was trying to be stoic, but I sensed his pain. "You need to take it to the sheriff," he said. "Have him run tests on it."

"And tell him what? That you broke into Costello's place and cut out a piece of his carpeting?"

His features twisted with confusion.

"What you did was stupid, Doogan. What if it *does* turn out that Dub's the killer? We can't use any of this. And when he realizes someone was in his place, he'll start covering his tracks. He'll destroy anything that points to his involvement in your sister's death. And what if someone saw you? You could get into serious trouble."

"Nobody saw me. The only trailer back there is old man Nevin's. He's hard of hearing and probably half scuttered by now. Likes his whiskey." He stopped pacing and met my gaze. His lips twitched nervously.

Or was that a sneer? I fumed inside. What was he implying? Yeah, so I drank. God knew I'd earned the right. The things I'd seen, my scars, the suffocating nightmares . . . all of it out of my control. *Let your training take over, go on autopilot.* That's how they trained us Marines to handle dire combat. If we didn't learn to disassociate under stress, then we'd bury our heads in the sand, get our asses blown off. *Go numb, ignore the fear, and you'll live through it.* No, I wasn't anything like old man Nevin. He was just another drunk Pavee. They came a dime a dozen around here. I'd survived combat and left the war; it's just that the war hadn't left me. Not yet. The booze and other stuff? It helped me go numb, just for a while. Just until I could get through the pain, get my head screwed on straight. That's all it was for me.

"Costello killed my sister." Doogan was pacing again. "I know he did. Her stuff's still there, in her closet, folded in her drawers. Even her toothbrush. Sheila didn't just up and run away. Costello murdered her. And I'm going to make him pay."

"Easy, Doogan. We need to get more evidence first." Things weren't always what they seemed, and assumptions could lead to a quick death. Or a slow burn. I tugged at the fringe of my scarf.

He pointed down at the photo. "That picture. The blood. What more do you need?" His expression tightened. "You're acting like them. Saying these things because you're a cop. You've been on the other side too long. We Pavees take care of things our own way. Or have you forgotten?"

Clan justice: an eye for an eye. Literally. Some Travellers, the *yonks*, or criminals or wayward among us, had no trouble committing sins against our settled neighbors. But no Pavee would cross the line of harming or stealing from a fellow clan member. The consequence was too high. All the more reason to make sure we were on the right track. I didn't want Doogan going off half-cocked without substantial evidence. "We don't even have a body," I said. "We can't be sure until we find a body. We'll start in the morning." I swallowed hard. The implication was clear, and so was my fate: Sheila was likely dead. And I had one more body to find. "I promise."

I motioned to Wilco, and we left, but the pain and anguish written on Doogan's face revisited me as I lay in bed that night. Between Dub's belligerence and Doogan's intensity, one or the other would end up dead for sure if they met up like this. I couldn't let Doogan lose his life too at the hands of Dub. Nor could I let Doogan land in jail for murder. As much as I suspected Dub had killed Sheila, there was no proof—not yet. And there it was: I *did* suspect Dub of murdering Sheila. And . . . I squeezed my eyes shut . . . maybe my mother too. The facts of the case raced through my mind: Dub's temper, a temper I knew all too well; the blood; the DVDs, which suggested a fixation on red-haired women . . . red hair, the same color as my mother's hair . . .

My inner monster awoke inside me and breathed fire. An angry heat took over my body. Next to me, Wilco whimpered and burrowed his head in the crook of my arm.

Doogan's right. I've been on the other side too long. Since coming back, I'd felt suspended between two cultures, my loyalties torn, my sense of belonging, here or there, eaten away like grub-infested roots. Rootless. That's what I was. Like a tree that, for all purposes, appeared steady and strong but would easily topple in the next heavy wind. I've always felt that way. An orphaned half-breed, sired by an unidentified settled man, abandoned by my Pavee mother . . . all these years, so many unanswered questions. And now . . . now, if what Doogan thought was right, if Dub was the killer . . .

The irony of it shocked me to the core . . . Dub—the reason I'd left the clan, my grandparents, my way of life—may have also taken away my one chance of ever knowing my mother, of ever knowing the whole truth.

Clan justice. An eye for an eye, a life for a life.
Dublin Costello deserves whatever he gets.

CHAPTER 8

The morning breeze ran through the treetops like a silent serpent. I inhaled deeply, sucking in and savoring the familiar scent of mossy peat and decaying leaves. Wilco was by my side, wearing a tactical vest and tethered to a lead, his head held high and proud, awaiting my command. He was glad to be back working. It surprised me to admit it, but I was too.

We'd set out before daybreak and had already walked a few miles into the woods. I wanted to start at the previous scene and work our way outward, my theory being that if the crimes were connected, the perp may have dumped the bodies in close proximity.

From the start, I laid down the ground rules with Doogan: Keep any talking to a minimum, follow my lead, and don't for any reason make eye contact or any other contact with my dog. You see, the hunt is just as much about the handler as it is the dog. The reason Wilco performs his task so well, why he's a decorated war hero, isn't because he's brilliant—although in my eyes he is—or because of the hours and hours of grueling training we've invested in developing his skills. No, Wilco works as hard as he does out of loyalty and devotion to me. Most people don't get it. Hell, most of my friends in uniform, including my superiors, didn't get it. They want to believe that it's the breed, or the training, or the inherited instinct that makes a dog so good. Of course, all of those things contribute to the making of a good human remains detection (HRD) dog. But it's the human/canine relationship that makes a *great* HRD dog. Unless you've truly loved a dog and that dog has loved you, it's hard to understand. In short, Wilco performs out of devotion and a strong desire to make me happy.

For that reason, if I'm not careful, he'll lie just to please me.

In handler lingo, we call it a *false alert*—when, for one reason or another, a dog reacts to a nonexistent scent. In the early stages of our training, Wilco and I had struggled with false alerts. Despite six weeks of grueling training at Lackland Joint Base K9 School and having it pounded into my head over and over by my superiors, I still screwed up. Especially those first few weeks after Wilco and I were matched. I found myself constantly enamored with my dog's capabilities and often made the mistake of stopping to admire his technique. But if I met his gaze or gave even the slightest hint of approval, he'd stop and go down on alert, thinking that if I was pleased, then he must have met his goal. My response spurred his actions. Left unchecked, that sort of thing could have become chronic and ruin his career. It's one of the most elusive aspects of our training, an emotional paradox: bond, love one another, yet learn to work independently of those emotions.

Rather than try to explain all this to Doogan, I just told him to keep his mouth shut and stay ten paces back.

About a half mile from the outcrop of rocks where we'd discovered my mother's body, Wilco lifted his nose for a deep sniff. His head twisted this way and that, his nostrils working first the air, then the ground. Some of Wilco's over 200 olfactory cells—or smellers, as I called them—had picked up my mother's scent. I had expected this. The last few days had been cool but dry, and her scent could easily still linger. So I allowed Wilco to press forward to the highest concentration of smell, the rock fissure where her body had been discovered. I kept him on the lead, though, not wanting him to incur a repeat injury. When we reached the fissure, he sat down and looked expectantly my way.

I unhooked his leash and signaled for him to continue. Behind me, Doogan paced impatiently. "We should have begun at Dub's place and worked our way from there. That would have made more sense."

"I know what I'm doing."

"If he killed her at his place, he wouldn't have been able to carry her out this far. He would have dumped her closer."

"He's got an ATV." *As does half the population in the area.*

"And a truck." Doogan swiped at his hair and scanned the woods. "She could be anywhere. He could have driven up north and dumped her off the Chestoa Bridge."

"I doubt it. The cab of Dub's truck is small, so he would have had to use the bed to transport her. Maybe at night. But still, he would have had to drive through the trailer park and out on the main road with a body in the back of his truck. His place backs up to the edge of the woods. It makes more sense that he would have chosen to hide her out here. Less risk." My theory was thin, at best, but it was the only thing I had. I did know that there was no way my mother's body just appeared this far out from any civilization. Someone had to have hauled her in by ATV, or maybe even horseback.

I'd kept one eye on Wilco. Off lead, he wandered back and forth aimlessly and became distracted by a fleeting squirrel before racing back and pawing at my leg. He was trying to engage me. "Playtime?" he seemed to say. My heart, which had soared seconds ago when he'd successfully hit upon the previous scene, now plummeted. Wilco, once focused and driven, was looking soft in the field. But what did I expect? When was the last time he'd trained?

When was the last time I'd *trained?*

Overhead, the morning light gave way to rolling gray skies. A thunderhead was building, and so was my disgust with myself. *Stupid, stupid, stupid.* I thought about my lapse of judgment in waiting this long to conduct my own investigation of the scene. I should have been out here earlier, looking for tracks. And what had I been doing instead? Drowning my sorrows in a bottle. I'd thought about it the day I found my mother's body. I'd wondered at the time if the sheriff had set the boundaries of the scene wide enough to encompass possible ATV tracks leading into the area. Only, at the time, I didn't know it was my mother. I felt no connection to the case. No reason to insert myself in the investigation. Then, with everything else going on, I'd let it slip through the cracks. My dog wasn't the only one who'd become soft.

I threw my hand up and issued a firm signal for him to continue working. This time he didn't balk but bounded ahead, deeper into the trees, with his nose down and tail held high. Rain fell. I kept my head down and forged ahead. Wilco, oblivious to the weather, was fully engrossed in the search now: back hunched, tail extended, nose to the ground. Doogan and I maintained an unobtrusive distance.

"What's he doing?" Doogan whispered a few minutes later. Wilco had stopped to sniff at some scrubby brush and then lifted his nose toward the boughs of a pine tree. "Why's he sniffing up high? If Sheila's out here, she'd probably be buried, or at least on the ground."

"Tree branches and dense foliage sometimes trap odors that travel in the breeze. Sort of like a filter."

Doogan's next question came at me almost as a whisper. "What will she look like? If we find her, I mean?"

I hesitated, trying to decide how much to tell him. Most peoples' only experience with dead bodies is what they see on television. Reality couldn't be further from the truth. It only takes a short time for gasses and pressure to render a body unrecognizable. I once saw the flesh slide off a soldier's face as he was being hoisted onto a bag for transportation. It pooled on the ground like a puddle of overripe squash. The memory still haunts me. As do so many others.

Sheila had disappeared over three weeks ago. If we found her, it wouldn't be a pretty sight. I glanced Doogan's way, wondering how to explain or, more accurately, how to protect him from the brutality of what he might see. I was used to recovering bodies, even helping in the identification process, but someone else handled the death notifications. Dealing with grieving families was something I'd been spared in the past. Something I'd worked hard to avoid. I wasn't even sure where to begin, so I told him, "You won't recognize her."

We continued on in silence for another thirty minutes or so. Rain fell steadily now. My clothes felt heavy, and my drenched scarf was chafing my skin. I wanted to take it off but couldn't stand the idea of exposing my scar to Doogan, or to anyone. War had changed me. High-collared shirts, scarves—no matter how I tried to cover my damage, I'd never look the same again. Some people never seemed to change. I couldn't envision that Doogan had ever looked any different. Or Colm. Especially Colm. I thought back to Colm, the way he looked, still so good after all this time. And his hands. Big and strong and gentle. I'd thought about his hands a lot over the years. The way they'd touched me, caressed me . . . but that was the old me. The pretty, young, innocent girl I used to be. I was none of those things now.

I stomped ahead, pushed a glob of wet hair off my face, and tried to swallow down the acid rising in my stomach. How did Colm see me now? *As a used-up, disfigured drunk. A sinner.*

Doogan grabbed my arm. "Hold up."

I stopped. Over the drumming of the rain, I heard voices, low and masculine, coming from somewhere in the woods. I looked Doogan's way. "Just hikers, probably. A branch of the AT runs west of here. Or hunters." My eyes scanned the shadowy trees.

His grip on my arm tightened. "Let's head back. The weather's not all that great anyway."

"It's just a little rain. It won't affect Wilco's ability to sniff out—"

"Let's go. Now, Brynn."

His eyes bulged against the sharp angles of his cheekbones. He was scared. I remembered his prior warning about the woods. "What's going on, Doogan?"

He pulled me back the way we'd come, then hesitated. The voices were getting louder, closer. The words seemed foreign. Doogan's eyes darted about. "We need to get out of here. Now."

"Okay. Let me get my dog, and we'll—"

"Leave him," Doogan hissed. "He'll find his way home."

I batted him away. "No. No way. I'm not leaving him." I wasn't sure what was up with Doogan, but something had him scared. And I sure as hell wasn't going to leave my dog behind to face whatever it was that had Doogan freaked out.

I started for Wilco. But Doogan lunged forward and clamped one arm around my abdomen and his other hot and salty-tasting hand on my mouth. He pulled me backward, against his own body, and dragged me toward a nearby ravine.

I struggled against his grip, pushing his arms and kicking my legs back toward his shins. Out of the corner of my eye, I could see the back of Wilco's body as he hunched over, sniffing under a nearby log. He was in his zone, engrossed in his task and oblivious to all around him, with the added hindrance of being deaf. I needed to get to my dog, but Doogan's arms felt like a vice grip around my body.

"I said leave the stupid dog!" His words felt hot against my neck as he strained to move me. "There's no time to—"

I rammed my head backward, connecting to his face with a sickening *thunk*.

Doogan dropped me instantly and sank to his knees, clenching his nose. Muffled cries escaped from his twisted mouth. I ignored him and went for Wilco. In a flash, I reached him, clipped his lead, and pulled him toward the ravine.

Hide!

I slid behind a fallen tree and pressed my belly into the muddy ground. Instinct and training had kicked in simultaneously as *danger* ignited my brain. I could handle Doogan, but whatever had a man like him totally panicked had to spell severe danger.

Wilco lay prone beside me. The voices were moving closer now, and the words were undeniably foreign. I looked for Doogan. He was off a ways, hunkered behind a low outcrop of rocks and still holding his nose. I pulled my eyes from him and scanned my surroundings in search of a weapon, a good-sized stick or a heavy rock. Something to even up the odds, just in case there was a confrontation.

The noise and commotion grew louder, and I realized the men were crossing through the trees about fifty feet away. They seemed oblivious to our presence, talking among themselves and moving confidently through the woods. They knew where they were going. They'd taken this path before.

Wilco caught sight of them and growled. I reached over and squeezed the back of his neck, silencing him, but not before one of the men heard the sound. He turned and looked in our direction. He was short, stocky, and clad in tactical rain gear. He carried a heavy pack and a military-style rifle, which he waved across the breadth of the woods. I prayed that Wilco wouldn't move. A few seconds passed. A wormy, sulfurous smell stung my nostrils. I fought the urge to shift position as gunk and mud oozed around the waistband of my pants and the legs of an insect prickled the skin behind my ear. Then another guy appeared. This one was taller, but dressed the same. The two men exchanged a couple of foreign words, glanced around, and continued through the woods.

The tenseness in my muscles drained. I dared a glance toward Doogan, who motioned for me to stay put. I did. It was another five minutes before we crawled out from our positions.

An hour later, Doogan and I were in his trailer, faced off across his kitchen counter. We'd walked the couple miles back in silence, Doogan casting furtive glances through the woods as we trekked, and me holding my tongue—and temper—until we got back to his place. My sweatshirt hung heavy with mud on my body, and thanks to Wilco, I smelled like a wet dog. "How did you know about those men?" I blurted out.

Doogan used a dish towel to wipe at a smear of dried blood under his nose. "I was at Mack's a couple weeks ago. It's a bar over in McCreary."

"Yeah. I know it."

"There were some guys there. Hispanics. I'd never seen them before, but I recognized their tats. Gang tats." Doogan tore off his soaked shirt and ran the towel around the back of his neck and down his torso. He had a "tat" of his own. A darkly inked serpent head, wicked and dangerous-looking, was visible just above the edge of his waistband. I found myself staring at the image, wondering if the serpent's tail coiled around his . . . I looked away. Despite the heat radiating through my lower body, I shivered.

Doogan was still talking. "I recognized the symbols. Surenos. They're a gang tied in with Los Zetas."

I knew next to nothing about gangs. "Zetas?"

"Mexican drug cartel," he explained. He poured what was left from this morning's coffee into a mug and popped it into the microwave. He offered me some.

I waved it off. "No thanks. Cartel? Are you sure? In this area?"

"They're everywhere." He grasped the mug with both hands. "I grew up in a small village in South Carolina, just over the Georgia border, maybe twenty miles from Augusta. I hated it there. Went a little crazy during my teen years. You know. Looking for excitement and all that. I left home and ended up taking to the streets for a while."

"And you got mixed up with a cartel?" Harris had said that Doogan had a criminal record. At the time, I didn't think it was any of my business. My mistake. I should have made it my business.

"No. Not directly."

Not directly. What does that mean?

Doogan fidgeted for a second, furling the dish towel through his hands a few times before tossing it aside. Then he opened one of the cabinets and pulled down a bottle of whiskey, adding a shot to his coffee. I stared at the cup and swallowed hard, swiping at the moist corners of my mouth. "Harris said you did jail time." I tore my eyes from the cup and met his gaze, waiting for his response.

He took a long sip before answering. "Harris has a big mouth." He put down his mug and threw up his hand. "Look. I did some stupid things. And I paid for it. It's over. Done."

"Okay. Fine. But I still don't understand how you knew about these guys in the woods. You heard them speaking Spanish, and you just assumed they were the same guys you saw at Mack's?"

"No. About a week ago, maybe a couple days before you got here, I was out in the woods."

"Why?"

His jaw muscle twitched. "I'd been watching Costello. I'd seen him wander out into the woods a couple times."

I remember seeing the binoculars on Doogan's windowsill.

"I got to thinkin' that maybe his trips into the woods had something to do with my sister."

"So you followed him?"

"Just once. At a distance. I stuck with him for a mile or so, but then lost him around Settlers' Gorge. I was on my way back when I heard something in the woods. Just like today."

"The guys from the bar."

"I don't know. I didn't actually see them. But I heard them talking. I recognized a name they mentioned—*El Tio*."

"El Tio." *Uncle?* Way back when, I took a semester of high school Spanish before dropping it midway through. No need for a Pavee girl to learn Spanish. That's what Gramps had said anyway.

"It's the name of a drug Lord. Out of Mexico. I think the thugs in the woods were drug runners."

"And you think Costello's mixed up with them?"

"I don't think so. I can't see the connection. What would a Pavee be doing with a Hispanic gang?" He raised his chin. "As much as I hate the guy, he's no wetback's flunky."

No matter where a group of people stood in society, they could always find someone else they believed were beneath them. For some Pavees, Mexicans held that honor. For that reason, I had to agree—the idea of any Traveller working with a Mexican drug cartel made no sense. But I didn't believe in making assumptions either. "How can you be sure?"

"Because I've spent some time with drug dealers." He angled his body away from mine and lowered his eyes. "I did seven years on drug charges."

CHAPTER 9

I found Zee behind the Sleep Easy's front desk beside a bored young desk clerk, filling two foam cups with coffee from a metal thermos. She handed one to me. "You're late," she said.

I looked at the wall clock. "No. It's just now noon." I took a sip and cringed: bottom of the pot sludge. Took me right back to MRE (Meal, Ready to Eat) coffee. Tasted like crap, but when you've been on twenty-four-hour standby, waiting on reconnaissance, bagged black joe was the day's salvation. I gagged down another swig. Hard telling how many toilets needed scrubbing today.

"Noon is when we start cleaning. Status meeting's at 11:45."

"What status? It's just us."

Zee glanced to the side. The young woman working the front desk slapped her magazine shut and came out from behind the counter. I looked her way and raised my brows. She was twenty something, with stringy blond hair pulled back into a low ponytail. She'd paired the requisite Sleep Easy polo with a skin-tight pair of leggings that left nothing to the imagination.

"Brynn, this is Maybelle." Zee's voice was tight. "She works the desk on weekends."

Maybelle chomped down on her gum and gave me a nasty once-over, her gaze stalling on my scarf. "Do I know you from somewhere?"

"Brynn's been away, in the Army," Zee offered.

"Marines, actually."

"Whatever." Zee shrugged. "Anyways, you don't know her, Maybelle."

Maybelle was still staring at me, her penciled-on brows knitted together. Her eyes popped, then narrowed to tiny slits, hate radiating from her pores. But I had no idea why. I looked away, shuffled my feet, and took another sip of the coffee. Anything to distract me from Maybelle's incessant glare. What was her problem?

Zee opened a cabinet behind the desk and lifted the laundry room key from the pegboard. She shoved it my way, casting a nervous glance at Maybelle. "Take this. I got the list already, so I'm goin' to start on the rooms. I'll be needin' the sheets that are in the dryers. And if you could put a couple more loads in, but be quick about it. Saturday's our busiest day. Then I'll fill you in on what needs to be done." She glanced out the office window. "Where's that dog of yours?"

"Same place as yesterday. Under the tree."

Zee smiled. "Good. Brought an extra treat for the fella today."

Maybelle was still glaring at me. "You brought a dog with you?" Her voice hardened. "That's against the rules."

Zee stiffened. "So is cuttin' out fifteen minutes early, or spending the whole day on social media. Doesn't seem to stop you none."

Maybelle's nostrils flared, her eyes still on me. "Wait 'til Drake hears about this. He won't like it."

I clenched my coffee cup. "He already knows. And he's fine with it." We locked stares. I tried to keep my face expressionless, but anger swelled inside me like a tidal wave.

The corner of Maybelle's mouth twitched. She liked getting to me. "We'll see."

Zee tugged at my arm, and I followed her outside.

"What the hell's her problem?" I asked.

"You don't know?"

"No. No, I don't know. What?"

Zee had trouble meeting my gaze. "She hates your type." She pulled aside her long dark braid and fingered the crystal hanging around her neck. "And my type. Most types, actually. Except her type."

"Fat bitches, you mean?"

Zee cracked a smile at that.

I glanced back at the office and then down at myself. "How'd she know? About me, I mean?" It wasn't like I was wearing a multi-layered crimson ankle-length skirt with a laced-up, off-the-shoulder peasant blouse—which I doubted any woman in Bone Gap even owned anyway. That was Hollywood's vision of us, as if we hadn't yet found shopping malls. I was wearing the usual: jeans, a bit worn, I guessed, but not trashy, the requisite polo work shirt with the collar turned up and a light scarf around my neck. My black hair hardly identified me with my red-haired Irish ancestors either.

Zee dipped her chin and raised her brows.

I sighed. "The news?"

"Uh-huh. They've been playin' it over and over. It's gettin' folks all stirred up. There's been talk."

"Talk? Of what?"

"Of running y'all off. Right now they're lookin' for legal ways to do it. Zoning and sanitation laws, that type of thing. Or maybe shutting down your access off the main highway."

"Shutting down our road?"

She tilted her head sympathetically. "It's just talk, Brynn. That's all. And not everybody feels the same way."

"Maybelle sure does."

"True. But I should warn ya, that new night manager that Mr. Drake hired is the same way. Maybe more hateful than Maybelle."

"I haven't met him yet."

"You probably won't. He doesn't come on 'til seven." She fingered her necklace some more. "You'd best stay clear of him. He won't like it much that you're one of them gypsies."

I forced a smile. "Thanks for the warning."

The laundry room was cramped, with no ventilation. I crammed a load into the washer and then opened the dryer to pull out the finished sheets. Less than a minute into folding them, I was half-buzzed on detergent fumes, and my temples throbbed from the whirring of the machines. The worst, though, was the sourness rising from my gut. Maybelle had caused that. Maybelle and Zee's dire warning about the townsfolk.

I'm not sure why it bothered me. I should have been used to prejudice by now. Sly looks, name calling, exclusion . . . I'd grown up with it as a Pavee in public school, dealt with it as a woman navigating male territory in the Marines, and still faced it from both sides, settled folks and my own people. My own grandmother even. "You're on their side," she'd said. *Their side. I'm so sick of sides.*

But in this rural area, ignorance prevailed, and prejudice ran as thick as blood in the veins of those who had rooted themselves in the backwoods hollers of these Appalachian hills. I'd run up against it my whole life, especially now as I dealt with the local sheriff's department. Like today, when I called to report what I'd seen out in the woods this morning. I was put through to Harris. As soon as I identified myself, he became abrupt and dismissive. Surely all I'd seen was some good ol' boys hunting. Never mind that they spoke Spanish or carried military-grade weapons. What did I know? In his mind, I was just a stupid gypsy.

I wrapped up folding just as the next load of sheets finished in the wash. I transferred them to the dryers and then gathered up a batch of soiled sheets from a nearby hamper. Like I had on the first load, I opened each sheet briefly so crumpled tissues, spent condoms, and half-empty lubricant bottles could fall out before they got laundered into shreds or oozed their contents into an ungrateful washer. Sleep Sleazy was the right nickname for this place. Thankfully, though, nothing gross was in this load.

But something else fell to the floor.

I bent down and retrieved a folded newspaper clipping, started to toss it in the garbage can, then stopped when the headline grabbed my attention: LOCAL MAN'S BODY FOUND IN NOLICHUCKY RIVER; BONE GAP RESIDENT SOUGHT FOR QUESTIONING.

That sour feeling from earlier now burned in my throat. *Another dead person? And the cops are looking for one of us?*

But this paper was old, yellowed and fringed around the edges. Smoothing it over the table, I leaned forward to read, my eyes catching on a familiar name: Drake. But not Johnny, my boss. This was Billy Drake. According to the article, the body of Billy Drake, eighteen years of age, was discovered by a hiker along the banks of the Nolichucky. Billy had been a suspect in connection with a local armed robbery of a drugstore and the shooting death of the store owner. Police were seeking the whereabouts of his girlfriend, an unidentified Bone Gap woman. She was wanted for questioning.

The article was clipped from the center of a page so there was no date, but there were a few ads on the back side. One was for a new Ford Taurus, listed at 10K. New car prices hadn't been that low since . . . when? Twenty, twenty-five years ago? So, if Billy was eighteen at the time of his death, that would have put him somewhere around forty now. Johnny had to be in his fifties. That meant Billy and Johnny could be brothers. Or paternal cousins, maybe.

But why did this clipping show up now? Maybe Johnny kept articles like these around, and this one just happened to slip out of his pocket. I glanced at the laundry hamper. But why then was it mixed in with the soiled bedlinens?

"Got those sheets ready?"

I turned to see Zee standing in the doorway. I quickly slipped the article into my jeans pocket, snatched up pile of clean sheets, and hurried back to work.

I whipped into the vet clinic lot a little after 6:00. Zee and I had run late on the rooms, not finishing until well after 5:00, at which time she left to go home and fix supper for her daughter.

The only other car in the lot was a sleek black Trans Am, a late 1970s model, but fully restored and in mint shape, with chrome wheels and custom painting. I couldn't remember what Styles drove, but if this was his, he had good taste in cars.

The closer we got to the front door, the more stressed Wilco became and the harder he panted. His tongue dangled like a wet pink rag from his mouth. I bent down to comfort him just as a young man stepped out of the clinic. He was what Gran would call a girly man, slight build, soft jaw, hair combed just a little too nicely. The braided leather bracelets and gold earrings weren't helping his cause either.

"If you're here for Doctor Styles, he's already gone for the day," he said. "Something I can help you with?" He carried a plastic crate in his hands. It jerked and hissed.

Wilco forgot his earlier woes and snapped into play mode. Or maybe kill mode. Wilco and cats didn't mix well. I tightened my grip on his leash. "We're here for a med refill."

"The doctor will have to take care of that." His brows furrowed. "Are you Brynn?"

I blinked. "Uh . . . yes."

"Eamon. Meg's boyfriend." He put the crate on the ground and held out his hand. His eyes slid toward my dog, who was eyeing the downed crate with too much eagerness for my tastes. "Wilco?" I nodded, and pulled Wilco back to a "sit" position, and he continued, empathy clouding his features as he noticed the nub that used to be Wilco's leg. Then his eyes settled on my neck with the same sympathetic look he'd just given my dog. "It's good to finally meet you. Meg's told me all about you and Wilco."

All? Like in everything? Prickles of sweat broke out under my scarf. *This is silly.* It was only natural that Meg shared stuff with him. Personal stuff. I tugged at my collar and rolled my neck. *My* personal stuff.

"Molly's going to a new home today." He picked up the carrier and stepped over to the Trans Am, slid it into the back seat. Wilco noticeably slumped in disappointment. "She's a rescue cat. Been here a while. Had a whole litter of kittens a month ago."

"How sweet." My voice sounded insincere, even to me. I wasn't a big fan of cats. Just another way Wilco and I were alike. "Is this your car?"

"Yeah."

"It's incredible." He beamed, making him look even younger. Somehow I wouldn't have put this guy behind the wheel of a muscle car, but whatever. It was his. And it was cool. I could kinda see what might have attracted Meg. She was always a sucker for a guy with cool wheels. Nomadic genes and all that.

"So, you're working for Doctor Styles?" I asked.

"Yeah. Winter mostly. Only after the travelling season. Been doing it for a couple years now."

"And Doc's okay with . . . ?"

"With us Pavees? Yeah. He's a good guy. I like working for him." He fiddled with his bracelets and cleared his throat. "I was at your place the other day. Paid my respects to your grandparents. How're they holding up?"

"It's difficult."

He lowered his gaze. "When's the funeral Mass?"

"Uh . . . I'm not sure. I don't think Gran's finalized the plans." Or maybe she had. I'd come in late after my conversation with Doogan the night before. All the lights had been out, and the house was still, except for the hushed sobs coming from behind Gran's bedroom door. I should have gone to her, but I couldn't. Our earlier confrontation still stung.

The sound of another car drew Eamon's attention. His face lit up. I turned to see Meg pulling up in her compact. She hopped out, still wearing her work uniform, but her face glowed, and her red curls bounced as she headed toward us.

"Hey, y'all." She leaned into Eamon. I glanced away as they kissed. "Thought I'd see if you wanted to take me to dinner." Then to me, "I didn't expect to find you here, Brynn. Glad you two have met. Want to go grab a bite with us?"

"Thanks. Think I'll pass, though." Nothing like being the third wheel. A dandy, his pretty Irish lass, and her maimed cousin. *Great fun.* "I just popped by to get some more pills for Wilco."

The pockets of her work apron jingled as she bent down and planted a smooch between my dog's ears. "Why, hello, sweetie." She straightened and met my gaze. "How's he doing?"

"Better. The medicine seems to help. He's been working hard, though. We're helping Kevin Doogan look—"

"Kevin Doogan?" Eamon's focus shifted my way.

"You know him?"

"Not really. He's new around here. But I heard he's trouble." He frowned and looked at Meg.

"I've heard the same thing," she said. "What are you doing with him?"

"Sheila's still missing. He's asked me to search the woods for her body."

Meg bristled. "And you agreed?"

"Wilco is a cadaver dog. It's what he does. It's what we do."

Their eyes stayed wide, unblinking. What was the big deal anyway?

After a beat or two, Eamon spoke up, his voice taking on a soothing cadence, like he was trying to pacify a crying baby. "I can imagine what you went through over there."

No, you can't.

He added, "It's gotta be tough being back here. I understand."

I hated it when people said that. They didn't understand crap. *Especially not this guy. He'd last all of two seconds in the sandbox.*

"And I know you've been struggling . . ."

Struggling? Meg must've told him about the drinking too. What else had she told him? I shot a look her way.

Her eyes widened. "But that's understandable. With all you've gone through . . . Don't be mad at me, cuz. I'm just concerned, that's all. It's been less than a week since you found your mom's body out there in those very woods. Now you're traipsing around out there with a . . . a *graansha*."

Graansha meant "stranger." I kicked at the stones under my feet. My own condescending cousin felt more like a stranger to me than ex-jailbird Doogan. But she was family, she was concerned, and I knew I should be glad for it. I looked up. "It's fine, Meg. He's fine. I don't feel threatened by him."

Eamon jumped back in, "He's had problems with some of the members of the clan."

I glared at him. I could understand Meg's concern, but what was it to him? And since when was the clan the deciding factor on who was dangerous? "Like who? You mean Dub? The man with a known mean streak? The man Doogan's sister was told *by the clan* to marry? Now she's missing. What would you do, Eamon?" I'd raised my voice a couple of octaves and sissified his name. "Just let your sister's body rot in the woods?"

Meg flinched, and a wave of regret washed over me. But it was too late. A bitter silence fell between us.

Eamon shifted and reached protectively for Meg's hand, giving it a reassuring squeeze. My eyes were drawn to the way their hands intertwined, palms together, fingers interlaced.

I felt all alone in the world.

Meg broke the silence. She spoke her next words softly; still the message hit home hard. "I think you need to give all this a break. Folks are talking, Brynn. They've seen you"—her voice was a whisper now—"out drinking. Gran needs you, Brynn. Gramps' illness and now the death of her only child. It's too much for her to bear alone. I think—"

I held up my hand. "Enough. I get it." I tugged Wilco's leash toward my car. "I'm going to go home now. Do my *duty*." I spit out the last word.

"Brynn! Stop. Come back. I didn't mean . . ."

But I kept going.

I drove toward Bone Gap on autopilot, my mind stuck on what they'd said. Not so much their concerns about Doogan. They were right. What did I really know about Kevin Doogan besides the fact that he had served time on drug charges? Nothing. But dangerous? A killer even? No way.

What hurt was that Meg had questioned my loyalty to Gran. And if what she hinted at was true, other people questioned it too. But what hurt worse was that look of pity on her face. I didn't need her pity. Anybody's pity. The poor damaged drunk, they were probably saying. Unable to pull herself from the bottle long enough to help her own kin. Meg and everyone else saw only part of the picture: two respected members of the clan grieving the loss of their only child; and Gran, poor Gran, bearing the burden of this unfathomable loss along with the certain, impending death of her terminally ill husband; and then there was me.

Me, the black sheep of the clan, the prodigal granddaughter returned as a washed-up drunk, looking for a handout to cover her own life's failings, but unwilling or unable to help bear the family burdens.

But what Meg didn't see, what nobody saw, was the history of betrayal and lies that had brought me to this point. My loyalty to Gran? What about her loyalty to me? Gran, the only person I'd ever loved, the only one who I felt had ever loved me . . . how could she have let her own daughter die in my young eyes? Only to have me find her body . . .

I shuddered, and a hard underbelly of anger tightened my gut. I could no more provide Gran with the comfort she needed now than I could grieve the loss of the mother I'd never known. And now the cousin who was like a sister was talking to someone like Eamon about me as if I were nothing but a . . .

I slammed my palm against the steering wheel. "Screw them!" I didn't need their pity. I swiped at my cheek and blinked away the hurt and betrayal. A sudden curve jerked me from my thoughts. My grip tightened, and my foot slammed against the brakes as I cranked a hard left. My back tires skidded dangerously close to the guard rail, and a sickening thump sounded as Wilco slid into the passenger door. He yelped and dove onto the floorboard, where he cowered beneath the dash. I slowed the car, my hands wet against the wheel, my heart pounding against my chest. The blood coursing through my veins turned my muscles into a thousand hot firecrackers exploding against my skin. I swallowed hard, forcing saliva down through my anxiety-constricted throat.

Managing another mile, I pulled into a scenic overlook and slammed my car into park. I tried to crank down my window, remembered it didn't work, threw open the door and gulped in the clean mountain air. I shoved my trembling hand deep into my pockets, where my fingertips brushed against a couple of loose pills. I kept them around like a kid would a security blanket. Sinking back into the car's seat, I popped one into my mouth and wished for a swig of Jack to wash it down.

Wilco crawled out from his hiding place and nudged me with his snout. I opened my arms and pulled him close, feeling his body tremble against my side. His wet nose worked its way behind my ear, cold and ticklish against the sensitive skin under my scarf. "Hey, boy, you're okay. Take it easy." But his nails clawed my front side as he struggled to wedge himself between me and the steering wheel. I reached down and pulled the recline lever, sending my seat collapsing backward with a *whoosh* and a *thunk*. Wilco clamored over the console and pressed the full weight of his body against mine. I put my mouth to his ear, willing his deaf ears to understand the mantra I repeated over and over. "We're going to be okay, boy. I promise. We'll be okay."

After a while, I felt Wilco's breathing quiet, and so did mine. The pill had wormed its way into my gut, softening the knot, threaded its way along my muscles, smoothing their taut anxiety. Outside, a hint of mist settled over the valley as the sun slipped toward the horizon, taking with it the last slivers of daylight. A dark purple curtain was descending on the world. And on my mind. A peaceful darkness. I welcomed it.

CHAPTER 10

"Sheriff's here. He wants to talk to you."

I jolted upright, pushed Wilco off my legs, stood, and blinked a few times. Gran stood in my bedroom. I was home and in my room, although I had no recollection of driving back the night before. I glanced at the clock: barely 5:00 A.M.

Gran hovered nearby in her robe with a scowl on her face as I kicked around a few dirty clothes looking for a sweatshirt to throw over yesterday's work uniform, which I was still wearing. The obvious question hung in the air: *Where were you last night?* But she didn't ask it, and I didn't offer any explanation. Mostly because I didn't want to admit—to her or myself—that I must've driven down Settlers' Mountain in a drug-induced fog. One of these days, for sure, I was going to get myself killed.

"Sheriff's here. He wants to talk to you," she repeated.

"Yeah, I heard you." I pulled on a gray USMC sweatshirt and ran my fingertips through the tangles in my hair. She stood still, frowning. I stared at her. "Could you tell him I'll be right out?" She huffed, spun on her heels, and shut the door behind her with a thud. I cringed. And cringed again when Wilco nudged his nose against my leg and let out a whine that rang in my tender brain loud enough to breach the sound barrier.

I gently pushed him aside and retrieved a cotton scarf from the same pile. I gave it a quick sniff, tucked it around the edges of my sweatshirt, and made my way to the front room. Gran was leaning against the wall with her arms crossed over her chest. Pusser was still outside. "You didn't ask him in?"

She mumbled something about no *muskers*—a not-so-polite word some Pavees used for "police"—allowed in her house. She glared as if blaming me for the early-morning intrusion from the settled authorities.

I ignored her and opened the door. Wilco shot out around my legs, barely making it down the steps before squatting in the front yard. Pusser looked on with interest. "Can't say I ever saw a three-legged dog take a dump." He turned back to me, a smirk playing on the edge of his mouth. "Guess shit's shit, no matter how many legs the dog's got."

"Do you have something besides my dog's shit on your mind? Like more news about my mother, Sheriff?"

His expression sobered. "No. Afraid something else has come up."

"What?"

He lowered his voice and leaned in. For a second, my eye got stuck on a gap in his shirt. He'd missed a button. "Just get your dog and come with me," he said.

My gaze snapped upward. "A body?"

He chomped down hard on his toothpick. "A hiker just found what we think is a human foot. Along the trail up by Dry Bone Creek. Harris is at the scene. He says it's small. Looks female. Could be Sheila Costello." He relayed this message in typical cop fashion, with little or no emotion.

Behind me, Gran made a little sound, like a cat mewing, and then shuffled away, probably to digest this horrible turn of events. Part of me wanted to excuse myself and check on her, just to make sure she was okay, but my work instinct had already kicked in, and my full attention became focused on the pending task, cataloging what I'd need to take and to do.

I took a half step forward, craned my neck, and looked toward Doogan's trailer. It was a little after 5:00 A.M. Doogan and I were scheduled to meet up at 6:00. I knew he'd be mad when I didn't show, but if he found out about this, he'd want to come along. That was the last thing I wanted.

Pusser shifted his stance. "You gonna help, or not?"

"I'll be right out. I need to get a few things together." I shut the door in his face and hurried to retrieve Wilco's vest and my field pack. When I passed back through the house, Gran was at the kitchen table, hunched over her coffee. I went to her, but she kept her head down, not looking my way. From the back, with her elbows pulled in and shoulders bent forward, she looked tiny and frail. A hollow feeling formed in my stomach as remorse washed over me. I leaned in, wrapped my arms around her, and brushed my lips against the back of her neck, that spot where course gray curls met her bare skin. She still smelled like sleep and yesterday's chicken stew and the same cheap floral-scented hair shampoo she'd used for years. I breathed it all in, as a plethora of a thousand tender memories threatened to reduce me to tears. I pulled back and gathered myself. "I gotta go, Gran. The sheriff needs me."

She didn't speak. Not even a nod. Nothing.

I shouldered my pack and headed for the door.

"Wait!"

I turned back.

"Doc Styles stopped by yesterday evening with these." She shoved a prescription bottle toward me. "Just in case Wilco needs some this morning."

I exhaled and smiled. "Thanks, Gran." I leaned in to take the pills, and her hand rose slowly to my cheek.

"*Lackeen*?"

"Yes, Gran."

"Be careful."

I kissed her cheek and headed for the door.

The interior of Pusser's Tahoe held a mixture of smells: bitter coffee, yeasty bread, and a slight undercut of stale cigarette smoke. And now hot doggie breath. I reached over my shoulder and pushed Wilco's head back.

"Want some?" Pusser pointed at two foam cups and a greasy bag on the middle console.

I eagerly took a drink of coffee, the hot liquid searing the grit off my tongue, and pulled a chocolate doughnut from the bag.

"Hung over?"

I tossed him a sideways glance. "What all do you know so far?" I liked to know what I was walking into. And subjecting my dog to.

"Hiker's name is Trent Stevens. Weekend warrior type. Working his way toward Greeneville on a branch of the AT. He left the trail to take a piss. Turns out he was urinating on a severed foot. Harris says he's freaked out."

"That's it. Just a foot. Nothing else?"

"So far. The trail runs through a gully. The trees and shrub are pretty dense, even this time of year. It's going to be hard searching."

"Usually is." Dense forests, windblown desert sands, blasted concrete and rebar . . . there was no such thing as an easy search.

I licked chocolate icing from my fingers. Good thing I'd packed a thirty-foot tracking lead. I extracted a plastic container of dog food from my pack, turned, and put it on the seat next to Wilco. Little bits of kibble peppered the seat as Wilco chomped away. Add the smell of slobbered kibble to the Tahoe's brew.

Pusser wrinkled his nose and glanced in his review mirror. "What are you doing?"

"Feeding my dog. He's not going to work on an empty stomach." And he couldn't take his meds on an empty stomach either.

Pusser grumbled but didn't protest. He asked about the guys I'd reported seeing out in the woods the day before. I spent the next fifteen minutes bringing him up to speed. Eventually, the road wound down into a valley, and we pulled off the main road and into the trailhead parking area. Harris's cruiser and a couple other civilian vehicles were already present. Hikers probably.

We parked, and I gathered my patrol pack and ran through a mental checklist: bug spray, nylon rope, basic first-aid supplies, water, water bag for Wilco, and a pair of gaiters, just in case, and an extra leg wrap for Wilco. I'd clipped my knife, a Smith & Wesson MP, to my belt. A good knife, but I wished it was my regular sidearm—a Beretta M9 pistol, standard issue. I'd fought it at first, the bulky grip a little too large for my smallish hands. But after hours and hours on the range, it'd grown on me. I became efficient—no, good. Damn good with it. But the Marines didn't let us take our toys home with us. Too bad, I thought, as my eyes skimmed over the trailhead and strained against the inky depth of the woods. I missed my gun. 'Course, they didn't always let us take our dogs home with us either. I looked toward Wilco. Thankfully, I'd won that battle.

I secured Wilco's orange work vest, double-checked his leg wrap, and slid one of the pills down his throat under the guise of a piece of jerky. He normally fought pills, but the work vest already had him focused. His ears pricked, his whiskers twitched, and he made long, drawn-out mewling sounds. Anticipation coursed through him. He was eager for the job. Normally, I would be too. Nothing was more rewarding than working a search with my dog. But overseas, in a remote location, I could keep my emotions disengaged. This was home. And there was a personal connection to the victim. Usually, the challenge of the hunt, the promise of a find, is what kept me going. Today, the only promise I could count on was that of pain and grief for someone I knew and had grown to like. I shouldered my pack and tried for a calm, confident composure despite the dread creeping over me.

Pusser didn't have a pack. He did have boots, though. But other than that, just khaki pants, a standard work button-down shirt, and a lightweight windbreaker. He pulled the radio hooked to his belt. "10-97. ETA twenty minutes."

"Roger that."

He turned to me. "Harris is about a mile and a half in. Let's get going."

It was easily ten degrees cooler inside the woods, and an early-morning mist still hung in the air, swirling around my head and clinging to my face like a cool mask. The familiar damp smells of the forest rose to my nostrils as I kicked up layers of decaying leaves and dry twigs. Next to me, Pusser gasped for air, the extra ten or so pounds of his utility belt adding to the already twenty-pound spare tire he carried around his midsection. He'd tossed his toothpick a quarter mile into the hike, his lips having gone slack from sucking air. Now his face was flushed, and despite the coolness, he shed his windbreaker, revealing growing sweat stains under his armpits.

"Stuff like this never goes down in town. Always out here in the middle of nowhere." He looked around. "Where's the dog?"

"Two o'clock."

Pusser's head swiveled to the right. "Doesn't know how to heel, does he?"

"You want some pom-pomed poodle show dog prancing at our heels or a trained HRD dog?" I didn't bother to look at Pusser. I was used to working with people who had some grasp of the job Wilco and I did. Obviously, that was not the case here. I'd kept Wilco off the lead on purpose. The trail we walked traversed a lower portion of the woods; the trees were thicker here. The ideal spot for hiding a body. A lazy murderer might have dumped the body close to the trailhead, where it could be ravaged by a bear or coyote and dragged deeper into the woods. I explained all this to Pusser. "Don't worry," I finished. "If there's something out there, he'll find it."

"You're awfully confident in that dog. You do know that the body's probably been out here for weeks."

"Wilco's trained for a wide spectrum of decomposition. He can trace it and handle it. Better than some deputies." That shut Pusser up.

And conditions were perfect for tracking. The sun was just beginning to heat up the ground, effecting a rise of any scent that might be present. A couple hours more and that same sunlight would be too intense, burning off scents and adding another obstacle to the search. We were working in the best possible window of discovery. If it was out there, Wilco would find it. Yes, I felt confident. Very confident.

About Wilco, that was. Not so much about me. Doogan, I figured, had probably waited for me back at his place. When I didn't show, he most likely went looking for me at Gran's place and learned that a body part had been found. His worst nightmare was about to come true, and I was going to be a part of it: the bearer of bad news and principal witness to his grief. That made me squirm, but I swallowed back my apprehensions and kept my emotions in check. Wilco could read me like a book.

I focused instead on my strategy. If Wilco couldn't pick up a scent trail from the crime scene, I'd have to make a decision. Guide his search to the thick underbrush or stick alongside the trail. It depended. Did the victim come into the woods alive? Was she on the run from her attacker? In that case, she'd likely be found not far from the trail. People being chased don't instinctively run into impenetrable woods. They want to escape.

The fastest, easiest escape route was the trail. If, however, she had been killed and dumped, her body would most likely be hidden in the shrubby undergrowth or buried in a shallow grave and covered by logs and other forest debris.

Then there were external factors: vultures, crows, raccoons, and, I was guessing in this case, bears, which meant dragging. Exposure weighed in too. Depending on how long she'd been out here, we might be looking for nothing more than minimal tissue and bones. I'd know more once we got to the foot they'd found. If they had found a foot, it meant at least she wasn't further gone, decomposed beyond recognition, and reduced to leftover acidic residue showing as nothing more than a brownish stain on the already brown forest carpet. Like soggy brown bread. *Brown bread.* Death was death, no matter where it happened, here or in a far-off desert. Death doesn't discriminate between young and old, Pavee and settled. We all boiled down to the same biological matter. Putrification had no prejudices.

I shuddered. Again, I was glad that Doogan wasn't with us.

"Up there." Pusser pointed ahead, to where Harris and another man sat on the ground.

The hiker was the picture-perfect outdoorsman. Ruddy complexion, but still handsome, with just enough facial hair to look rugged but not sloppy. He was dressed in expensive, brand-name gear. His boots weren't even scuffed. One of those types who carefully cultivated and maintained their image. Or at least he did before discovering a rotting appendage. As soon as he saw the sheriff, he blubbered like an idiot, pointing behind him toward the ground and near where Harris now stood. Pusser ignored him and pushed by to a clump of tree trunks wound in crime-scene tape. "Anyone move anything?"

"No, sir."

"Did you puke this time?"

Harris's eyes darted to me, then focused on Pusser again. "No, sir."

"Good to hear."

A ways down the trail, Wilco broke through the cluster of trees and came toward the crime-taped area with his nose high in the air. He'd hit on the scent of the foot, but not before coming to this site. I looked to where Pusser stood and then up the steep ravine beyond. Wilco went straight to the foot, sat down, and looked at me expectantly—his alert. I motioned for him to come to my side, to avoid stepping into the taped area myself, clipped his lead, and pulled him away before rewarding him for the find.

Dropping to my knees in front of him, I rubbed my hands back and forth along his head and placed my face alongside his. Then I worked a hand down to his chest. He rolled to the ground and onto his back for a generous belly rub—Wilco's ultimate reward.

Harris observed our ritual of playful tussling with a hardened expression. Undoubtedly, he still held a grudge from our last encounter. His attitude worried me. A man so set in his prejudices could easily jeopardize even the most cut-and-dried cases.

Pusser was still looking at the appendage. "It looks female to me. The bones are too small to belong to a man."

I tethered Wilco's lead to a nearby tree trunk and joined Pusser. We squatted just outside the crime-scene tape and examined the body part. A black, thin layer of skin clung to the bones. I'd seen enough dead bodies to have a general idea about the decomposition cycle, and I knew this type of preservation of skin usually occurred in dry climates. I'd seen it a lot in the Middle East, where the hot, arid air sucks the moisture out of the skin so fast it shrink-wraps the bones. Sort of like those vacuum sealers they sell on late-night infomercials for meat and fresh food preservation. It'd been cooler since I'd arrived home. But if she was killed back when she went missing, then dumped, that would track with the typical hot, dry spells of late summer. Her skin might have lost its moisture more quickly than it could decompose, a sort of mummifying by heat. We'd know more after the pathology exam.

I stood. "This foot was probably fresh when it was dragged here."

Pusser stuck a toothpick in his mouth. "How's that?"

I pointed to the patch of dead vegetation outlining the foot, like a brown chalk line. "The fluids that purge from our tissues are nitrogen heavy. The nitrogen kills off plants. That happens somewhat early on, especially in an exposed corpse. Plus, there's tissue intact. I'm just guessing, but I think whatever had ahold of it didn't get a chance to finish it off. It must've been interrupted."

"Coons?"

"No, raccoons don't normally drag their prey. They eat at the kill spot."

"Bear?"

"Maybe. More likely a coyote." I glanced around. We were in a ravine, and the trail ran along a seasonal creek. It was dry now, but there was probably a small current in the spring and early summer. On either side, tree-packed hills ran upward, with craggy rocks and boulders jutting out here and there. "Bears can drag a whole body. Especially a smaller female frame. A coyote would be more likely to carry a single limb."

Pusser rocked back on his heels, shifting a fresh toothpick from cheek to cheek and nodding. "That so?"

I pointed upward. "There's probably a coyote den or two in those rocks up there."

"Okay. Let's say you're right. A coyote dragged it here. All good to know, but where's the rest of the body?"

I frowned. "A typical male coyote's territory can extend up to thirty square miles."

"You got any good news for me?"

Wilco whined, his leash taut against the tree as he pulled, pushing the edge of his boundary, ready to go again. There was

a chance he would pick up on a scent trail leading from the severed foot. Still, it was a long shot, further complicated by the
tree density in this area. "Afraid not. But we'll get started." I
checked my phone. No service. "I need to get word to Johnny
Drake, my boss. Looks like I won't be in to work today."

"Don't worry. I'll see to it." Pusser walked over to Harris,
giving him various instructions.

I refocused on my task, squatting down for a closer look at
the forest floor, searching for any signs of tracks or distur-
bances. A man on the run in the woods leaves behind telltale
traces. Obvious things like shoe prints, broken twigs, and disturbed leaves. And less noticeable signs like slightly depressed
stones and pebbles that have been trampled upon, or shoe rubs
left behind on fallen trees that the person climbed over, and
something called transfers: material that has been moved, usually in the tread of a boot, from one area to the next.

I looked for anything that didn't belong, anything that didn't
fit, but saw nothing.

Pusser had finished giving Harris instructions, so I unclipped
Wilco's leash and gave him the go-ahead. In an instant, he was
off, moving up the ravine at a good clip. He was lower to the
ground and agile despite having only three legs and recouping
from a minor injury. The ascent was effortless for him. His
head bobbed excitedly from side to side, and his fur bristled.
By the time I caught up, he was already on the ridge, holding
his nose low, scooping up scents here and there. I maintained a
disengaged distance, observing, but keeping my emotions neu-
tral. I held a hand up to Pusser, signaling him to do the same.
Another fifty yards later, Wilco jerked and flipped back on
himself, bending over a low spot on the ground where leaves
had drifted and piled. He sniffed, spun a circle, sniffed some
more, but didn't look my way. An area of interest, or perhaps a
spot where scent had wafted and accumulated, but not actual
human remains.

On we went, for a couple of hours, Wilco relentless in his quest.

Pusser had been following about twenty yards behind me, but now he fell even farther back. I too slowed down. My legs, unaccustomed to physical exertion, grew wearier by the minute. My body vacillated between hot and cold as the terrain changed from the cool shelter of dense tree trunks to the more open grassy areas washed in the late-morning sun. I worried that we'd already missed our window of opportunity. Odor rises and moves on currents of air, but too much sun will burn off the scent, confusing even the best canine nose. I'd been so confident earlier; at this point, I wondered if we weren't on a bit of a wild goose chase.

I needed a break. And although he'd go until he dropped, Wilco needed a break too. I was just getting ready to call a temporary halt, time to cool down and get some fluids into both me and my dog, when I saw Wilco lift his head and straighten his tail. He'd hit on a positive scent. Something stronger, denser, more telling than what he'd smelled so far. He quickly moved across to the far side of the meadow and along the distant tree line. His tail grew even more rigid, like a pipe cleaner, but with a little hitch at the end.

He'd hit on a cadaver scent.

Jogging, I crossed the grassy patch, cockleburs and thistles clinging to my boot laces and the outer edges of my pants, somehow working their tiny claws into my bare skin underneath. Pusser was way behind us now, I wasn't even sure where. I'd lost track of him a while back. I didn't care. I was intent on catching up to my dog and finishing the task. Whatever that finish might bring.

I pushed into the woods. My eyes adjusted, and I caught sight of him to my left, pawing at the trunk of a tall hemlock. He scratched viciously at the bark for a second, then dropped down again on all threes, and pressed his nose back to the forest floor. He zigzagged for another thirty yards, tunneling through the leaves, his snout pressed into the ground like an aardvark. I followed, my heart rate kicked up, my eyes zeroed in, my breath came in quick spurts—all signs of my own adrenaline rush in anticipation of the pending discovery.

Everything around me blurred and faded into the background, except my single focus: my dog and his every move.

Then he stopped and sat down.

A body lay in front of him. He turned his head, his eyes bright and alert, bored into mine, as he barked.

"Found her!" I yelled. My voice echoed through the woods. I yelled out a few more times as I ran to Wilco. I clipped his lead and pulled him away from the body, all the while smiling and flailing my spare arm animatedly. He'd done his job. The promise of a reward lured him to a place a safe and unobtrusive distance from the crime scene.

Some twenty yards away, I dropped to the ground, rubbed my face alongside his, and brushed my hand rapidly up and down his back. He lifted his face, rocked back on his haunches, and lifted his front paws onto my shoulders. "Good boy! Good boy!" I pushed forward, tumbling down to the ground, where we rolled like a couple of playful puppies. Then the tummy rub. Wilco flipped, opened his legs, playfully growling while I scratched the soft underfur of his belly. Pure delight.

And, I had to admit, I felt it as well. The downpour of success, like a rush of water cascading over my whole being, the lightness in my half laugh, the warm reassurance of his fur squiggling beneath my hands. Then the outpour of thrill ebbed and washed away, and exhaustion flowed through us as we both released the morning's tension through our private celebration.

After he'd had his fill of my attention, I sobered. It was time for me to do the rest of my task now. A task that would not end in any celebration.

I stood up and brushed off my clothing. I poured Wilco a full container of water and watched as he lapped it up. Pusser had yet to show. Cupping my hands around my mouth, I yelled out again. This time I got a response. After more back and forth shouting, Pusser found us.

"Female?" he asked, coming our way.

I pointed to the body. "I think so. I didn't take a close look."

Pusser went in the direction I pointed. I joined him. We approached the vicinity of the body carefully, stopping a few feet away, where we stood shoulder to shoulder. Neither one of us spoke. Out of the shock of finding the body, or out of reverence, I couldn't be sure. In our silence, I heard the harsh caw of a crow and a rustling sound of rodents disturbing dry leaves. A ray of hot sun broke through the tree branches and warmed the sudden chill that had come over me. I hadn't prayed for years, yet I found myself remembering my childhood prayer: *Our gathra, who cradgies in the manyak-norch . . .* Our Father, who art in Heaven . . .

Decomposition had rendered her an unrecognizable heap of bones and black leathery tissue, which splayed away from her body in long strips. Remnants of faded clothing still clung here and there, but much of it had been ravaged away by the same rodents that had feasted on her tissue. Her chest cavity was exposed, a hollow cage of rib bones jagged and frayed from flesh-picking vulture beaks. One shoe, a synthetic leather flat, lay off to one side. Red, I thought. It was hard to tell because it was caked in mud.

Pusser's deeply flushed face did little to mask the combination of anger and sadness that clouded his features. When he spoke, his voice was low and somber. "Suppose you're used to seeing this type of stuff. All those soldiers dying over there. Probably doesn't bother you much anymore."

I squeezed my eyes tight against the scene before me. When death settles in, it evicts the soul and devours the flesh, and reduces a whole life to nothing but dry bones and a mere smudge of bio matter. Back in the Marines, I liked to pretend it was just a job and that I could handle it. I'd been lying to myself. Each and every one of those recoveries had stuck with me. This one would too.

"When I go," Pusser continued, "I don't want nobody to be puttin' me in the ground to rot." He removed his hat and swiped the sweat on his brow. "Nope. Just pop me in the oven and flip the switch. None of this rotting crap for me."

I looked on. My throat grew thick. Pusser was right. There was nothing pretty about death. And considering the extent of decomposition involved here, identification might take a while.

"You see that?" Pusser indicated toward her skull, where a key-shaped hole was evident about five centimeters above the right eye socket. "Could be from a bullet. Exit wound maybe."

A connection to my mother's murder, maybe? "The body's been here a while." I scanned the trees. "Any tracks in and out of here would be long gone." I recalled yesterday's rain. "Did you find tracks at the last scene?"

"Just a partial. One of the crime-scene techs found an imprint in the area. Could be from our guy. Though it could be from anybody. Lots of recreational ATVs out on these trails."

"True." But if an arrest were to be made later, the imprint could tie the perp to the scene. "You think this is Sheila Costello?"

"Probably."

If so, that made two now. Both females, and both connected to our clan. "I want to know what you've got on my mother's case. Show me the file. No one has to know about it."

He didn't respond.

"I helped you out here today. You wouldn't have a body if it weren't for Wilco."

"You're right. Thanks."

"I missed work. Probably ticked off my boss."

"I said *thank you*."

"Look, what's the chance of two females, both shot in the head, both during the same month, and then both dumped within the same five square miles?" Certainly he saw that. "And if this turns out to be Sheila Costello, then you can add another connection. They're both Pavees."

"What are you saying? A hate crime?"

"It hasn't crossed your mind?"

"What about the guys you mentioned seeing out in the woods? Could be that has something to do with all this."

"Drugs?"

"We don't have enough to rule out anything at this point."

I asked again to see my mother's file. He blew me off again, telling me to stay put and not disturb anything while he radioed in our location and got the ball rolling with the crime-scene unit.

Frustrated, I watched him pace as he talked. Pusser hadn't considered the hate crime angle, or maybe he had, but either way he preferred to ignore it and opt for an easier solution, pinning it on one of us Pavees. As far as I knew, that'd always been the local law's MO for any crimes involving Bone Gap residents. We were easy targets. No presumption of innocence. Just guilt by association and prosecution by the media. This most recent body, especially if it was Sheila, would simply be another nail in the clan's coffin.

Pusser finished his call and sat next to me. "Everything's in motion, but it's going to be a while before they can get out here." He leaned in closer. "Look, Callahan. You and your dog did good today. I'm grateful. And I don't need to tell you that tensions are running high around here. This ain't going to help things neither." I agreed, and he continued, "Dealing with you gypsy people is like banging my frickin' head against the wall. I need your help."

I looked away. I sure as hell wasn't going to be his informant. I didn't turn on my own. That's not how I operated.

When I didn't respond, Pusser sighed heavily, stood up, and

said, "Let me get this area secured, and then we'll talk about your mother's case."

I shot a glance at him, but he was busy now, determining the crime-scene area to cordon off. And I felt the boundaries of my own loyalties, of my own needs, being redefined and marked with every step he took and with every turn in this case.

CHAPTER 11

It was late Sunday afternoon by the time Pusser drove me back home. My body ached, and a gritty coating of sweat-soaked dirt covered my face and hands. I rubbed my palms up and down the sides of my jeans, but the grime stuck. The stale energy bar I'd scrounged from my pack earlier sat like a lump in my gut as my stomach rolled with anxiety over the pending task of telling Doogan his sister was dead.

Pusser shot me an odd, sort of sad smile. "I'll break the news to Doogan. It's my responsibility."

"Thanks. But I know him. I should be the one to tell him." Sheila's driver's license was discovered in the back pocket of the victim's element-eaten jeans along with a small baggie, believed to be some sort of narcotics packaging. Both findings needed further substantiation, and the ID of the victim wasn't a sure thing until more tests could be run, but Pusser felt it prudent to tell Doogan that the body we found most likely belonged to his sister. Although he already suspected she was dead, I knew Doogan would take the news hard. I dreaded telling him.

"Fine. But I'm going to need to talk to both of you about what you saw out in the woods yesterday."

"There's not much to tell. Males, foreign, Spanish-speaking, and carrying what looked like semi-automatic rifles. We only saw them at a distance, and they wore full camo and rain ponchos."

"Doogan thought they were drug runners?" The ME's finding of the narcotics-like package on Sheila's body had swung Pusser's focus toward the drug angle.

"That was his impression."

"Based on what?"

Experience, I wanted to say. But I didn't. They already knew about Doogan's stint in prison. Harris had told me as much. He was just playing me, trying to see how much *I* knew. A part of me wanted to trust Pusser, but he was making it difficult. "You'll have to ask him."

He grunted and moved on. "About two years back, a couple of Sullivan County guys down in the Cherokee National Forest found heroine in drums buried in the woods. A big bust. Feds, DEA . . . you name it, they all got in on it. The stash was part of a drug pipeline that runs from south of the border up through Kentucky and West Virginia. Ended up that the whole operation was tied into a cartel."

"So you're thinking they've reestablished themselves here?"

"Could be."

"And you think my mother and Sheila were somehow connected to this pipeline?" I shifted in my seat. "I don't know. I'm not really buying it. Seems too coincidental."

"I think your mother may have been an addict. Toxicology is still outstanding. You know the drill. We have to send it to the state labs. Results could take four to six weeks before we know what was in her system. But the coroner found needle scarring on her arms." He looked over, checking for my reaction, I supposed. But I didn't react; I wouldn't allow myself to, not in front of him.

"Scarring. Not fresh tracks?"

"Hard to be sure, considering . . ." He didn't finish, and I nodded. The degree of decomposition would make it hard to determine. This new development brought up more questions. I'd been stuck on the premise that Dub had something to do with both crimes. The possibility of a larger narcotics connection just muddied the waters.

Pusser continued. "It'd help if we could get a history on your mother. We need to know where she's been, why she came back. I can't seem to get anything from your family." I knew what he was asking, but even if I was willing to pump them for information, I wasn't sure if they knew, or would tell me, much more. They thought I'd gone over to the other side. Maybe I had. Regardless, the trust was gone between us.

Pusser raised his brows. "There's also Dublin Costello. The husband. What do you know about him?"

More than I ever wanted to know. A shudder scrabbled its way up my spine. "He's got a hot temper and has a history of violence. Rumor has it that Sheila wasn't happy in the marriage. Doogan told me that she wanted to go home to South Carolina."

"Why didn't she?"

"Even if Dub was abusive, her family would have encouraged her to stay to try to work things out. Divorce is uncommon in our culture. Women rarely leave their husbands."

"Even if the guy's beating on them?"

Beating and more. Again I refused to react to the repulsion churning in my gut. I tried to think of a way to explain it to him, then decided against even trying. He probably wouldn't understand anyway. Most settled folks didn't, or couldn't. Our cultures were so different. "That's just the way it is."

"Sounds stupid, if your men—."

"Dub is an exception, not the norm." Irritation crept into my voice. "It's not like all *our men* are wife beaters." I rolled my eyes. Yet another stereotype Pusser probably bought into.

"Just like not all backwoods sheriffs are uneducated, dough-nut-eating bigots."

I heard a few stiffened muscles pop as he rolled his neck and cleared his throat. He switched topics. "Hopefully preliminary ballistics will come in tomorrow. I'm curious to see if the bullet in Sheila matches the one they dug out from your mother. If so, that'll cinch the connection between these two cases."

I wanted to tell Pusser about the stained carpet fibers, the DVDs, and the other stuff Doogan had found in Dub's mobile home, but doing so would implicate Doogan in a crime. So I kept my mouth shut. We were nearing the entrance to the trailer park, and outside, the number of news vans had doubled since yesterday, and what looked like a small crowd of protest-ers fanned out near the main entrance. As Pusser's Tahoe passed by, they waved signs with crude logos, their hateful chants de-manding "Evict the gypsies!" One of the protesters noticed me in the passenger seat and snapped a picture. That triggered a massive swarm of reporters, who aimed their cameras my way like firing squad assassins.

Pusser swerved out of the way. "Damn reporters. They're like flies to shit."

I was more worried about the protesters than the reporters. "Those people with the signs are calling for our eviction." I re-membered Zee saying something about a group organizing against us. Seeing the hate in these peoples' expressions made me realize just what we might be up against. "Can they do that?"

Pusser turned down my road. "They're laying pressure on city council to do something. They want you folks out."

"We own the land. Have for a long time." This area was orig-inally a *halting*—or a resting spot—chosen by my ancestors for its seclusion. Families temporarily migrated here to winter over or wait and regroup for the next cash job opportunity. Aging Pavees, unable to tolerate the demands of the road, stayed for longer stints. Then, when the government began tracking children's schooling, demanding inoculations, medical records, paid taxes . . . many of us found it easier to set up base camps. Aging clan members often traded their RVs and campers for roomier mobile homes, like my grandparents' place. They were still moveable, if push came to shove; it was just not as easy to pull up stakes. But sometime early on, clan elders collected money and bought the deed to the land. We weren't squatters. We owned the land. Still, what Pusser said made me worry. I'd heard of people losing their land through eminent domain laws and other such things. If these people wanted us out badly enough, they'd find a way, lawful or not.

We pulled up in front of Gran's mobile home and parked. Doogan was there, outside, sitting on the steps with Gran and Colm.

"Sure you don't want me to inform Doogan?" Pusser asked again.

"No. I'll tell him."

"Fine. I'm going to break the news to the husband. Tell Doogan I'll be back later with a few questions."

I steeled myself before stepping out to open the back door for Wilco. Pusser drove off. When I looked over again, Doogan was coming my way. Gran and Colm were right behind him. "Sheila? Was it Sheila?"

I swallowed hard and took a tentative step toward him, but before I could say anything, he crumpled into himself and withdrew from my reach.

"There'll be an exam and more tests . . . but they found her driver's license on the clothing . . ." I let my voice trail off. He lowered his face into his hands and quietly sobbed. I looked to Gran for help, but she simply stood there, her arms at her sides, her face pale and drawn. Even Colm seemed at a loss. Everything seemed to grow silent and still, except the heart-rending sound of Doogan's grief.

Colm stepped up, his gaze trained on the reporters coming our way. "Let's go inside. Can you make us some coffee, Anne? Or some hot tea."

"Of course, Father."

Doogan didn't answer. Instead, he was looking down the street to Dub Costello's place. Pusser was there, along with another police officer now, out in the front yard, caught up in a deeply animated conversation with Dub. Doogan looked on, his sadness quickly changing over to anger. His hands rolled into tight, compact fists, and the veins on his neck, taunt with adrenaline, pulsated like plucked guitar strings. A low, guttural sound—an audible mixture of anguish and hostility—emitted from somewhere deep inside him. With a sudden jerk, he took off sprinting toward Dub's mobile home. We went after him, Colm ahead of me, Wilco on my heels, Gran hurrying the best she could.

Before we could catch him, Doogan made contact, slamming his palms into Dub's chest and sending him to the ground. Spit spewed from Doogan's lips as he leaned over and screamed, "You killed her! You killed my sister!"

Pusser pulled him back, struggling to subdue him. The other officer joined in, and between the two of them, they slapped cuffs on his wrists. But Dublin popped up off the ground and crowded in. "I didn't kill your sister, Doogan. She brought it on herself, the way she was whoring around."

Pusser inserted himself. "Back off, Costello."

Doogan twisted against the officer's hold, and even with his hands cuffed, charged after Dub. The officer strained to pull him back. "You lie, Costello! You lie. My sister's no whore."

The two of them butted chests. Wilco barked. Behind me, someone let out a loud whoop, and I turned to see that the crowd of protesters had closed in on us. They chanted something, but their words were muffled by Wilco's barking. People poured out of their trailers and into the street. Pusser turned to the crowd, waving them all back, but with little effect.

"You didn't know nothing about her," Dub's voice cut through the chaos. I whipped back around. "She was a druggie and a tramp. You don't believe me, just ask Rooney. The bitch was sleeping with him and a half dozen other guys."

Doogan ripped out of the officer's grip and rammed his forehead against Dub's chin. I heard a sickening *thunk*, then saw Dub crumple to the ground. The next thing I knew, Doogan was standing over him, kicking, each strike harder than the next.

I lunged forward. "Stop! Stop, Doogan!"

"Stand clear!"

I instinctively stopped. The shot came: a loud crack followed by a faint buzzing sound. Doogan arched his back, screamed in pain, and fell to the ground, where he erupted into convulsions. I jerked back, shocked. Horror and confusion followed. *He shot Doogan!* Then I noticed the barbed electrodes that had sunk into Doogan's skin, one in his back and the other under his rib cage. Thin wires led back to a Taser devise, not a gun, in Pusser's hands. A wave of relief washed over me.

But I didn't have much time to think about it. The reporters were on us now, cameras clicking, excited voices swirling all around. Protesters waved their signs and clashed with the Pavees in the street. Accusations and insults spewed from the crowd, rising through the air like acrid smoke. A small scuffle broke out, temporarily diverting at least some attention from us.

"This isn't good," Colm said. His voice was laced with panic.

"You think?" I snapped, instantly realizing—and grateful—that my words hadn't even registered in his shocked face.

Wilco let loose with a high-pitched whine, followed by a series of sharp barks, his eyes taking in the chaos. I frantically scanned the crowd, hoping Gran was safe.

I heard Pusser talking to the officer. "Backup better get here fast, or we're gonna have a full-out riot on our hands." I looked back to see him holster the Taser and grab one of Doogan's arms. "Let's get him loaded." They double-teamed him, one on each side of his cuffed arms, and dragged him into the cruiser.

I knelt down by Wilco, calming him or calming me, I wasn't sure which. Again, I searched the crowd for Gran, hoping she wasn't caught up in the chaos, but instead my eyes landed on someone else—Maybelle from work. She brandished a crudely fashioned sign with some sort of anti-gypsy slogan. Her T-shirt clung to her ample breasts, which bobbed up and down with each upward thrust of her fist. Our eyes connected. Hers were full of hostility. Hostility that seemed to be directed solely at me. Behind her stood someone else I recognized. It was Al, the jerk from the bar with the cheesy Fu Manchu, the one who wouldn't take no for an answer. He was also eyeing me—not with lust this time, but with unmistakable hatred.

I shivered and broke eye contact as two more police cars screamed onto the scene. Lights flashed, sirens wailed. Pusser ushered Dub toward another cruiser while barking out orders to the new officers, but the presence of additional police seemed to agitate things more. A rock flew out of the crowd and hit one of the cop cars. Someone yelled. Off to the right I heard a loud crashing sound and looked to see a man repeatedly slamming his sign against someone's garbage can. *Gran. I need to make sure she's safe.* I pulled at Wilco and turned back toward our trailer when I caught a glimpse of Colm coming my way. Gran was with him, and her hand was pressed to the side of her face.

I ran to them. "What's happened?"

Colm's gaze penetrated mine. "She's okay. Just get her out of here." I grabbed Gran's elbow and headed toward the trailer. Colm headed back toward the chaos. I yelled after him, told him it was crazy, futile, but he ignored me and kept on going. I was grateful he'd focused his efforts on Gran; priests were good at one-on-one situations, but I doubted he was up to a frenzied mob. At this point, I didn't care. I needed to take care of Gran.

*   *   *

The chaos raged on. It wasn't until late that night that things calmed down outside. After it was all said and done, a half dozen people had been arrested, mostly Pavees, and several others were taken to the hospital for minor injuries. Colm had stopped by to check on Gran, then left again. He'd asked me to bring her by the church tomorrow, to finalize burial arrangements for Tuesday. I had a feeling he had wanted to discuss something else too, but I didn't want to overtax Gran, so I'd hurried him along.

Gramps had been characteristically miserable about everything: Gran shouldn't have been out there; we Pavees needed to stick together better; those settled ones were scum; the law always favored the townsfolk; and the litany went on. It took all the strength I could muster to put up with his intermittent glares at me, as if I somehow had instigated or approved of the brawl. All I wanted was to care for Gran, but right now, her tending to Gramps seemed to be the best medicine for her.

After we got Gramps fed and situated in his recliner in front of the television, I lured Gran into the kitchen, where we could speak in private. Wilco was there too, curled up and snoring soundly in front of the still-warm oven. His eyelids flicked, and his paws moved in time with his dream, probably a rehash of today's successful search. He was smiling in his sleep. A second "task well done" for him in less than a week. A second dead body, a second murdered woman.

"I need some answers, Gran." I placed a hot cup of tea in front of her and sat down, scooting my chair in close so we could speak quietly together.

She looked down and fidgeted with the frayed edges of a dish towel. A lengthy silence ensued. I remained quiet, determined to wait it out. She abandoned the towel, picked up her tea, and took a quick sip, only to put down the cup again and go back to worrying the dish towel. An undercurrent of anxiety ran below her sadness. Something heavy weighed on her mind.

She fixed her gaze on me. "I never wanted to hurt you, child. Never. Everything I did, right or wrong, I did out of love for you."

My gut knotted, both from resentment and out of pity for her, but I didn't dare react, so I said nothing.

She rubbed the muscles in the back of her neck.

"Are you sure you feel okay, Gran?" Earlier, she'd been caught up in the ebb of the crowd and gotten bumped on the head. It didn't seem serious at the time, certainly nothing that warranted a trip into the doctor, but at her age . . .

"Fine. I'm fine, please don't fuss over me." She looked about, and I realized she was concerned that Gramps might overhear our conversation. What could be so terrible? Dread filled me. I shifted away and folded my arms tightly around my chest, a subconscious shield against whatever was coming.

"Your mother was independent," she started. "Much like you, and wild. A free spirit, I used to say." She chuckled. "Stubborn and disobedient is what she was. Still, I loved her more than life itself. Perhaps that was the problem. I tended to indulge her, you see. Which left your grandfather as the disciplinarian. Of course, he was on the road, so Mary often ran wild and out of control. Once she got older, I realized the need to reel her in, place more boundaries and stricter rules. But it was too late by then. She rebelled. That's when the trouble began. She met a boy . . ."

"My father?"

Gran's mouth drooped. "Yes. A settled boy. We didn't know his name. She wouldn't tell us." Her eyes darted away, then back again. "Or she didn't know. She had a lot of boyfriends. All settled boys."

Dub's previous words screamed through my mind. *Whoring around.* Suddenly chilled, I rubbed at my arms and tried to shut out the previous events of the day: the long trek through the woods, finding another body, then Doogan twitching and convulsing in pain, the angry crowd, Dub's ugly words about Sheila and someone named Rooney . . . the name clicked: Eamon Rooney, Meg's boyfriend? Unless there was another man named Rooney in Bone Gap. Yet somehow I doubted it. Poor Meg. I lifted my chin. I'd put that off for later. One worry at a time.

Gran continued. "We'd hoped she'd calm down after you came along. But instead, she took up with a bad crowd in town. Staying out all night, or coming home drunk."

Like mother, like daughter.

Gran's hands worked over the dish towel some more. Her eyes took on a faraway look. "I remember that awful night like it was yesterday. She came rushing back home—you were just a baby, maybe a month old—and she was hysterical, crying and blabbing on about how someone was going to kill her. I couldn't soothe her." Regret tinged her voice. "My own baby, and I couldn't comfort her."

I leaned closer. "Someone was going to kill her? Why?"

"I wish I knew, child. I only know that she was frightened. So terribly frightened. She packed up her stuff. Said she had to leave. Your grandfather was home. He tried to talk some sense into her, but there was no stopping her."

"What about me?"

"She asked me to watch over you. Said she'd come back for you when it was safe."

"But she never did."

Gran's gaze met mine, then fell back to the dish towel as she continued. "Later, maybe a couple weeks after Mary left, the police came around, harassing our people. Said they were looking for a Pavee girl with a baby."

Looking for a Pavee girl? I thought back to the article I'd found at the motel. The timing would be just about right . . .

Gran was still talking. "The *muskers* were asking all sorts of questions. We got scared, so we took to the road for a while."

"Why didn't you just tell me all this? Why lie and tell me she was dead?"

She hesitated. But a slight tilt of her head gave it away.

"It was Gramps' idea, wasn't it? But you agreed to it. Why didn't you try to find her? Bring her back. Help her?"

She squeezed her eyes tight and pinched the bridge of her nose. "We did. We found her in Memphis. She wasn't herself. She was living like an animal on the streets, taking drugs, selling herself . . ."

Gypsy whore. If the moniker fits . . . images of Sheila's picture at the Sleep Sleazy, of the slimy condoms I'd shaken out of the motel sheets, and of my mother's blood-soaked hair all came together in an ugly reminder of the taunts we'd heard all our lives. But it didn't have to be that way. "She wasn't *dead*. Maybe you could have helped her."

"We did everything we could. You have to believe that, Brynn. But she was lost. We'd lost her to the settled world." She met my gaze with dull, wet eyes. "All we knew for sure was that we couldn't bear to lose you too. But you wouldn't let it go. Even as a youngster, you asked about her all the time. And then when you got older, you became obsessed with finding her. You spent all your time on the computer, searching her name. Guess you could never let a question go unanswered."

"And suicide covered all the bases, didn't it?" I was growing angry again. "Because otherwise, I would have wondered why we didn't have a wake. Instead, you convinced me that her death was shameful. That we had to hide it, keep it a secret. And I believed you."

"We did what we thought was best at the time. That's all any of us can ever do." She looked away.

"When did she contact you?"

Nothing.

"When did she contact you, Gran?"

Gran exhaled. "Last month. She wrote a note, just a brief note, saying that she was still alive and that she . . . she loved us. She had her parish priest send it."

She pulled a small white envelope from her pocket and passed it to me. I took out the note, carefully unfolded it, and read the simple message: *Dear Mam, I want you to know that I'm still alive and miss you. All of you. Love, Mary.*

"All of you?" That's it? I was nothing more than one of the "all of you."

I flipped the paper over, looked at the blank back side, and flipped it back again. Two short sentences. That was it. Nothing more. "The priest sent this to you?"

"No. To Father Colm. He brought it to me."

"Father Colm?" That explained Colm's recent connection to my family. Guilt. He'd helped bring my mother back here, back to her death.

"Yes. I begged him not to tell the police about it. I didn't want them involved in our personal matters. Nothing good ever comes from the police." She lifted her chin defiantly, her eyes sliding my way. Then she blinked, and a tear streamed down her cheek. "It was such a shock to hear from her after all these years. I wrote right back. Told her about your grandfather's sickness. Told her all about you. I begged her to come home."

"Did she mention me in her reply? Did she . . . did she want to see me?"

Gran's features clouded over. "I never heard back from her. I thought she'd changed her mind. It wasn't until . . ." She pressed her lips tightly, her chin trembling. Tears flowed freely now.

I covered her hand in mine. "It's okay, Gran. It's okay."

She swallowed back a sob and forced a small smile. Leaning forward, she brushed back a strand of my hair and tucked it gently behind my ear. All of a sudden, I was seven years old again, upset and hurt after a brawl at school. I'd taken on a fifth grader after he'd said something nasty about my family. The fight hadn't gone well for me. I was small; he wasn't. It wasn't the physical pain, however, that needed to be assuaged, but my injured pride. It was one of the first times I realized that I was different. My family was different. We were fringers, as I'd grown to think of us. Living on the edge of what was considered normal. It was one of those pivotal points of childhood. From that day forward, I defined myself as different. I'd even somehow prided myself in that fact, at least until I grew old enough to disobey my clan's basic rules. Then? I became a disgrace.

And now? I wasn't just an alienated bastard but a whore's maimed and drunken bastard. A total misfit. An outcast.

Except at home. At home, there was always Gran.

I closed my eyes, exhaled the hurt and pain, and let her touch console me. Just like then. Just like I needed now . . .

"I'm sorry, child. Can you forgive me?"

I nodded my head and cried.

CHAPTER 12

I tossed and turned in bed, unable to get to sleep, my mind churning over everything I'd learned about my mother. The old newspaper clipping kept popping to the forefront of my thoughts. Was it merely a coincidence that the timing of that decades-old crime and my mother's departure from the clan coincided? I doubted it. Now I'd heard from Gran's own lips that the police had been looking for a Pavee girl with a baby soon after my mother disappeared. The article stated the authorities were seeking Billy Drake's girlfriend, a Bone Gap girl. Could that have been my mother?

What did I *really* know? Just that sometime back around the year I was born, Billy Drake's body was found, and he'd presumably been involved in a theft and the drugstore owner's murder. And he had a Bone Gap girlfriend. I also knew my mother had birthed me by a settled boy and then, frightened for her life, had run off. That didn't necessarily mean these incidents were connected—certainly my mother wasn't the only one of our clan girls to be chummy with settled boys. *I mean, look at me and Colm.* I cringed. *Don't go there, Brynn, stay on track.*

Facts, I needed dates and facts.

I rolled over and snapped on my nightstand light, pushed Wilco off my legs, and got out of bed. After kicking through the dirty laundry, I found the jeans with the article still in the pocket. I skimmed over it again and found myself wondering about Billy Drake. Was Billy my mother's boyfriend? Or was it like Gran had said, my mother had a lot of boyfriends? Was I his child? After all these years, I wanted to believe that I'd found my father, but I could be grasping at straws here. But how could I really know?

I shuffled across the room to my dresser and pulled out the bottom drawer. Would it still be there? Yes! Gran had kept my things for me. I withdrew an old shoebox and settled back on my bed. My fingertips traced along the worn cardboard edges of the box that held my first pair of heels—white, sparkly two-inch pumps—bought for my First Communion. Gran was so sure I'd love them. I told her I did, of course, but in the end, I'd switched them out for my more comfortable sneakers. There'd been a gasp or two from the ladies in the pews, when I knelt for communion and my black sneakers peeked out from under the billows of white taffeta. First Holy Communion was akin to a wedding; little Traveller girls were garbed in princess-style white gowns complete with long flowing trains, white gloves, and puffy veils, their hair done up in elaborate styles and makeup garishly applied. It was a grand pageant, and the little girls were put on display like beauty contestants or mail-order brides. In fact, many of the arranged marriages occurred soon after this display of our too-young and too-innocent girls. Our souls sanctified to God in our First Communion and our bodies sold off to the highest bidder, all in one fell swoop.

Backroom deals were the order of the day; it's when Gramps and old man Costello, Dub's grandfather, shook hands and negotiated my future like a used car salesman would with someone interested in a Buick. Bitterness crept over me. One "test drive" was all Dub got from this Buick before I crashed and burned. The phrase caught me off guard, and I smirked at the irony, rubbed my neck. *Get over yourself, Brynn; you've got a task to do.*

I removed the shoes and lifted the tissue under them, where my little treasures nestled beneath it. I skimmed the memories I'd squirreled away over the years: a squished penny Gran and I had placed on the train track, a dried meadow flower from a walk with Colm, ticket stubs from a rock concert I'd snuck out to see . . . and at the bottom, tucked between the pages of a forbidden paperback novel, my mother's picture. The only one I'd ever found. While I expected Gran had an album somewhere, most of my mother's pictures were removed from the house when I was an early teen. Out of sight, out of mind. I'd found this one by mistake, and I'd treasured it.

I stared at her image. My mother had been beautiful. Large green eyes, dark auburn hair, fair skin and soft, even features. I looked nothing like her. My dark hair and strong features, I'd always assumed, came from my father. Again, I found myself wanting to know more. The whole story. Ugly or not, I needed to know about her life if I wanted to solve her death. Was that old crime somehow connected to her? And could it also be connected to her murder these many years later?

I thought of the clipping and how I'd found it, tangled up in the bedsheets. Dropped by someone? I'd thought of Johnny Drake at first, since it named someone related to him. But what sense did that make? Johnny wouldn't have been sleeping in one of the motel rooms. Or had my mother checked into the Sleep Easy on her return trip here and had it with her? It was the only lodging on this side of the mountain, so it'd make sense that she might have booked a room there. But . . . why check in at any motel at all? Why not just come home?

I glanced at the clock on my nightstand. Only a little after 9:00 P.M. I snatched up my cell and punched in the number for the Sleep Easy, hoping to get Johnny Drake's personal number from the clerk. No one answered. *Great way to run a business.* I hung up and dialed Meg's number, thinking she might know how to get hold of him, but she didn't answer either. Frustrated, and intent on getting some answers, I pulled on some clothes and gave Wilco a quick hug. "Stay here, boy. Rest up. I'll be back in a jiff."

Twenty minutes later, I pulled into the Sleep Easy parking lot and whipped into one of the empty spots outside the row of rooms and a couple doors from the office. I'd barely put the car in park when a motel door farther down the row from me swung open and a woman stepped out, dramatically struck a match against the door frame, and held it to the tip of her cigarette. After a long draw between full, crimson painted lips, she tilted her chin high and blew a silver stream into the air. Captivated by her flamboyant mannerisms, I sank back into my seat and watched as she crossed her muscular legs and leaned against the door frame, smoking like a fifties film star. She looked like one too. Maybe a cross between Marilyn Monroe and . . . and, I didn't quite know. She was unusual-looking: long platinum curls, strong features, model-tall with broad shoulders. And the short, silk robe she wore left little to the imagination.

Just as I realized what was so different about this Marilyn look-alike woman—she wasn't a woman, but a man—another male emerged from the shadows of the room, zipping his fly. He snatched the cig from the she-man's hand, took a long drag, then handed it back, along with a couple of folded bills, and walked away with a stupid grin on his face. No sooner had he driven away when my old buddy, Al, stepped out of the motel office, and—dear, God!—he was wearing a Sleep Easy shirt. *He works here?* Then I recalled Zee warning me about the new night manager. Al was the night manager. Talk about bad luck.

Shrinking even farther into my seat, I watched as Al sauntered along the walk in front of my car, swagger on, chest puffed out, like a cock in a henhouse. His slicked-back hair gleamed with a greasy sheen every time he walked under one of the room lights. He headed straight for the woman—I mean man—who quickly stomped out the cig. The two of them exchanged a couple of words, then the she-man handed over the money and watched, wide-eyed, as Al flipped through each bill. Al must not have liked the way it added up, because he waved the money in the she-man's face. She-man backed away. Al was working himself into a rage. With a swoop of his hand, he snatched a handful of she-man's platinum curls—which must've been real, not a wig—and jerked her back into the room. The door slammed shut. I shuddered. I felt sorry for that person. Really sorry.

And for me. Because two things were evident: Al was the night manager Zee warned me about, the one who meant trouble for my clan. And he was a pimp. My eyes slid down the line of peeled-paint doors, wondering how many more were full of Al's workers. *Oh, great!* Like I needed to know where the multiple stains on the sheets I'd be laundering came from. A slither of repulsion inched down my spine. He was making a nice sideline profit at Drake's expense. Another chill hit me. Maybe Drake was in on it? I had no idea.

I groaned. As if learning about my mother's "many boyfriends" wasn't enough, potentially my father's brother was now running a brothel! I pushed away that line of thinking. Way too many facts still had to be uncovered. I couldn't afford to have my personal angst color the findings. I needed some answers, and fast.

Either way, there'd be no getting Drake's number from Al. I shot another glance at the closed door and made a break for the motel's office.

Al hadn't bothered to lock the motel office door. My heart pounded as I slid inside. How much time did I have? How long did it take to . . . well, I didn't want to think about what Al was doing to, or with, the wannabe woman.

Finding Drake's personal number was fairly easy; it was

listed on a sheet of emergency numbers posted by the desk phone. I glanced through the window. My car was closer to the office than to the motel door, but only barely. I refocused and turned my attention to the computer. I wanted to see if someone under my mother's name had stayed at the motel, but the computer was passcode protected. Seconds later, I was back in my car, slumped down, cell phone in hand.

Drake picked up on the third ring. "Mr. Drake. Brynn. I need to speak to you."

"If this is about yesterday, it's fine. Zee was able to handle the rooms."

A low din of tinkling glass, country music, and rambunctious voices filled the background. His words were slightly slurred. Guess I knew where Johnny spent his off hours. "No, this isn't about missing work yesterday. This is important. Can I meet with you?"

"I'm busy. It'll have to wait until—"

"It's about your brother. Billy."

He fell silent. I waited, listening to the muted tones of a Toby Keith song, while Drake's drunken mind churned out a way to handle the little twist I'd thrown his way. "What about Billy?" he asked.

"It's about his murder."

There was another long pause. I jumped back in before he could ask any more questions. "I'm at the motel. I'll wait for you."

Twenty minutes later, Drake pulled up next to me and got out of his car. He looked ticked.

I stepped out of my vehicle. "Thanks for coming." I tried to keep my tone light.

He frowned and took a sip from the foam cup in his hand. The bitter aroma of coffee floated in the air along with the stale smell of beer. "Just cut to the chase, will ya? What's so important that it couldn't wait until tomorrow?"

I hesitated, trying to figure out how best to approach things.

He shifted his stance. "You said you had information about my brother's murder."

"At the time, the police were looking to question a woman. A Bone Gap woman. They thought she was involved with your brother."

"Could be. I don't know for sure. Billy was a few years younger than me. I was already deployed when it happened. I have no idea who he was involved with."

"But there were rumors."

"It's a small town. There are always rumors." He chuckled and took another sip of coffee. "What are you getting at?"

"I believe the woman they wanted to question was my mother, Mary Callahan. If he was involved with her, then your brother could have been my father. Which would make you my uncle."

I saw him flinch, but he recovered quickly enough. "Maybe. Maybe not."

"Did you know I was Mary's daughter when you hired me?"

He met my gaze. "Meg told me who you were. I have no idea who my brother was hanging out with back then. Or your mother. Like I said, I was gone at the time."

I studied his features. His eyes were round like mine, and we both had a bump on the bridge of our nose. But eye shape and nose bumps didn't necessarily make us kin. "Do you have a picture of Billy?"

"Not on me." He pushed his glasses up. "All this could have waited until tomorrow."

"Did you know my mother had returned to the area?"

"No. Not until after they found her body out in those woods."

"Did she stay at your motel?"

A small nerve twitched along his jawline. Was I making him nervous? "Hell if I know. Like I said, I didn't know your mother. Never met her. I wouldn't know her if she was stand-ing right here with us."

Standing right here . . . I envisioned the picture Doogan had shown me of his sister. She'd been standing in one of the motel doorways. Just like the hooker I'd seen earlier. Maybe I'd over-looked something. Maybe this wasn't about an old crime, or drugs, but about a prostitution ring run right out of this motel.

"How about Sheila Costello. Did you know her?"

His brows shot up his forehead. "Sheila . . . ?"

"Sheila Costello. The other woman they found out in the woods."

"What are you getting at, Callahan? If you think I'm some-how involved with all this, then you're barking up the wrong tree. I'm a pillar of this community. A good Christian man—"

"I saw an old picture of Sheila. She was here, at your motel." That cut off his pious assertions, and fast. I looked over to the motel office. Al was staring out the window, watching us. I turned back to Drake.

Anger flashed over his features. "A lot of people have stayed at my motel. I don't know all of them. What's your problem anyway? I've been good to you. Hired you even though you're one of them people from Bone Gap."

So we were "them people" to him. No wonder he'd flinched at the idea that one of us might be a blood relation to him. I avoided rolling my eyes at his hypocrisy, but just barely.

Then he leaned in for what he must have considered the kill. "Don't you value your *job*?" It was surprising how quickly he'd changed from a good Christian man to the big boss man, lording it over his underling.

No matter. I was about to wipe that smug look right off his face.

"Maybe she worked for you."

"No. I'm familiar with all my employees, and no one named Sheila Doogan has ever worked for me."

"Maybe not legitimately, but in some other . . . *capacity*?"

He squinted. "What are you talking about?" He reached for his car door. "You know, I'm tired of this little game you're playing. I'm heading home."

Al was still watching us. I was taking a chance that Johnny, the good Christian man, didn't know anything about the prostitutes operating out of his motel. I put a hand on his car door before he could open it. "This is no game, Johnny. Two women are dead. One of them is my mother. The other was a young Pavee girl, desperately trying to escape an abusive marriage. She needed money. Maybe you helped her earn a little money on the side." Our faces were only inches apart—no jawline twitch in the motel's neon light this time, no blink, only a blank stare of incomprehension. Either he was a good actor, or he had no idea what I was talking about.

He pulled open his car door. "I don't know what you're getting at."

I leaned down as he slid into the driver's seat. "Your night manager is running prostitutes out of your motel."

His head snapped my way. "What?"

I waved my hand toward the motel rooms. "Check it out. Not more than five minutes ago, the brunette in fifteen greeted the second john I've seen her with tonight. So you might want to give them a few more minutes. But room ten? You'll find that one particularly interesting. Al's pimping them right out of your rooms. If the cops find out, you'll be shut down."

The smug look melted from his face. His eyes snapped toward the office, where Al quickly stepped away from the window. Drake squirmed, his jaw clenching over what that sleazeball's sideline business might do to his motel.

I took advantage of his distress and showed him the newspaper clipping. "I found this."

He grabbed it from my fingers, held it in the glow of his car's dome light. "Were you in my office?"

I looked toward room 13 and blinked. "No. I found this when I was doing laundry. It was mixed in with the sheets. Why?"

"I have a bunch of clippings from Billy's case." He skimmed it. "I'm pretty sure I have this one too." The way he fingered the edges and frowned, it didn't appear that he thought this was the same clipping he had in his keeping. He looked as perplexed as I felt.

"Your office is in room thirteen?"

"Yup."

"Does everyone have access to the room key?"

"No. Just me. I had a special lock installed a while back."

I considered what he'd said. If this wasn't his clipping, then maybe my mother had kept a copy of that article too. Then if she'd stayed at his motel, she might have left this article behind by mistake when she checked out.

"Can you get that file for me?"

"Sure." He looked over at the motel office. "Then I'm going to take care of this other issue."

A little after eight the next morning, I slid into a chair across from Pusser's desk. Wilco settled in at my feet. There was no offer of coffee and doughnuts this time, which disappointed me. I'd been conditioned already, like one of Pavlov's dogs, to associate Pusser with doughnuts.

"What are you doing here, Callahan? Aren't you supposed to be at work or something?" He pushed aside a stack of papers and looked at me over the rim of his glasses. He didn't seem happy to see me.

"I have Mondays and Tuesdays off. Not many people in on those days." Unless we counted Al and his entourage, but I figured that Drake had cleaned house by now. I didn't mention the prostitutes to Pusser. Better to keep Drake on my good side for a while. Besides, I did need my job.

Pusser's toothpick dangled in shreds from between his lips. "Bad day already?" I asked.

"What do you think? I'm up to my eyebrows in complaints about you people. City council's breathing down my neck, wanting me to make an arrest."

"A Pavee arrest, you mean."

He grumbled and shot me a look.

"How's Doogan?" I asked.

"He was released earlier this morning."

"No charges?"

"He cooperated. Told me what he knew about the drug runners and whereabouts you were when you saw them. I've got a call into the DEA. I should hear from them soon. We'll organize some manpower and search that area of the woods." He stood and came around the front of his desk, leaning against the edge with his arms folded over his chest. He stared down at me. "The ME identified a slug found in our victim's brain. It was a .380."

"The same as they found in my mother."

"The complete ballistics report won't be available for a while. But preliminary results show a likelihood that they were fired from the same gun. I'm having one of my officers run a random stats check through TIBRS." I didn't know what those letters stood for exactly, but probably some sort of database of crime statistics. He continued, "If there's been another recent crime using a .380 in this area, we should know about it soon." He paused. "What do you know about Eamon Rooney?"

"He's dating my cousin, Meg."

"Costello thinks Sheila and Eamon were having an affair."

"I gathered that." I shifted in my chair. "If it's true, I don't think Meg knew about it." I'd planned to stop by the diner and talk to her later that day.

He raised a brow. "You sure about that?"

I didn't like where this was headed. "I'm sure. We're close. If she thought Eamon was cheating on her, she would have told me." I glared at him. "She's not involved in this."

"She had motive."

"So do a lot of people. Costello, for starts. Don't you always look at the spouse first? And maybe Eamon, if they really were involved. And how about all those protesters? You were there yesterday. You saw how they hate us." Then it hit me. "But you're not looking at any settled folks for this, are you?"

He shot me a look. "I'm sick of you accusing me of improprieties. I go where the evidence points, and that's it."

"Is the evidence up your ass? Because that seems to be where your head is."

I braced myself, waiting for an outburst. Instead, he smirked. The tension in the room dispersed, and I found myself once again trying to figure Pusser out. He was a hard one to read. "Look, Sheriff. Even if you thought Meg was involved in Sheila's death, what connection would Meg have to my mother's murder? None, I'm telling you. She's family. Clan." Dublin and Eamon were clan too. Pavees rarely killed their own, but there had been stories . . . past crimes, incidents when a clan member had fallen at the hand of another. We'd always handled those things ourselves. The cops were never involved. "You just don't get it," I added.

He trudged back to his chair. "You're right. I don't. I can't get anywhere with you people out there. But you could help, you know."

"I *have* helped you. What do you think yesterday was?"

He pulled back and lowered his voice. "Tell me more about your mother."

I bit the inside of my lip. I'd come in prepared to discuss my mother's past with him, yet I still wrestled with how much to reveal about what Pusser called "you people." Still, I had information for him. After my little talk with Drake the night before, we had met at his office in room 13, where he handed over a small file of newspaper clippings, which included his own copy of the article I'd found. Most of them, I could've likely found myself in the archives of the newspaper or library the next day. But he also gave me a key piece of information: a photograph that he'd found mixed in with his brother's belongings. It was young Billy, black-haired, with bright blue eyes, strong features, and a carefree smile. Much like mine. The photo was taken down by the river. He had his arm around a young girl. My mother. And she was definitely pregnant.

Billy Drake was my father. He was murdered. And so was my mother. And I needed Pusser to connect the dots for me.

"Your mother?" Pusser asked again. "Where had she been all this time? Do you know?"

"Memphis." I reached into the knapsack I was carrying and pulled out Drake's file. It shook in my trembling hands. Guilt chewed at my conscience; still, I handed it to him. "This belongs to Johnny Drake. His brother was—"

"Billy Drake." Pusser opened the file and pushed up his glasses. "I know the name. I worked his murder case years ago." His eyes skimmed the articles. "Billy's killer was never found."

"No leads?"

He closed the file and discarded his toothpick. "We suspected his murder was tied to a local drugstore robbery. The owner was killed, some money stolen, drugs missing. The way things went down, it seemed there had to be more than one perp. But not much evidence was left at the scene. Whoever did it was smart enough to clean up and remove the security tapes. We tried to locate Billy's girlfriend, but . . ."

"My grandmother told me that my mother left because someone was threatening her. She was scared, so she packed and left." *And left me behind.*

"Why didn't they go to the police?"

I met his gaze but didn't answer.

He cleared his throat. "She never contacted them again?"

"I don't believe so. My grandparents somehow tracked her down, though. They found her in Memphis. She was working as a prostitute, supporting a drug habit. That's what Gran told me anyway."

"When did your grandmother tell you all this?"

"Last night."

"All this time, they'd told you that—"

"She'd committed suicide. They made it up. All of it. They thought it was best that I believed she was dead, rather than have me know she was a prostitute. They were trying to protect me." I was surprised by how quickly I jumped in to defend their actions to Pusser. And how their actions, their years of lies, made some perverted sense to me now. There had been a kindness, at least to their intentions.

He picked the photograph out of the file. I watched while he studied it.

"Your mother?" he asked, eyeing me over the rims of his glasses.

"Yes."

Silence fell over the room. I leaned over and petted my dog. Pusser watched, his expression pensive.

Finally, he spoke. "I don't see how it fits for Sheila Costello. She's not even from this area. What possible connection would she have to any of this?"

"I don't know. The only connection between Sheila's case and my mother's is the gun caliber and the fact that they're Pavees." Was Sheila also a prostitute? That could be another connection. Although I'd seen that photo of her at the Sleep Easy, that didn't prove what she was doing there—or if money was passing hands. And I didn't want Pusser to nail Doogan for theft by telling him about that photo. I paused, then asked, "Can you look in your files and see what caliber of gun was used to kill Billy Drake?"

"I don't need to look it up. I remember the caliber. It was a .380. That's how we tied Billy Drake's murder to the drugstore owner's. Striations on the bullets were a match."

"And you never recovered the weapon?"

"No. The weapon was never recovered." He snatched up his phone. "Sally. I need you to pull a cold case file . . . Billy Drake . . . Bring it to my office, will ya? And then see if you can get someone on the line from Forensic Services."

He hung up and looked my way. "I'll check into it."

CHAPTER 13

A two-story white clapboard house next to the church served as both the parish office and the priest's rectory. The church secretary, a pleasant woman with short-cropped silver hair and thick-soled shoes, met me inside the door and, after pausing to fawn over Wilco, showed me to Colm's office, located in what would have been the original parlor of the house. We'd passed a wide oak staircase on the way, which I assumed led to the priests' private living quarters on the second floor. She announced my arrival and slid the heavy paneled pocket door shut as she exited.

Colm stood from his desk. "Your grandmother's not with you?"

Those dark eyes of his shot to the now-closed door before landing on me. Was it me, or did he seem uncomfortable that I had come alone to see him? Or maybe I was the one uncomfortable about that. My mouth went dry. I swallowed hard and took a seat in a chair across from him. Wilco curled at my feet. A certain tenseness buzzed in the air around us. I wondered if he could sense the way I felt, the way my body involuntarily reacted to him, even after all these years and even though he wore a collar now. "She didn't feel well this morning. She asked me to come and finalize the details."

He looked concerned. "Nothing serious, I hope."

"No. Just a little roughed up from yesterday. She's sore, a bit bruised."

"Then I'm glad she stayed home to rest." His gaze fixed on me for just a beat too long, before he cleared his throat and searched through a pile of papers on his desk. "There are just a couple more details she needed to decide on. I've got it all written down somewhere."

Our traditional wake called for the deceased's body to be laid out in the front room of their home—in this case, Gran and Gramps' home, so friends and family could gather to pay their respects. But that tradition didn't allow for a bullet hole in the brain and insect- and rodent-ravaged flesh. So instead Gran had opted for a simple Mass and burial.

"Here it is." He held up a piece of paper. "Your grandmother already chose the music, but if you could let me know which readings you prefer." He came around to my side of the desk and handed me a Bible. "I've got a few suggestions."

He pulled up a chair and leaned toward me to show me what he'd marked. I felt the heat from him sitting so close. Then I wondered, again, if it wasn't my reaction only and not his at all. I glanced at him as he opened the Bible to point out each marked passage. His gaze followed his fingers as he gently, almost lovingly, traced the lines he'd chosen. Clearly the tingles of warmth he felt emanated from these printed pages; it was not flowing toward me but being offered to me through the words he so fondly read. I'd never pegged the old Colm as much of a churchgoer, but as he guided me through the decisions, his enthusiasm and knowledge of faith was evident. I struggled to reconcile this new Colm with the man I remembered from before, the wild, uninhibited Colm who liked to party and have a good time. My mind drifted from the page, and my eyes slid sideways and lingered on his profile. Ten years had changed him: a softer jawline, deeper creases, but his eyes were the same, as was his mouth—full lips curved with a hint of a grin—and I wondered if the old Colm was still there, lurking underneath the collar.

"I think your grandmother will be happy with these choices," he was saying.

I snapped back into focus and agreed. He jotted down a few notes while we discussed a couple more things. After we'd finished, I brought up the letter from my mother. "Gran said that you delivered the letter from my mother."

He gave me his full attention. "Yes. It came to me from a priest in Memphis."

"Do you know him personally?"

"No. Never met him. The letter came in the mail. It was in a plain, sealed envelope inside another envelope addressed from his parish."

"Which parish?"

"St. Louis Church on the east side. A separate note was also included, instructing me to deliver it in secret to your grandmother."

"Did you talk to anyone about it?"

He looked down. "Not exactly. But Father Donavan got to the package first and opened the note. Not that he meant to pry, he just got . . . confused."

"So he read the note?"

"I'm afraid so." Colm looked at his palms. "And it seemed to upset him."

"It did? Why?"

"Father Don isn't doing well. He's having memory lapses. He gets agitated easily. The beginning throes of dementia or Alzheimer's probably. That's why I was appointed here. He's having difficulty tending to his duties."

Difficult. Easily agitated. Sounded like my own grandfather. I quickly dismissed the idea. He'd always been quick-tempered and easily agitated. Nothing new there.

Colm was still talking. "The note triggered something in his memory. He keeps insisting that there's something important that he's supposed to do, but he can't remember what. Every time I mention it, he gets upset again."

"Do you think he's told someone else about the note?"

"I doubt it. He doesn't get out much these days." His eyes drifted to the floor and skimmed the oak boards, as if tracing the past string of events. "I regret that I helped bring your mother here . . . to her death."

I swallowed back my grief. "No. You didn't cause this. You only did what you were asked to do. You had no way of knowing."

Pain crimped the corners of his eyes. "Still, I brought a lot of sadness into your life. This and . . ." His eyes settled on my scarf. I bristled. "When I left McCreary all those years ago, I made you a promise."

I squeezed my eyes shut. I didn't want to go here. Not now. There were too many other things I needed to work through; this was something better off left undiscussed. "It's okay. We were just kids."

"No, it's not okay. I want to explain. I need to explain."

I opened my eyes and pleaded with him. "Please don't, Colm." I didn't want to rehash it all now. My grandfather's betrayal, the way he acted after Dublin . . . I clutched my stomach. *No, no, no . . .*

But Colm continued anyway. "When I left for college, I told you I'd be back on break. I promised to come back for you, but something changed in me. I can't explain it, but I felt drawn to the priesthood. A strong draw, but then there was this little doubt." He looked to the floor again. "You were that doubt, Brynn. And I was advised to cut off all contact with you. That's why I ignored your phone calls. I realized later how wrong that was. You see, it was easier to turn away from you than to go back and tell you that I'd changed. Especially after what we'd shared together . . . I was a coward."

My mind screamed for him to stop. I'd spent the last ten years running from all this, avoiding the pain. What right did he have to force open the dam and flood me with vile memories that I'd worked so hard to escape?

My mind plunged back to that time . . . I'd been promised to Dub, in a deal made long ago, back when I still played with dolls and wore my hair in pigtails. It was a good deal for my family by clan standards. Dub Costello came from one of the clan's founding families, a pure bloodline, good stock and well respected. Yet he'd chosen me, a half-breed, a nobody. Other Pavee girls envied me. But I'd already met Colm. I'd loved him. Always had. Still did.

"I eventually came back, you know, and looked for you," Colm was saying. "But you'd already left. Enlisted and out of the country. I can't blame you. Not after the way . . ."

"Dub raped me." The words were out before I could stop them.

Colm's hand shot to mine, his grip tight and protective. "What?"

I released a long, jagged breath and told him the whole story. How when I'd gone to Dublin to ask for my freedom, to be released from my obligation to marry him, he'd become enraged. Things got out of hand . . . I couldn't stop him . . . then afterward, I ran home, bloody and bruised, my body torn and brutally invaded. Gran was gone at the time, helping her newly widowed sister, but I ran to my grandfather and I told him everything that Dub had done. Every single, horrible thing. But instead of comforting me, instead of coming to my defense, he grew angry. He told me it was my fault. That I'd deserved it. That I was no better than my mother. My mother: single, knocked-up by a settled boy . . . *the gypsy whore.*

Colm moved closer and took both my hands. His face filled with sorrow. "I . . . I didn't know. If I had only—"

"No." I couldn't leave Colm with yet another guilt. Leaving me without a word was one thing—unforgiveable in my eyes for years, yet we *were* young and confused. But even if Colm had been around, Dub would have had his way, forced his "promised due" on me—I knew that. I blinked hard to push the memories back and focus on the present. Colm's hands, they felt good. Warm. Comforting.

"Have you forgiven him?" he asked.

"*Forgiven?*" My jaw tightened. Hate cursed through my blood and echoed in my voice. "I'll never forgive Dublin for what he did to me. Never."

"Not Dublin," he whispered. "Your grandfather. Have you forgiven your grandfather?"

I looked away. No. No, I had not forgiven the only father figure I'd ever had, the one man I'd thought would protect me. The very idea that Colm believed he deserved my forgiveness rankled me.

"He's dying, Brynn. You need to make peace with him before it's too late." He looked down, his eyes softened. "If I'd known . . ."

"It wouldn't have changed anything. We had already chosen different paths, both of us," I lied. He'd chosen his path. The priesthood. I didn't really choose the Marines. I didn't have a choice. I was eighteen, no longer welcomed at home. I had no work skills, very little education, and no money of my own. The only man I really loved had abandoned me. The military was my ticket out. My only choice, really.

"And *your* path almost led to your death." He was looking at my scarf again. "Is it bad, Brynn?"

I glanced away. He'd seen me before the scars, all of me, what would he think now? The explosion had seared the skin on over half my body. I kept myself well-covered these days. Skin grafts could only do so much. But still, my scars served as a constant and public reminder, an unwanted souvenir, of the war I preferred to leave behind. The whole left side of my torso was a reddish-purple mess of puckered, shriveled skin, pieced back together like a patchwork quilt.

His eyes were still on my scarf. *Show him. Show him how ugly you are.* It would certainly repulse him. It would serve him right. Because, yes, he did abandon me, with no word, no hope, no recourse. And it would serve *me* right to let him see the ugly creature I'd become, let me see the disgust in his eyes. Then maybe I could banish the feelings I still held for him.

I pulled my hand back and reached up to loosen the fabric, removing it from my neck. Air hit my bare skin, and a shiver ran through me. I stretched my neck downward and pulled back the edge of my sweatshirt. "It's here and on my shoulder, and my back, and . . ." My eyes fell over the front of my body. *And my left breast.* What was left of it after the explosion, was so damaged, it had to be surgically removed. It'd taken three reconstructive surgeries to give me even the semblance of a normal shape.

He'd fallen silent. I dared look at his face, expecting disgust, but instead found pain and sadness and something else. Something I'd seen before, out on those rocks all those years ago. Desire. And I felt it too. And before I could think better of it, I leaned inward, reached out, and touched his face. Our eyes locked. I drew him to me, his lips to mine. Heat spread throughout me, melting away years of resentment. He pressed closer; his hands found my face, then my neck. His fingers traced a line along my damaged skin. It felt right, safe, like it always had before. A moan escaped my lips, low and primal, then something shifted. I felt him tense. He stopped and pulled back. He pushed my hands from his face and stood. He looked surprised, shocked, angry . . . I stood too. Guilt washed over me. "I'm sorry," I said. "I'm so sorry."

CHAPTER 14

I swiped the back of my sleeve over my cheeks and looked around the diner's half-empty parking lot. After leaving the rectory, I'd driven around aimlessly, eventually parking down by the town branch of the Nolichucky River, where I sat for an hour or so, letting Wilco sniff his way along the water's edge while I sat in my car, rehashing the whole scene with Colm. What had I done? Hot embarrassment crawled over me as I thought back to our kiss. Was it all me? Or was it him too? Not that it mattered. There would never be anything between Colm and me. Never again. He'd made his choice.

It felt as if someone had pounded a thousand nails into my heart.

Why am I even here at the diner? Earlier that morning, I'd left the house intent on seeing Meg at some point during the day. I did need to talk to her about Eamon and Sheila. Still, maybe now wasn't a good time. She was at work, and I should really be home helping Gran prepare for tomorrow's funeral and spending time with family. But there was Pusser and his eagerness to pin this on a Pavee, and the way he'd focused his sites partially on Meg. "She has motive," he'd said. Did she? Assuming that Dub's accusation was true, did Meg know about Eamon and Sheila? Even if she hadn't before, she probably did now. I thought of all those people gathered around yesterday when Dub spewed his hateful accusations. Poor Meg. I reached for the door handle. *I'll just see how she's doing.*

Inside, the tang of spicy beef kicked my stomach into action. It rolled with hunger. The place was pretty much empty, so I headed straight for the corner booth, noticing Doc Styles sitting alone at one of the tables. I stopped to say hello.

"How's my patient today?" he asked, scrutinizing Wilco's front legs.

"Much better. Thanks for getting the medicine to me."

"No problem. I was in your area anyway." He gave Wilco a pat. "He's looking good. I don't think I saw any limping as you walked in here."

"No. And we were out in the woods all day yesterday."

His expression turned somber. "I heard. Terrible thing about that girl."

Meg approached with a couple of hot plates in her hands. "Hey, Brynn. I didn't expect you in here today." She glanced over at Doc's empty plates. "I'll get your bill right out," she told him.

"Then do you have time for a break?" I asked. "There's something I need to talk to you about."

She dipped her chin toward the plates. "Sure. Let me get these out and take care of Doctor Styles, then I'll be right back." She lowered her voice, her eyes gleaming. "I have something I want to tell you about too."

I watched her shuffle off, thinking she seemed awfully chipper. Maybe she hadn't heard about Eamon and Sheila. I said good-bye to the doctor and settled into the booth. A couple minutes later, Meg came back carrying a tray with two cups of coffee, a bowl of chili, and a plain hot dog for Wilco. "Chili's on the house. The cook overestimated the lunch crowd. There's a ton left over back there." She set the tray aside and slid into the vinyl bench across from me. I slipped Wilco the hot dog, wiped the slobber off my hands, and dug into my chili. Meg jabbered about this and that, the conversation moving along pleasantly while I struggled for a way to bring up Eamon.

As it turned out, she brought him up first. "Look what Eamon gave me." She shoved her hand in front of my face. There was a ring on her finger.

"What the hell's that?"

She shriveled. "A ring. That's what I wanted to tell you. Eamon and I are engaged." She pulled her hand back and scowled. "You don't like him." She glared at me. "I knew you didn't. I picked up on it the other day."

"I hardly know him."

"Then what?"

"Haven't you heard what Dub Costello said?"

She cringed. "I don't believe none of that."

"Come on, Meg. He accused Eamon of sleeping with his wife."

"Eamon says it's a lie."

"And you believe him?"

"Of course I do! He told me there was nothing between them. They were acquaintances, that's all."

"Dub made it sound like much more." There was that picture too. The one Doogan found at Dub's place. It showed Sheila at the Sleep Easy with some man. Eamon? Or was Sheila one of Al's girls, turning tricks on the side. Maybe trying to earn enough money to leave and get away from Dub?

"Dub's full of crap. You know that. You've always hated him. Why would you take his word over Eamon's? Over mine?"

"I'm not, it's just that—" I paused. "Don't you think you're rushing things? You've gone through a lot. How long has it been since—?"

"A year, Brynn. I've been widowed for a year. And I'm lonely. Sick of working this stupid job, waiting hand and foot on a bunch of settled folk. What's wrong with wanting to be happy?"

"Does Eamon make you happy?"

She looked down and twisted the ring on her finger. "Yes." But something in her hesitation and expression belied the affirmation. She looked up and met my gaze. "I'm happy, Brynn. Really."

I sat back, taking a couple bites of chili while she sipped her coffee. I decided to change topics. "Sheriff Pusser considers you a suspect in Sheila's murder."

"Me? Why?"

"Don't be dumb, Meg. The whole love triangle thing. He thinks you found out Sheila was sleeping with your boyfriend and killed her in a fit of jealousy."

"That's just ridiculous! How can you even say that?"

"I'm just telling you what's going through Pusser's mind."

"Look, Eamon knew Sheila, but they were just friends, okay?"

"Okay." Just a few seconds ago, she'd described them as acquaintances, now they were friends. My cousin's story was changing by the second. I squinted. *What's going on with her? Is she so lonely that she's willing to settle for anything?*

Sensing my doubt, she leaned forward and bit out her words. "He wasn't screwing her. He gave her one of the kittens from that stray cat's litter. He said she was lonely, and he thought it would make her happy. That's all there was to it."

Yeah. Now they were friends enough that he was giving her things to "make her happy." "I'm worried about you, Meg."

"Well, don't be. You've got enough of your own problems to worry about." She began to stand up.

I reached out and stopped her. "Hey. I'm trying to help you, that's all."

She broke my clasp and slammed her palm on the table. Wilco felt the vibration and sprang up under the table. Meg leaned in, tears glistening along the edges of her eyes. "All I wanted was for you to be happy for me. But you can't do that, can you? You're a lonely drunk, and you'll stay that way until you face your own problems and get some help. In the meantime, stay out of my life."

Out in the diner's parking lot, I shut Wilco in on the passenger's side and walked around my car.

"There you are, bitch."

I wheeled around. *Great, first a fight with Meg and now this jerk.* "What the do you want, Al?"

Al glowered as he stepped forward, then jumped back as Wilco pawed at the window, barking his head off. Slobber spewed from my dog's curled lips and smeared the glass. Al snorted, blocking my way back to the passenger door. "Stupid crippled mutt can't help you this time." He stepped closer. The stench of overripe BO and sickeningly sweet marijuana hit my nostrils. "What do I want? I'd like to see all you knackers wiped off the face of the earth, that's what."

"Yeah, well, I want a giant lollipop and a free trip to Disney. Ain't gonna happen."

His eyes narrowed. "You better—"

"Better what, Al? What's your problem anyway?" I headed around the front of my car, but he came up right behind me.

"I saw you talking to Drake."

"So?" I turned to face him as I reached my door.

"You ratted me out. I'm out money because of you, lady." He'd moved in closer, forcing me just beyond my door, then blocking my way.

I grasped my key but couldn't reach the lock beyond the bully. "You're a pimp. You should be in jail. You're lucky I didn't call the cops."

He snatched my arm. "You callin' the cops on *me*?" He laughed. "A thievin' gypsy calling the cops on me?" His eyes bored into mine. "You're actin' like you think you're better than me."

I tried to shake him off. "Let go!"

His grip tightened. Wilco was ramming his snout against the driver's side window now, the glass reverberating with his barking.

Al leaned in even closer. "You filthy gypsies don't belong around here, livin' like trash out there in your trailers, drinkin' and whorin' around. Sleepin' with your own cousins. And you . . ." His eyes glazed over with hatred. "Threatenin' *me* with the cops."

I'd positioned my key between my fingers, ready to shish-kebab his eyeball. His fingertips dug deeper into the flesh of my left arm. *One more move, Al, just one, and you're a blind man.*

He went on. "Listen to me. Nobody threatens me. And nobody screws me over and gets by with it. 'Specially not some pikey slut like—"

Crunching of gravel. We both turned. Another car pulled into the lot, and he dropped my arm. But he turned his rheumy eyes back on me, his spittle spraying my face as he said, "Folks don't want your type here no more. We're gonna get you out of here one way or the other."

"We're not going anywhere."

"We'll see."

He turned and walked to the diner entrance. I watched him, his shoulders hunched, his fists clenched, his gait solid and determined. I'd known guys like him in the Marines. Hot-headed lunatics with something to prove.

I looked down at my white knuckles still clutching my key ring, one metal key end protruding, ready.

Al could be dangerous.

I tightened the grip on my keys. Then again, so could I.

*   *   *

Al's threat hung with me on the drive back to Gran's place. And so did Meg's words. Pikey, slut. Crippled mutt. Lonely drunk. When did the insults ever stop? It was one thing to confront a settled jerk like Al. Another entirely to be called names by the one relative in my life who had been my steadfast friend. I reached across my seat and patted Wilco. I had only one friend now.

Then there was the heat that lingered from my encounter with Colm. It was as if someone had flipped a switch and turned on a part of me I'd suppressed all these years. I squirmed in my seat. Wilco turned my way, let out a little whine, and pushed his nose against the car door.

We were parked outside Gran's mobile home watching the buzz of activity: neighbors and friends coming and going with food and flowers. Preparations for tomorrow's service were in full swing. And more family had arrived: two more of Gran's siblings from Texas and some relatives on Gramps' side that I'd never heard of until this week. Some were overnighting at our place, and earlier Gran had asked if I wouldn't mind giving up my bed, maybe sleeping on the couch or in my vehicle, which I often did anyway, so that Great Aunt Tinnie, who suffered from sciatica, could have my bed. I didn't mind. My eyes slid toward Doogan's trailer. But maybe I didn't need to sleep in my car . . .

There'd be no rejection this time.

All I had to do is knock on the door. *Knock and you shall receive.* Scripture, something a man of God would say. I laughed at the irony of it all. Colm may not want me, but Doogan did. I'd sensed it a while back. The way he watched me, held my stare just a little too long, stood too close . . . I sat back in the seat and squeezed my eyes shut, imagining what it'd be like. His hands on me, his lips exploring me. Would it be gentle and slow or aggressive? The thought of it made my heart pound in my chest; blood coursed throughout my body. The heat in my belly spread lower, grew hotter . . .

I couldn't take it any longer.

I slid out of the car. Wilco followed, his head and tail low. He sensed my mood and probably couldn't decipher the emotions pouring from me. I couldn't; how could he?

Inside Doogan's trailer, the air was warm and humid and laced with a clean soapy smell. He'd answered the door with wet hair and a towel draped over bare shoulders. "Brynn?"

We were standing mere inches from each other, and I could feel my chest rise and fall, my breasts pushing against the fabric of my sweatshirt. His gaze travelled from my face to my body and back again. He blinked, his eyes searching mine with uncertainty.

I reached out and brushed a wet strand of hair from his forehead. With the tip of my finger, I traced a line down the side of his face, across his angled jaw to his full lips. He grabbed my hand and pressed it against his mouth, kissing my fingers, then my palm, his gaze holding mine as he captured my other hand and raised both my arms above my head, stepping in closer, forcing me back against the door and pressing his body against mine. He removed my scarf and lifted my chin, and I felt his tongue move along my jawline and under my earlobe. I closed my eyes and enjoyed the heat of his lips as they touched my neck, tender at first, then little nips that grew into stronger, more ravenous kisses. He grabbed my hair, pulled my head back, and took his fill, his lips not differentiating between my good skin and my damaged skin. Rough, calloused hands moved down my back, under my sweatshirt, and roamed freely. Nerves I thought were long ago dead, burned up and shriveled away, sprang to life. I pulled him closer, shifting and maneuvering until our bodies fit together. Maybe I wasn't what Colm wanted, what most men wanted, but Doogan wanted me.

He broke away, stepped back, and lifted my sweatshirt over my head. I watched as his eyes surveyed my body without a hint of repulsion. My wanting for him grew. His lips found mine again as he gently lifted me and guided me to the floor. The weight of his body on mine felt right, safe and good. I ran my hands along the long lines of his back muscles as our bodies rocked together. His breath hit my skin in hot, rapid spurts, and sensing my need or unable to control his own, his moves became more aggressive, faster and harder.

Then something happened. Whether it was his sudden urgency, or the familiar feel of the floor against my bare back, I don't know, but I was seventeen again, back in Dub's trailer, pinned against the floor, screaming and pleading while he forced my legs apart, forced himself into me. And before I could talk my mind out of it, my body tensed. I trembled.

"Brynn?" Doogan pulled back. "What is it? What's wrong?"

"No. No, please . . ." I tried to pull him back, make myself go back, back where we were just a minute ago, back to when it felt right.

But something had shifted between us. "Are you cold? You're trembling." He covered my arms with his and pulled me closer. Then something dawned in his eyes. "You're scared?" I hesitated, and he pulled back again. Concern or maybe anger flashed in his eyes. "You're scared of me?"

"No." Yet the trembling held its grip on my limbs; even my voice quivered with my objection.

He sat up and looked down at me. I felt horribly exposed. I folded my arms and covered myself.

He whispered something in Shelta, heavily brogued, and abruptly stood. I sat up and watched as he retrieved a blanket from the back of a chair. He came back to me, knelt down, and covered me. "Tell me," he said. "Tell me everything, Brynn."

And I did. The words and the tears poured from me as I told him about my childhood, my abandonment, my arranged engagement to Dublin, how I refused, and then how one month before my eighteenth birthday, Dublin Costello brutally and mercilessly beat and raped me. How I never thought something like that could happen, here, where I felt safe, surrounded by friends and so close to the family I trusted. And how afterward, Gramps blamed me. Ostracized me. I went on to tell him about the town boy I'd trusted, confided in, gave myself to, and who eventually abandoned me without any explanation. How all this led to my enlistment, and even though scouring desert sands for decomposed bodies seemed undesirable to most, I didn't mind the work, not really. It was easier to deal with the dead than the living, and it was rewarding to bring answers to families who'd lost someone they loved. How I'd never had the type of answers I needed. My regrets, my fears, my hopes, my dreams . . . they all tumbled out . . . and he listened.

And when I was done, emptied and exhausted, I could barely move, couldn't think another thought, the numbness in my soul was a deafening roar. I felt Doogan's solid arms as he lifted me and led me to the back of the trailer, to his bed, where he tucked me into his sheets and held me until I fell asleep.

CHAPTER 15

Sometime later, sirens jerked me awake. I sat up, alone in Doogan's bed, my eyes straining to adjust as the darkness strobed in bright flashes of red and blue. "Doogan!" My voice sounded flat and alone, tiny, like a child's, even in the small confines of his trailer.

I heard Wilco whining. I sprang from the bed, flipped on the lights, and found him facing the far corner, his back curled and tail tucked as he stared at nothing and shivered. *Wilco!*

I crossed the room and reached out to touch him, jerking my hand back when he snapped at it. I backed up, shocked at his behavior. A flashback. Still he needed immediate correction. For his sake and for our relationship. I grabbed him by the scruff and tugged his head up, making eye contact and letting displeasure show in my features. He demurred, his dazed eyes blinked back to reality, and he lowered his gaze, his muscles relaxing. I let him go, and he lowered his snout and eventually lay at my feet. I followed up with a quick pat on the head, a small token of trust and a little positive reinforcement. Still, he whimpered and whined, his eyes darting from shadow to shadow as police lights danced around the room.

I moved toward the front window when someone pounded on the door. "Police! Open up!" I'd barely snatched my sweatshirt off the ground and pulled it over my head when the door burst open. Harris rushed in, his weapon drawn. "Hands up! Hands up!"

I complied. Harris's weapon was pointed straight at my chest. Two more officers rushed in behind him and fanned out with their own weapons drawn. Behind me, Wilco snarled and barked at the intruders.

"Where's Doogan?" Harris shouted.

"I don't know."

"It's clear," an officer yelled out. The same was echoed by the other officer.

Pusser shuffled inside, his weapon secured in his holster. He eyed Harris right away. "Take your gun off her, you idiot." He mumbled something else and stepped toward me, keeping a leery eye on Wilco. "We're looking for Doogan."

"You and me both." I'd turned my focus to my dog, calming him the best I could.

Pusser was giving me a once-over, taking in my disheveled hair, crumpled clothing, and bare feet. He spoke into his radio. "Parks, I've got a 429. She's fine." Then to me. "Put some shoes on and follow me."

After some searching, I found one boot by the door, the other under a chair. All the while, Harris's eyes bore a hole in my back. The other officers stood off to the side, shifting anxiously as I worked into my boots and locked a still freaked-out Wilco in Doogan's bedroom.

My gut churned as we headed out the door. Outside, it looked like every emergency vehicle in the county was on hand, their throbbing lights piercing the darkness. Onlookers stood around in tightly cinched robes and slippered feet. I glanced toward Gran's place. "What's going on, Pusser? Are my grandparents okay?"

"They're fine. I sent Parks to tell them you're here. Your grandmother was worried about you."

I looked from him to the other officers. A putrid, wet burnt smell hung in the air. "What's burning?" I strained my neck, but my vision was blocked by cop cars and fire trucks. "Would someone tell me what's going on?"

"Dub Costello's place burned down."

My head snapped toward Dub's place. I headed that way, Pusser taking the lead and escorting me through the horde of onlookers and inside the cordoned area. Costello's mobile home had been reduced to a burned-out, smoldering carcass of corrugated steel. I looked to Pusser. "Costello?"

"No trace. So far. It's too hot for a thorough search."

Doogan! Doogan did this! He'd already thought that Costello was responsible for his sister's death; then I told him about the rape. *Stupid! Stupid!* This was my fault. I'd pushed him over the edge . . .

"What is it?" Pusser asked.

"Nothing."

"Where's Doogan?"

"I don't know."

"What do you mean? You were at his place. Where'd he go?"

I coughed and swallowed hard against the slimy smoke coating the back of my throat. "I fell asleep around nine. I woke up when I heard the sirens, and he was gone."

"So you have no idea when he left?"

I coughed again. Pusser's voice grew distant, like he was talking to me from down a long tunnel. My eyes stung. "No. I don't know when he left." I struggled to draw in air.

Pusser went silent and stared at me. I avoided his gaze, taking in the scene: fire trucks were on standby—useless at this point—as the cops pushed back the crowd that was quickly gathering. I saw a few familiar faces, all Pavees, no townspeople. Al's threat from earlier popped into my mind, and I searched the crowd again. I didn't see him. One of the officers was off to the side, questioning Old Man Nevin. "You're assuming arson," I said. Again, I thought of Al. He hated us enough to burn down one of our trailers, but why Dub's? No. That seemed too coincidental. This was personal. This was Doogan.

Pusser tipped his head toward the tree line. "We found an empty gas can a couple hundred feet into the woods."

This time of night, the woods behind Costello's place were inky dark and dangerous and nearly impossible to navigate. "A lot of stuff gets dumped back there." It was true. We lived too remotely for sanitation services, and although we burned or hauled off most of our trash, still people inevitably dumped things just inside the edge of the woods. Trash. Bodies. My mother's body. Sheila's body. Now maybe Doogan was out there somewhere, on the run after killing Costello. Clan justice. I shivered.

Pusser turned to face me straight on. "It seems you know Doogan better than I thought."

I didn't answer.

He continued, "What do you know about this?"

"Nothing." The cold, thin night air. The smoke . . . I coughed and sucked in deeply, but my throat was closing, my ears wooshing . . . I just couldn't get a deep breath.

Pusser didn't seem to notice. "You were there yesterday when your boyfriend kicked the crap out of Costello. He would've killed him if I hadn't stepped in."

"I don't know anything about this, Sheriff. You'll have to take my word on it." Sweat broke out on my upper lip. Now Pusser took notice and narrowed his eyes suspiciously, probably thinking he was onto something, sweating the truth out of me.

He was wrong.

Panic consumed me. Exhaustion, the cold air, the smoke, the sounds . . . I needed to get out of here. Back to Wilco, back to Gran's place, anywhere but here.

"You okay, Callahan?"

His voice was swallowed up by the buzzing in my ears. My heart kicked into jackhammer mode inside my chest. Clouds slipped over the moon, a breeze kicked up, and I shivered. From somewhere close by came the sound of a car door slamming. Then another, the noise echoing in the cold night air like the report of a rifle. I flinched. I was slipping again. My flashbacks were coming more often, getting worse . . . I shoved my sweaty palm into my pocket but felt nothing. My pills were gone. How many had I taken today? *Relax, Brynn. Just a car door.* I raised my hood to tuck the edges of my scarf closer to my neck, but it wasn't there. I felt the gnarled skin under my fingers, felt exposed, naked. A chill seized me and ran over my body like an icy shower. A tightness gripped my chest, I felt the sensation of a black curtain descending, and I knew what was coming. Not here. Not now. Not in front of Pusser. I inhaled and exhaled slowly, one . . . two . . . three. *Stay in the present. Stay in the present.* But the curtain fell, and suddenly I'm outside Falluja and . . .

I'm running. My heart pounds against my sternum, artillery fire hits all around me, the sound echoes through my skull, and debris pelts my skin. This area is supposed to be clear! Where's my unit?

"Kolwalski? Grady?"

I dive behind a large rock and cover my head. I want to stay here until help comes, but Wilco pulls me forward.

"No, boy. Stand down!" A mortar explodes. Dust blinds me; it cakes my nostrils and coats my tongue with an acid-tinged grit. I can't get any air. My dog's lead goes limp. "Wilco! Wilco!"

"He's here." Pusserss's voice sliced through the fog. "He's right here."

A familiar warmth pressed against my thigh where I crouched on the ground. I grabbed for my dog, worked his fur through my fingers. Reassuring him . . . reassuring me. "There you are, boy." I placed my head against his. He ran his tongue over my face as if to lick my wounds, invisible wounds only he recognized. The ones I tried, but never succeeded, to keep hidden from the rest of the world.

I realized that Pusser was hovering nearby. And another officer. "Sorry, Sheriff," the officer said. "We were searching the trailer like you said, and the dog got out and bolted this way. Couldn't stop him."

Pusser regarded me strangely. "It's fine," he said, waving the officer off. He shifted his weight, still looking at me, unsure of what to do, uncertain of what had happened. Good. Maybe it wasn't so bad. Maybe what had seemed like an eternity in my anguished mind was, in reality, only a few seconds. I could never be sure. The best I was ever able to do was take my cues from those around me and try to cover my absences. "Sorry. I was surprised to see him, that's all."

Pusser didn't look convinced. "You okay, Callahan?"

"Fine. Tired." I shifted. "Actually, I don't feel all that great. Tomorrow's my mom's funeral . . ." I swiped at my upper lip and let my words trail off. As cold as I was just minutes ago, I was sweating now. My scar felt like it was on fire. "I should get back home and check on my grandparents."

"Go ahead. I know where to find you. You see Doogan, call me. He's wanted for questioning."

The next day came all too soon. The day of my mother's funeral. The day I would say good-bye yet again, only this time for real.

I dressed with care, slipping on a simple long-sleeved black dress and a pair of lace-up ankle boots. I picked out a brightly patterned silk scarf and adjusted it around my neck, my thoughts drifting back to the day before, the way Doogan traced his fingers across my scar and the way I let him, without reservation and without shame.

And then I thought about Colm, and how he'd accepted me

as I am—damaged, broken . . . I stared at my reflection . . . ugly. But I'd seen it in his eyes. In that one stolen moment, before everything changed. He had wanted me . . . just as I am.

I untied the scarf and carefully folded it across the top of my dresser.

"Brynn." I turned to see Gran standing in the doorway. Her dress swallowed up her small frame. Was it simply too big, or had she lost weight recently? "I need your help," she said. "Your grandfather's fallen."

I followed her a few steps down the hallway and into Gramps' room. He was on the floor next to his bed, struggling to get to his feet, his oxygen bottle hissing, its tubes a spiderweb over his head.

"Gramps!" I rushed over, knelt down, and touched his arm. "Hold on, we'll help you." I glanced back at Gran. "What happened?"

"I don't know. He must've tried to get up without his walker."

"Someone get me off this damn floor!"

My head snapped back to Gramps. His arms flailed about, slicing the air like he was swimming against an unseen current. I leaned in closer, trying to settle him, and took a blow to the jaw. The strike stunned me and, instinctively, my hand rose in retaliation. I stopped myself, cursing my knee-jerk reaction. *Get ahold of yourself, Brynn. This is your grandfather.*

Gran stepped forward, shot me a scornful look that softened as she turned back to Gramps. "Calm down, Fergus."

Gramps opened his mouth to say something but coughed instead. He finished and collapsed weakly against the bed. I heard a wet gurgling sound from somewhere deep in his throat. Wilco shoved into our circle and sniffed at Gramps' face. I gently pushed him away. "Where are the guys?" I asked Gran.

"They've gone to the church, helping to set up for the luncheon."

I looked back at Gramps. "Are you hurt? Can you move?"

He'd gotten his arm tangled in his oxygen line. I gently worked it free.

He struggled, fighting my efforts. "Just get me the hell off the floor."

Gran stooped on his other side and together we hoisted him up to the bed. I tucked the sheets around his legs. He glared at Gran. "Where'd you hide my walker?"

"I didn't, Fergus. It's right here by the bed."

His cloudy eyes wandered around the room. I jingled the bell attached to his walker. "Over here, Gramps. On this side. Gran always puts it on the right side. Remember?"

He didn't even look that way. Instead, he narrowed in on Gran. "I heard talking outside my window last night. It was you, wasn't it? Talking to another man. Can't even wait until I'm in the grave."

"Gramps!"

Gran's eyes rounded with concern. "You're confused, Fergus."

"I ain't confused. I know what I heard."

"It was probably Aunt Tinnie," I said. "Talking to one of the fellows. All your brothers are here, you know. They've all come for the funeral."

His head bounced between us, his attitude swinging from anger to panic. "Funeral? What funeral?"

"Mary's funeral, Fergus." Grans's voice was barely a whisper.

"Mary. Our Mary?" A deep purple flush settled in the hollows of his cheeks.

Gran and I exchanged a look. Gran knew already, of course, she'd been with him night and day. But I'd not seen this part of his illness firsthand. As if the body's painful dying isn't bad enough, the mind slips out first, causing even more misery for both patient and everyone around him.

Gramps let out a little cry. "How can this be? How can this . . . ?" He pushed his torso a couple inches off the mattress, shook his head in frustration, then sank back into the pillows. He clenched his fists, clamped his lips tightly together, and, with flaring nostrils, drew deeply from his oxygen tube. I watched his chest rise and his lungs expand with air, only to collapse again in another spasm of wet coughs. I adjusted his pillows, trying to get him more upright, but my actions agitated him and spurred even more coughing. A glob of green phlegm oozed out the corner of his mouth.

I stepped back.

Gran snatched a nearby tissue and gently wiped at his cracked lips. "You need to calm down, Fergus." She looked my way and dipped her head toward the dresser. "Get me his pills."

The dresser was littered with spent tissues and prescription bottles. I fumbled around until I found a prescription for morphine. I held it up.

"That's it. He gets two."

I emptied some into my palm, one eye on Gramps. Just the sound of rattling pills seemed to calm him. I handed two over to Gran and, as soon as she looked down, slid a few into my own pocket.

"I've got your pills, Fergus," she was saying. Gramps' eyes eagerly searched the air in front of his face, and he opened his mouth like a baby bird eager for a worm. Gran popped them in. I grabbed his water bottle and bent the straw to his lips. Some dribbled out of his mouth. I dabbed at it with a wadded tissue and looked Gran's way. She was hovering nearby, watching and wringing her hands. She knew, we both knew: Gramps didn't have much time.

Colm's words echoed in my mind. *Forgive him.*

But I couldn't.

I turned away and left the room, quietly shutting the door behind me. Gran came out a few minutes later. "He's resting." She glanced at her watch. "Meg said she'd be here by now. She offered to sit with him while we go to the funeral."

"I wonder what's keeping her?" Although I thought I knew.

Our argument the night before. She was still mad. *No. That's not right.* Meg wouldn't let a disagreement between us get in the way of helping Gran. Would she?

Gran stared pensively at the family pictures that lined the hallway wall. Her and Gramps. Me as a child. A few of her immediate family and Gramps' too. Any pictures of my own mother were absent, taken down and hidden away long ago. Maybe that would change now that there were no more lies between Gran and me. I hoped so.

Gran reached up to straighten a lopsided frame. Her sleeve crept up her arm. I noticed a scratch. "What happened there?" I grabbed her arms and gently turned her wrists upward, revealing not just one, but several long scratches along the soft white flesh of both forearms. "Gran?"

She chewed on her lip. "I don't know. I don't remember."

"Did Gramps do this?" The scratches were deep, but thinly scabbed over.

She shrugged.

"We're going to have to call in some help soon."

"Let's get through today first. Then we can talk about all that." She turned back to the pictures, her expression taking on a faraway look. "I was thirteen when I first met your grandfather."

"Thirteen?"

"Yes. My mother and his mother were cousins. We'd come here to Bone Gap before them. My father wanted us kids to get some schooling, so we wintered over here, my brothers and me taking our learning at the schoolhouse. There weren't many of us here at the time. After my First Communion had come and gone, my folks got to worrin' about my future, so my mother sent a note to her cousin and told them about this place." She smiled. "Afraid she might have painted a much prettier picture of what Bone Gap was really like. All in hopes of luring her here, you know."

"Because of Gramps."

Gran chuckled. "Fergus's mother had five children. All boys, you understand. Mam was hedging her odds, betting that one of them would take a liking to me. She was right." She raised her eyes to the window. "Fergus was almost ten years older than me. Handsome and strong. And quiet." She looked my way. "He was the kindest, gentlest man I'd ever met."

Kind and gentle? Gramps? "Did your families arrange the union?"

"Not exactly. My father had a different notion. He and Fergus's father thought I should go to Fergus's older brother. But Mam understood."

I raised my brows. "Understood what?"

"That in my heart, I'd already chosen Fergus."

My jaw tightened. Where was that same understanding all those years ago when in my heart I'd chosen not to marry Dub?

Gran continued, "Mam stepped in for me. Convinced my father to let Fergus and me get married." Her gaze met mine. "Mam was a strong woman. Much stronger than I've ever been."

Something in Gran shifted, and a dark shadow crossed her face. This was all too much for her. My mother's funeral, Gramps' illness, the investigation. I reached out, touched her shoulder. "That's not true. You're the strongest woman I know, Gran."

The lines around her eyes deepened. "I haven't always been strong for you, *Lackeen*. And I'm sorry. That's changed, though. I want you to know that." I waited for her to explain what she meant, but she didn't. Instead, she glanced at her palms and changed the subject. "Quite the crowd gathered down the street."

"Mostly townsfolk," I said. I'd seen them first thing that morning when I crawled out of my car to come in to get dressed. After the fire, I'd finished what was left of the early-morning hours trying to catch a few winks out in my car. But the lights, the smell of smoke from Dub's burned-out trailer . . .

all of it had affected Wilco as much as me. I'd spent most of the night trying to keep him calm. Not that I really minded. Sometimes it was easier to stay awake than to fall asleep and face the nightmares that lingered in my mind, waiting for the opportunity to nibble away at my sanity. "The fire will be in the paper today. And all over the news channels." I'd seen plenty of reporters in the crowd, and a few troublemakers too. Namely Maybelle. "I'm sure this will stir things up even more."

"Did that *musker* know anything about Dublin?"

"His name's Pusser. Sheriff Pusser. And no. He didn't know anything last night. I haven't talked to him yet this morning."

Gran pursed her lips and turned away. I followed her to the front-room window. She pulled back the curtain and peered outside. "Where's that Meg? I've got to be getting to the church soon."

"I'll give her a call." I went back to my room and found my cell phone. No answer. Irritation pricked at me. *You can be mad all you want at me, Meg, but don't take it out on Gran.* I pocketed my phone, grabbed my keys and a sweater, and found Wilco. "We're heading over to Meg's place," I told Gran on the way out the door. "I'm going to go see what's keeping her."

The corners of Gran's mouth drooped. "Do you think something's wrong?"

"Nothing I can't fix; don't worry. If you have to leave before I get back with Meg, have one of the neighbors sit with Gramps. I'll meet you at the church."

Meg's trailer was on the other side of the mobile park, tucked back off the road on a double lot. When her husband was alive, the place was well kept and in pristine condition. Now weeds choked the front yard, and rust dripped from the corners of her metal window frames. Her car was parked on the concrete pad next to the trailer. I got out and moved toward her door.

My cell phone erupted. It was Pusser. "Costello's still missing, but there's no sign of human remains inside the trailer."

"What about his vehicle?"

"Parked next to the trailer. Not much left of it." He paused. "An accelerant was definitely used. That gas can I told you we found in the woods behind Dub's trailer was wiped clean, but we got a partial print inside the cap. It's a match for your boyfriend."

My grip tightened on the phone.

Pusser was still talking. "He's wanted for arson."

"I understand."

"I've put out a BOLO on him. I'll find him. But if you know something about this, now's the time to come clean."

Pusser didn't trust me. Not that it mattered. The feeling was mutual. "If I knew something, I'd tell you. I don't. I have no idea where Doogan is and . . ." I glanced toward Meg's trailer. "I've got my own things to deal with right now." I told him I'd be in touch and disconnected.

I stomped through the weeds and banged on Meg's door. "Meg! It's me, Brynn. I need to talk to you."

Loud music thundered through the thin metal walls of her trailer: flutes, fiddles, and tin whistles. Despite my anger, I grinned. Meg was crazy for the traditional Irish stuff. When we were kids, she had lived for the parties, coming alive with the music, drinking and dancing, laughing . . . I banged louder. "Come on, Meg!"

I gave up and tried the knob. It was open. I stepped up and inside her trailer. Maybe the outside looked trashy, but the inside was neat and tidy. "Meg! Meg!"

Wilco had come in behind me. Now his nose twitched excitedly along the floor. He moved about, taking in the new scents. A kid in a candy shop.

The place seemed empty. Maybe she had walked to our trailer, I thought, or maybe Eamon had picked her up in his car.

But why would she leave the music on? I crossed to the stereo, flipped it off, and listened for any sign of Meg. Instead, I heard Wilco lapping at something. I looked toward the kitchen. Nope. No Wilco.

I groaned. The toilet. Gross. I scurried toward the bathroom in the back of the trailer and, as expected, found Wilco folded into Meg's tiny bathroom. I pushed inside, reached for his collar, but stopped short when my feet sloshed on the wet floor. The shower curtain was heaped in the corner of the shower. Water was everywhere, the bath mat soaked through, and the tiny mirror over the vanity was spotted with water marks. A shampoo bottle was on the floor next to the toilet.

My gut clenched. I yanked Wilco by the collar and dragged him out, using my sleeve to shut the bathroom door. Ten steps later and I was inside Meg's bedroom. "Meg! Meg!" My foot hit on something on the floor. A hairbrush. I bent down and picked it up. Long red hairs wound through its bristles. Red hair. My mind flashed back to my mother's red hair camouflaged against the russet hues of fall leaves, and then the long thin hairs clinging to Sheila Doogan's nearly skinless skull and now . . . Meg's hair. I remembered the porn flicks Doogan had found in Dub's trailer. Dub had a thing for redheaded women. A perversion. I knew him to be controlling, violent . . . and I knew firsthand what he was capable of when a woman disobeyed him. I thought back to that photo Doogan found of his sister at the Sleep Easy. Evidence of an affair? His red-haired wife had cheated on him—the ultimate betrayal. Enough to tip him over the edge and create a monster determined to make every redheaded Pavee woman pay for his wife's sins?

I grabbed my dog and ran back outside. I hit RETURN on Pusser's last call.

"What is it, Callahan? You decide to come clean on Doogan?"

"Meg's missing." A long pause ensued. "Pusser. Did you hear me? My cousin's missing."

"Where are you?"

"At her place." I gave him directions, but he already knew where she lived. "Something's not right," I said. Panic set in. "It looks like there was a struggle."

"I'm not far. I'll can be there in ten."

He hung up. I called Gran and caught her before she left the house. "Hey." I kept my voice calm. "Is Meg there by chance?"

"Here? No. I thought you were getting her." Anxiety zinged over the line. "Where is she? Has something happened to Meg?"

"Please don't get upset, Gran. I'm sure everything's okay."

"But it's not like her to simply not show up."

"She's probably with Eamon. I'm going to check his place, okay? I just wanted to let you know that I might be late getting to the church." *Keep calm, Brynn. No need to get Gran all upset.* "How's Gramps?"

"He's sleeping. I called Mrs. Black. She said she'd come sit with him until Meg gets here."

"Good. I'll see you soon." I hung up before she could ask any more questions.

Wilco and I circled around to the back of Meg's trailer. There was no sign of a break-in; nothing seemed out of place. A chill ran up my spine. I pulled my sweater tighter and folded my arms across my chest. *Where are you, Meg?*

I looked at Wilco. Maybe he'd picked up on something?

But Wilco hadn't picked up on any scents—thank God. Instead, oblivious to the sounds around us, he'd wandered over to a truck parked along the curb, one of those jacked-up units with big tires and a frame that sat high on a lift kit. He half-squatted his single back leg, lifted the stump of his lost one, and peed. Big-time. A look of relief washed over his face. He had this thing about tires—the bigger the tire, the bigger the relief.

Back out front, I checked Meg's car. It was locked, and the hood felt cool. I scanned the immediate area. There was another trailer on the lot next to Meg's, but it looked vacant. No cars were parked outside the mobile home down the road either. I looked back and forth—Meg's car, the neighbor's place, up the road, and back to Meg's car. *What the hell's taking Pusser so long?*—I was getting antsier by the minute.

I turned to head back inside the trailer when Wilco perked up, his eyes zeroing in on the tree line. I followed his gaze. A dark shadow darted between a nearby electrical pole and the edge of the forest. I blinked. A trick of light? An animal?

Wilco's reaction told me differently: ears back, tail high, lips rigid. I went to him and squatted, placing my hand on his neck and leveling my gaze with his. *What do you see, boy?*

I caught another flash of movement around the edge of the transformer box. A figure wearing a dark brown hooded camo suit, boots, and a ski mask. Not an animal. A man.

A man lurking behind Meg's trailer.

My muscles tightened and coiled like a snake's body. I sprang up and struck out across the backyard, running full speed. Instantly, the man broke from cover and ran toward the neighbor's trailer. I hiked my dress to my thighs to free my legs and ran harder.

Wilco ran next to me, almost playfully, keeping pace with my pace, his eyes darting from the ground to me and back to the ground again. Wilco was the best human remains detection, or HRD, canine around, and if I was being attacked or threatened, he'd kill to defend me, but he wasn't conditioned to attack on demand. So, while I had no doubt this mysterious person was a threat, or maybe even our killer, to Wilco this was just a fun romp in the neighborhood.

The man had a least a forty-yard head start and was moving fast, dodging between parked vehicles and trailers, quickly making his way deeper into the trailer park. A metal garbage can seemed to spring up out of nowhere, blocking my path. It crashed to the ground, clanging like a thousand cymbals.

The front door of the trailer swung open. The owner stepped out. "Hey! What the . . . ! Who's gonna clean up this mess?"

My foot hit on a paper plate slimed with blobs of potato

salad and a half-eaten ham sandwich. I skidded and hit the pavement, gashing my palms and knees.

I righted myself and kept going. Blood dripped into my boots, my lungs stung with exertion, and, for a second, I lost him. I stopped and listened, straining to hear something other than my own heart pounding in my ears.

Who was this guy? Did he have something to do with Meg's disappearance? Possibilities flew through my mind. He wore camo. A hunter? A stupid hunter, perhaps. I hadn't seen any orange, and it was shotgun season. What type of idiot does that? And why run? Maybe an unlicensed hunter, a poacher. Or one of the Mexicans we'd seen before. Or maybe it was Dub. I already knew he was a psychopath. Was he lurking behind Meg's trailer, stalking yet another red-haired Pavee woman? Neither my mother nor Sheila were killed where they were found. Did he hold them somewhere in his mobile home, maybe in that horrible room Doogan had described, making them wait in terror for the end . . .

Meg. Oh, Meg.

A distant crashing sound drew my attention to the right. Dogs broke out into a rapid chorus of barking. I hesitated and looked in the other direction. The mobile home park was now a symphony of echoes, as sounds banked off the metal-sided trailers like balls in a pinball machine. *Where'd he go? Where is he?*

Another crashing sound. A neighbor shouting. I swiveled and looked behind me. Then, refocusing on my task, I scanned the neighborhood for any sign of the intruder: sounds, a flash of color, anything. Nothing. *Crap.* I'd lost him. And maybe my only chance of finding Meg alive . . .

The sound of a grinding engine cut through the air. My head snapped to the right. I heard it again. Definitely coming from the right.

Breaking into a full sprint, I tore down the street, checking every parked car I passed. Nothing.

I heard it again. This time, I pinpointed it a couple streets over. I ran between two trailers, over the next street, and through the side yard of a mobile home. Up ahead, an old Ford pickup, brown and yellow with a topper, struggled to start up. I ran faster, but I was too far away. With the next crank, the truck's engine roared to life. Tires squealed and smoked as it peeled away from the curb and raced down the road. I yanked out my cell and got off a couple shots before it completely disappeared, then jogged back toward Meg's trailer, my pulse in my ears.

Wilco, still feeling playful, darted back and forth in front of me, stopping here and there to sniff out an interesting odor.

"Callahan!"

Pusser was in Meg's side yard, waving me toward the trailer. "Where the hell were you?" Two more cop cars screeched to a halt in front of the trailer. "I saw your car . . . I thought . . . I called in every unit in the vicinity."

I passed by him, hitting SEND on the photo as I made my way to the front of the trailer. "Check your texts," I said. "There was a guy here earlier. He ran. I chased him through the neighborhood. He had a truck parked a couple roads east of here. I just sent a picture of the truck."

"Got it."

"Think you can get a license plate number from that?"

"I'll send it in to the department. Get an analyst to enhance it."

He motioned for his officers to stay put and followed me inside the trailer. "The door was open when I got here," I explained. "Her music was playing."

He followed behind me. I headed for the bathroom, stopping at her bedroom on the way. I stopped in front of the dresser. Pusser came up next to me. "What is it?"

"Her purse and phone are still here. There's no way she left without them. And check out the bathroom. Water's all over. I think . . ." My voice cracked with fear. "I think someone snatched her from the shower."

"Take it easy. Maybe she's at work."

"I don't think so. Johnny gave her the day off for the funeral."

He crossed to the bathroom and used a handkerchief to open the bathroom door. An unrecognizable emotion flitted across his face as he peered inside, but he recovered quickly. "Was this door closed when you came in?"

"No. I shut it to keep my dog out."

His brows shot up, but before he could say anything, I started in. "I think it's Dub."

"Dublin Costello? How's that?"

"His trailer, the fire . . . I don't think it was arson. I think Dub torched his own place. To hide evidence."

"What brought you to this conclusion?"

"Doogan found some stuff in Dub's trailer the other day." I had no choice now but to come completely clean with Pusser. Meg was missing. I told him about the blood on the carpet fiber, the photograph of Sheila at the Sleep Easy, and the porn videos. I emphasized the porn videos. "Think about it. My mother and Sheila were both red-haired Pavees. Dub has a thing for red-haired women. He also has a thing for power and control. I think he's gone off the deep end."

Pusser listened, chomping on his toothpick like a crazed man. "That doesn't explain Doogan's disappearance."

"All I know is that Meg's missing."

"Is your cousin into drugs?"

"What? No!"

"How about you, Callahan?"

I took a step back.

"Last night, when we were talking, you seemed . . ." He hesitated. "I don't know. Spacey. Were you and Doogan shooting up earlier that evening?"

My flashback. I'd hoped that Pusser hadn't noticed it, but he did. And he'd taken it for something else. For a drug-induced episode.

I gritted my teeth and shot my hands deep into my pockets. "I don't do drugs." But even as I bit out the words, my fingertips hit on the morphine tablets I'd stolen from my grandfather's prescription. Medicine, though. Not drugs. This was different. Just a little something to get me through until I could hook up with a new doctor. "What are you thinking, Pusser? That all us gypsies do drugs? Or maybe that the whole clan is tied in with a cartel?"

Before Pusser could answer, his phone rang. A minute later, he pocketed it. "They ran the plate on the truck. The vehicle's registered to Al Lambert."

"Al Lambert . . . Al?"

"You know him?"

"Yeah. He works at the motel. He's part of that protest group trying to get us evicted." I gave Pusser a quick rundown on my confrontation with the guy. "We had some problems at work the other day, and he ended up getting fired. He blames me."

"He threatened you?"

"Yeah. Pretty much. Said he wanted to wipe us gypsies off the face of the earth."

"Okay. I'll have him brought in for questioning, but I don't see a connection. But Doogan"—he narrowed his eyes— "Doogan did a stint in prison."

"Yeah. Drug charges. He told me." I glared at him. "People change, you know. He's not involved with a cartel, believe me. Not some gypsy drug operation either. Or whatever it is you've conjured up in your mind."

"Then where is he?"

The million-dollar question. "I don't know. But he's not high on my priority list right now." I pushed past him and headed for the door. "I need to find my cousin."

He cut me off, his arm crossing in front of me, his face a

mixed bag of authority and frustration. "Look, Callahan. I'm looking at two murders, arson, drug trafficking, a cold-case murder that may be connected, or not . . . I've got every resource possible working around the clock. I've even brought the feds in on this drug stuff. And all this stuff going on between you people and those protesters—"

"You're feeling pressure. I get it. But you're wrong about us. We're not all criminals." I pushed past him. "You pass on any idea of a settled guy, like Al, being involved, even though he just ran off like a scared jackrabbit from an obvious abduction scene. It just never dawns on you that it could be *you people* involved, does it? Do whatever you want, Pusser. I need to find my cousin."

CHAPTER 16

Fifteen minutes later, I whipped into the parking lot at the vet clinic. There were only two cars in the lot, and neither of them was Eamon's Trans Am. I stepped out of my car, attached Wilco's lead, and made my way to the entrance, passing a woman leaving with a beady-eyed Chihuahua in her arms. Just inside the door, a sharp-smelling mixture of animal urine and piney disinfectant hit my nostrils. I held back a sneeze, my eyes watering as I looked around. Except for Doc Styles, the waiting room was empty.

He looked up from his desk and smiled; then his gaze dropped to my dog, and his expression sobered. "Is everything okay with Wilco?"

"I'm not here for my dog. I'm looking for Eamon."

"Eamon. Why?"

"I'm trying to find Meg, my cousin. He's dating her."

Recognition registered on his face. "That girl who works at the diner?"

"That's right. Have you seen her this morning?"

"No, and I haven't seen Eamon either. He was supposed to be in earlier this morning."

"He didn't show for work?"

"Nope."

"Is that like him?"

"No, but . . ." He blew out a stream of air. "I'm sorry I can't be of more help, Brynn. If Eamon does shows up, I'll tell him to give you a call." He dismissed me with a quick glance toward the door, then busied himself with some papers.

I shifted my weight and blurted, "Meg's missing." He looked up, his eyes rounding with surprise. I continued, "I can't find her anywhere, and I was just at her trailer, and it looked like there'd been a struggle."

"You think something's happened to her?"

"I don't know what to think."

His eyes darted toward the backroom and then to me again. He knew something. "What is it?" I asked. When he didn't answer, I stepped closer, leaned over his desk, and spoke a little louder. "If you know something, tell me."

"I'm not sure—"

"Listen, Doc. There's been two women murdered, and now my cousin's missing. This is no game. Tell me what you know."

"There's some meds missing from the supply area."

"What type?"

"Ketamine. We use it as an anesthesia. But some people abuse it. The street name's Special K."

I'd heard of Special K. "The date rape drug?" I stared at Styles, sickened.

"That's its reputation, but addicts use it to get high. I receive controlled shipments monthly. They're strictly regulated and kept locked up in a refrigerated storeroom." His gaze fell. "Eamon and I are the only ones with keys."

I clutched my stomach. Was Eamon an addict? "How much is missing?"

"I'm just now going through inventory records. The numbers are off by several dozen units. It comes packaged in cases of ten-milliliter vials." He cleared his throat. "And that's just in the last couple of months."

I didn't know the dosages for that drug, but Styles's clenched jaw told me all I needed to know: Eamon might be an addict, but those numbers hinted at much more. More than likely, Eamon was a dealer, or maybe he was somehow tied into Al's prostitution business. Ketamine could be used to subdue young girls, eventually forcing them into sex trafficking. My mother had worked as a prostitute. Sheila too, maybe. Was Sheila really seeing Eamon as a lover . . . or was he pimping her out? Was this tied into their murders? And now Meg. *Oh Meg! Where are you?* I knew Eamon didn't live far from Gran and Gramps, but I'd never paid attention to where exactly. I leaned over Styles's desk. "Get me Eamon's address."

He retrieved the address from his files, jotted down the information, and handed it to me. "I hope she's okay."

A sickening feeling settled in my stomach. Time was ticking down on Meg's life.

"Me too," I whispered. "Me too."

I dropped Wilco's leash, leaned against my car, and dialed Pusser.

"Where are you now?"

"I'm at the vet clinic, looking for Eamon. I thought he might know where Meg is, but he's not here. And, get this, Styles thinks he's been stealing ketamine from the supply closet."

"Ketamine? How much?"

"Enough to make half the county high as a kite."

Pusser let out a low whistle.

"Styles says Eamon's a no-show for work today. I'm heading by his place now."

"No need," Pusser said. "I'm at his trailer now. No one's here."

That pulled me up short—so Pusser was also worried about

Meg. That should have made me feel better, but it only meant the danger for Meg was clear to the sheriff as well. "He drives a late-model Trans Am."

"Nope. Not here. Think they're on the run?"

"Meg and Eamon?"

"It makes sense, you know. The two of them stealing ketamine from Styles, selling it to locals. Maybe the Costello woman was in on it. Your mother too. Or she could have been one of their customers. It could all be connected."

"No. Not Meg." So Pusser wasn't worried about Meg but targeting her. I should have known.

"You've been away for a long time, Callahan. She's widowed. Times are tough. Maybe she's desperate."

"No!" I banged my hand against my car. The sudden movement startled Wilco, or maybe he felt the vibration. "Get off it, would ya, Pusser? Something else is going on here." I tried to quell the anger and panic growing inside me. Bottom line, I needed to find Meg, and getting Pusser angry wasn't going to help my cause. "I'm heading to the diner. Maybe someone there knows something."

I shifted the phone to my other hand and reached for Wilco's leash. It was gone. Wilco was gone. *Crap!* He'd taken off again. *This is the last thing I need right now.*

I got off the phone with Pusser and searched for him. I cursed myself. I should have bought that vibration collar I'd seen online for out in the field, or times like this when he wandered away. I could simply press a button and zap him into obedience. But a couple hundred bucks had seemed like too much to spend. What was that anyway? Two days, maybe three of toilet scrubbing? I bit back a chuckle. *Forget it, Brynn. It ain't gonna happen. Shouldn't need it anyway, if my dog would just do as he's supposed to do.*

A cool breeze swept over me; I pulled my sweater tighter and circled my vehicle, glancing under the carriage. Wilco wasn't there. Then I caught sight of a familiar bushy tail poking out from behind a storage building set back by the tree line—a Quonset hut that rose from the earth into a rusty half-circular arc of corrugated green metal. I headed over there, glad to have found him and eager to get on my way. But any relief I felt melted away as I drew closer. I stopped, my feet rooting in horror as I watched my dog working across the ground. That hitch in his tail, the way his ears perked forward and his nose quivered, first working the ground, then the air—it all indicated one thing:

Wilco smelled death.

Not Meg! God, please . . . I broke into a jog, heading his way, then pulled up short, remembering not to interfere with his work. He was moving at a good pace now, zigzagging along the edge of the woods. I shifted from foot to foot. The burden of waiting for him to finish his task was becoming nearly unbearable.

Maybe he'd hit on a rotting rodent or a larger animal. This was an animal clinic, after all. Things happen. Animals die. Their remains need to be disposed of. How was that done anyway? Cremation? But this is a small country operation. Would the doctor have a crematory, or . . . my eyes skimmed the nearby tree line. The woods, the same woods that ran for miles along this mountainside, from Bone Gap down to McCreary. Cove woods was the scientific term—a dense almost tropical foliage in the summer—which even at this time of the year made for a nearly impenetrable covering and an easy dumping ground. *Sure, that's it.* Styles probably buried animals back there. Nothing wrong with that. And the scent of all those animals . . . well, it would be overwhelming to Wilco's several hundred olfactory cells. No wonder he was going crazy.

As I looked again at my working companion, an automatic switch turned on in my mind. It was a transformation I'd experienced with every search: a numbed resolve as my brain mapped the terrain, planning potential routes that would take us to "most likely" sites while avoiding inherent danger. Debris-strewn buildings had been the worst, with every step a potential danger to my faithful companion as he relentlessly searched. Even open areas posed dangers; scorching desert winds had scrubbed my skin like sandpaper, but Wilco never flinched. How many scent trails had we followed in the past, him in the lead, me in command of our safety?

Memories of one search sprang to mind: a camel's decaying carcass, flies swarming thick around it. Wilco had passed its fetor without a glance.

Now another chill dug into my soul.

Wilco never reacted to the scent of a dead animal.

Or the scent of a live human.

He was trained for cadavers—only for the death stench of human decay.

Not Meg. Not Meg. Not Meg . . .

I continued watching as Wilco moved on to the storage shed, his nose working the weed-covered edges. Parts of the shed walls were rusted and jagged and formed a useless barrier against weather and whatever rodents might wish to burrow their way inside. The north side was covered with blackish-green speckles of mildew. The whole thing looked like it was on the verge of collapse. I lost sight of Wilco as he darted around the corner, only to return a second later and sniff some more at the large double garage door. He hesitated, pawed at the bottom edge, and growled. He was clearly agitated. I crossed to him and squatted down, my vision of sight now level with his.

That's when I saw the tracks.

Parallel lines, with a three- to four-foot tire stance, leading up to and disappearing under the garage door. I'd seen these tracks before, across desert sands and war-engulfed terrain. Made by government-issued all-terrain vehicles, the very same type that I'd ridden in and used to transport recovered human remains. Corpse wagons, we called them—filled to the brim with dead soldiers, whole and in pieces, making their last journey back to base camp.

Corpse wagons.

Springing to my feet, I placed my palms flat against the garage door and pushed upward. It creaked open, about a foot off the ground. Wilco was pacing now, running his nose along the outer edges of the barely raised door, stopping here and there to bark at me. "Get inside, get inside," he seemed to say. My mind zinged back and forth, vacillating between fear and panic, dread and urgency. I bent, put my knees into it, and hefted the door a couple feet higher.

Wilco bolted inside. I crouched down and followed, the back of my sweater snagging on the rough metal as I maneuvered underneath. It was dark inside and smelled like wet cardboard and gasoline and something coppery sweet.

Blood.

I stood stock still, waiting for my eyes to adjust. As I suspected, a four-wheeler sat in the middle of the dirt floor. Then I saw Wilco bouncing on his back leg and clawing at the side of the vehicle. He was clamoring to get inside, to where the scent must've been the strongest. His leash trailed behind him. I grabbed it, led him safely away from ATV, and tethered him to the leg of one of the workbenches that lined the far wall of the shed. Once he was secured, I quickly rewarded him with a few long strokes before turning back to investigate further.

The blood smell was intense, even to my non-canine nose. I turned on my phone and activated my flashlight app, shining it around the interior of the vehicle. A dark stain smeared the entire back cargo box of the ATV, streaking the metal sides and the back of the bench seat. The natural assumption would be that an injured animal had been transported in this vehicle. But Wilco's nose told me differently.

This was human blood.

My limbs trembled. Sourness burned the back of my throat. Then my phone light caught something that set panic coursing through my veins—long strands of red hair wrapped around a bolt in the floorboard. My mother's hair? Sheila's? Meg's?

And there was something else. Just on the edge of my awareness, like a nearly invisible spider's thread that connected one thing to another, but what? I forced fear aside and commanded my brain to enter that dark place.

My vision narrowed, fading along the edges and intensifying on the hair—long, wavy strands of red hair. I recalled sitting across from Meg at the diner the day before, watching as she'd tucked a loose strand of her beautiful hair behind her ear, hair as curly as these strands, but there was something else . . . I closed my eyes and saw it: the light from the nearby window catching on the stone of her engagement ring.

I'd seen that ring before. In Doogan's kitchen. It was the same ring his sister wore in the photo hanging on his fridge. Tendrils of white gold, almost a filigree, at the sides of a square-cut diamond.

I grabbed for the edge of the vehicle, steadying myself as the facts permeated my shock-racked mind. Not Dub. Not Al. But Eamon. Eamon had access to the ketamine. Eamon had access to this ATV.

And Eamon had access to Meg.

A sudden growl from Wilco jerked me back to the present. *Wilco?* I turned his way, and something dark flashed in the corner of my vision. I flinched, grabbed for my knife. Not there! I raised my hand to strike out, but too late. The sharp stab of a needle penetrated my shoulder. I flung my arm up and back to fight, but heat oozed through it, and my arm crumpled, useless. I tried to turn, but the burn snaked through my limbs, liquefied my muscles. My knees buckled, and I plunged forward into darkness.

CHAPTER 17

I came to facedown on a wood floor with my hands bound behind my back. Razor-like plastic ties gashed my wrists. Blood trickled onto my palms, turning them both sticky and slick at the same time. Yet my brain didn't register pain. Not yet. *The aftereffects of the drug probably still coursing through my system.*

Sounds were distant and muffled, but I heard voices coming from somewhere . . . deep and low . . . masculine . . . agitated . . . I didn't really care. I was wrapped in a warm, drug-infused cocoon. My body was loose, relaxed, my mind free-floating, a welcome respite from the normal zing of anxiety that undercut my every sober moment. I gave into the feeling, glad for the comfort. I sank lower and lower . . . happy to forget about everything . . .

Meg. Where's Meg? I've got to find Meg.

I forced open my swollen eyelids and turned my head toward the voices, my mouth brushing against the filthy floor. Dirt and dried bug parts and God knew what else stuck to my lips like lint to masking tape. I squinted at my surroundings. I was alone, in some sort of old shack converted into a drug lab. A shop light hung by chains over a wooden table lined with butane-fueled torches, beakers, and ceramic bowls, pots, mixing and measuring supplies. Empty glass vials littered the top of the table next to a small microwave. There was a gas-powered generator in the corner of the room. It hummed softly. The air smelled hot and strangely acidic and a little like an oily gas station. Again, low murmurs of voices came from outside the thin walls of the shack—somewhat muted, but distinctly male and Hispanic. I knew those voices. The men from the woods. Cartel, Pusser had assumed, ruthless and heavily armed.

Then another voice. Male also. But without the Spanish accent. Eamon. So Eamon was mixed up with a Mexican drug cartel.

My body broke into a cold sweat. Time was limited. *Think. Think!*

I tried to turn over, but my muscles were like warm Jello. Squeezing my eyes tightly, I focused my efforts. Side to side, side to side . . . finally I landed on my back, biting back a cry as my weight crushed against my bound wrists. Pain shot through my forearms up through my neck and radiated throughout my body.

Good! Pain is good. The drug is wearing off.

Folding my legs, I pressed upward to a seated position and searched for anything to use as a weapon. But my gaze hit on hair. Red and curly and protruding from under a tarp in the corner of the room. *Meg's hair!*

Meg. I have to help Meg.

Folding my body, I worked my hands down over my buttocks. My shoulders strained and nearly pulled from their sockets. My dress was bunched, the fabric hindering my movement. The irony hit me—wearing a dress for my mother's funeral and now dressed for my own.

No! Not my own, but Eamon's. He'd pay for what he'd done to Meg.

I wriggled until my wrists slid over the back of my bare

thighs. A couple more bends, some twisting, and my hands were in front of my body. Exhausted, I fell back to the floor, closed my eyes, and drifted back to the warmth and comfort of the drug . . .

Come on, Brynn. You're almost there.

I worked back up to my knees, then to my feet, searching the tables for something to use to cut my ties. Nothing. Nothing but drug-making equipment and none of it sharp enough to cut plastic.

My eyes darted back and forth, frantically searching, searching . . . then my gaze caught on a knife lying on top of a stack of boxes in the corner of the room. I hurried over and picked it up with my bound hands. It fell to the ground with a ping. I glanced at the door. The voices were still talking. I crumpled to my knees, picked up the knife again, and rocked back onto my bottom. I positioned the handle between my feet and frantically sawed the plastic back and forth over the blade.

Come on . . . come on!

It wasn't working. The ties needed to be tauter. Time was running out.

Determined, I braced my wrists as far apart as I could, forcing the tie to cut deeper into my flesh. I grimaced from the pain as the plastic tie tightened between them. I ran it over the blade again. Back and forth, back and forth. My fingers swelled and tingled. Blood now flowed freely from large gashes around my wrists. Tears burned my cheeks.

Outside, an engine roared to life. Someone shouted in Spanish. The voices grew louder, more animated.

If I don't free my hands, I'm as good as dead.

Back and forth. Back and forth. *Come on . . . break!* I bit my lower lip and sawed harder. *Snap!* Cool air rushed over my raw wounds. I stared incredulously at my liberated hands. *I'm free!*

A sound outside the shack's door jerked me back to reality. Eamon? The Mexicans? My throat constricted with fear.

I slid the knife into my boot, snatched up the broken pieces of zip tie and dove back to the floor, clasping my hands behind my back and closing my eyes just as the door opened. I kept my eyes closed. Noises penetrated the stillness: footsteps thudding against the wood floor under my ear; behind me, the clinking of glass shoved aside; the *thunk* of something heavy hitting the table. A click. The sound of fanning money. A low, barely audible chuckle. Another click. Then footsteps again. They came closer. Closer and closer until I felt someone standing directly over me. My heart hammered against my ribs. I forced my mind elsewhere.

Stay still. Stay still.

The footsteps retreated. Relief washed over me.

Then I heard the scraping sound of the tarp against the floor. Slowly, I raised one eyelid.

It wasn't Eamon moving about the shack, but Styles. *Styles?*

I blinked as he bent down and peeled back the tarp. There were two bodies: Meg and Eamon. They lay next to each other, both facedown, his blood-crusted arm draped over her body. Meg's face was turned toward me, and except for the paleness of her skin, she looked peaceful. Her eyes were closed, her head resting in the crook of one of her arms, the other arm protectively tucked under her body. Looking at her, I could almost believe she was simply asleep.

Then Styles jerked her leg, pulled her from Eamon's embrace, and rolled her belly up. He slid the engagement ring from her finger, pocketed it, and dropped her arm. It hit the floor like dead weight.

Dead weight.

Please no . . . not Meg . . . Memories flooded my mind: her standing beside me, unafraid, in schoolyard confrontations; her lilting laugh; her infectious optimism; how she twirled her crimson ringlets around her finger . . . our last fight. Cries threatened to escape my throat. I swallowed the agony rising within me and felt the cold blade in my boot. Styles was going to pay for this.

My inner monster swelled. I struggled to temper it. *Wait. Wait for the right opportunity.*

Styles moved quickly now, his back to me. He extracted a pistol from his waistband, wiped it clean, and placed it in Eamon's hand. He readjusted it twice. He was setting a scene. A scene that would frame Eamon for three murders: Meg, Sheila, and my mother.

Patience, Brynn. Wait.

Styles was too close to the gun and too far from me. I'd be dead before I reached him.

He stopped, shifted his stance, and turned my way. I quickly shut my eyes. His footsteps thumped closer, closer, then he passed by me. A few seconds later, I heard another noise. A faint hissing. This time from across the room. An odor, like rotten eggs, filled the air. I dared a look. Styles was opening the valves on the propane tanks. What . . . ?

He's is going to blow up the place!

Time was running out.

I rose from my position, forcing my limbs to comply, but two steps in and Styles's head jerked my way. We faced off. Surprise flashed in his eyes, then rage. Gone was the gentle, caring country doctor who'd treated my dog. His eyes blazed, his nostrils flared, and every ounce of me shivered from the evil that exuded from him.

"Hello, Brynn." He moved toward a briefcase on the table.

I took a step forward. "You're a drug dealer. And a killer." Five more yards. That's all I needed. He shrugged, disinterested. I had to distract him, keep him talking. "Did you kill my mother too?"

His lips twitched. "We were old friends, your mother and me."

"Screw you, Styles. My mother would never be friends with you."

His eyes grew flat. "You sure about that? We all grew up to-gether, you know. Mary, Billy, and me, friends one and all." He sneered.

Billy. My mother's boyfriend. My father. Murdered all those years ago. And then my mother, afraid for her life had run—from Styles. "You killed her. And Sheila Costello. Why?" My voice caught. "And . . . and Meg."

"Meg?" His gaze slid to the tarp. "I did no such thing. Your cousin isn't dead." He looked back at me, his eyes glistening. "Not yet."

I gasped and turned toward my cousin's body. *Not dead?* I looked closer. *Could it really be that she's not dead?*

The pinging sound of a microwave drew my focus back to where Styles was setting the timer on the microwave. *What's he doing?* I looked closer. There was a butane cylinder inside the microwave. Butane and microwaves equaled the perfect recipe for a small bomb. I'd seen it before, in my explosive breaching course. Styles must have researched this. He'd planned this all along to hide evidence of his drug scheme.

It'd take about twenty seconds for the microwave to break down the outer cylinder of the canister, releasing the gasses and causing a small explosion, a catalyst for the massive one to fol-low. With propane already thick in the air, we'd blow sky-high.

Styles had set the timer for thirty seconds, his finger moving for the START button.

"Stop!" I lunged forward and knocked him in the back. We hit the ground hard. In the background, I heard the sound of the running microwave. He'd turned it on!

I raised up, went for the microwave, but out of nowhere, Styles's elbow flew at my face. The sickening crack of bone on bone echoed through my head. I sank back down. The room swam before my eyes. I blinked. Styles was on his feet now and halfway to the door.

The microwave!

I stood again, then saw a dozen or more tangled cords behind the table plugged into a large power strip that led to the generator. I scurried on all fours, grabbed the entire bunch, and ripped them from the receptor.

The microwave stopped. *Thank God.*

I turned toward the closed door—Styles was gone.

The air hung heavy with gas now; the thick taste of it clung to my nose and mouth. Any sort of spark and the place could still blow. I quickly closed the propane valves, threw open the door, then darted back to where Meg lay crumpled on the floor. I knelt down beside her. She was pale and very still, but her chest rose and fell with short shallow respirations. She *was* alive.

My heart soared, then hardened. I ripped the gun from Eamon's hand and checked the magazine. Empty. I racked the slide. One round in the barrel. There'd be no room for error.

I tightened my hand around the grip. Styles killed my mother. He killed Sheila Costello. And he almost killed Meg.

He was not going to simply walk away.

My legs were still wobbly, but adrenaline propelled me forward. I ran outside. Then stopped cold. Styles stood, facing me, about five hundred feet from the door, his hands raised, briefcase on the ground at his feet, and the muzzle of an AR-15 pressed against his chest. He was pleading for his life. Urine ran down his leg. A drug runner, his back to me and his full focus on Styles, yelled something in Spanish and tightened his grip on the gun.

I lifted the pistol and aimed for center mass.

Styles reacted, his eyes darting my way. The drug runner spun his head. His gun followed. I pulled the trigger. His body jerked from the bullet's impact, and he went down.

I kept the gun raised and pointed it at Styles. "Stay where you are."

He tensed, looked at the gun, squinted, and then loosened,

his fear quickly morphing into arrogance. I'd spent the only round of ammo on the Mexican. And he knew it.

He dove for the AR-15 still in the dead Mexican's hand.

Oh shit!

Tossing the empty gun, I broke into a run and hit him in a full-out frontal attack, wrapping my arms around the crazy SOB and using my momentum to push him to the ground. We hit hard, my full weight on top of him. The rifle landed a few feet away.

Air expelled from my gut and lungs. Spots clouded my vision. I sucked at the air, recovered a little, but out of nowhere came Styles's palm. It connected with my chin. My neck jerked back, and muscles and nerves ripped and tore. Blood filled my mouth. Hot pain scorched along my spine and radiated through my neck. I rolled to the side, gripped my head, and brought my knees to my chest.

I drew deeper into myself. *I'm going to die. I want to die.*

Styles's voice came low and somber. "Poor Brynn. You're like her in some ways, you know. Stubborn, idealistic . . . stupid."

I stayed curled up but forced my eyes open. The black steel of the rifle's muzzle was inches from my nose. Styles's dirt-streaked face was on the other end of the gun, his eyes harried and wild.

He continued. "Only she was beautiful. Red hair, haunting eyes. And her body . . ." He ran his tongue along his bottom lip. "The things she did with her body." The rifle bounced awkwardly in his hands. His voice tightened, turned high and thin. "I couldn't believe she was back. Waiting for me at the hotel. I thought . . . but no. She didn't want me. You know what she wanted? She wanted me to *repent.* She'd found religion." He laughed. Shivers crawled up my back. "She was nuts. I told her to go to hell. But she insisted. Said she couldn't live with what we'd done. She was going to go to the cops. Clear her conscience." His voice hardened again, the tone deep and determined. "So, you see, she had to die." He thrust the gun closer. "Just like you have to die."

Acid rose in my throat. I swallowed and kept my hand low; my fingers trembled along the upper edges of my boot. My nails scraped the handle of the knife.

His grip tightened on the gun. "On your knees, Brynn."

I pulled my knees in closer. My body was a tight little ball curled in the dirt. "No."

"Get up!"

My fingers clutched the knife.

"Get up now!"

I sprang from the ground, ripped the knife from my boot, and thrust upward, sinking the blade into the meaty portion of his thigh. Blood erupted from the wound, spewing over the front of my body, droplets splattering on my face. At the same time, I wrapped my free hand around the barrel of the rifle and pushed upward. Styles squeezed the trigger. Shots exploded. Rapid bursts of air hit my face. The report whipped my eardrums, sending pounding pain through my jaw and throbbing temples. A couple dozen searing-hot brass casings pelted my face and slid under the edges of my sweater.

He grappled to free the gun, but I gripped the barrel harder, extracted the knife, and thrust it again.

Voices of the past echoed in my mind:

Marines!

Aye, Drill Sergeant.

What's the spirit of the bayonet?

Kill, kill. Kill without mercy.

I can't hear you.

Kill, kill. Kill without mercy!

I sank the knife deep into his abdomen. He screamed in agony. His hold on the gun loosened. I yanked it from his slackened fingers, flung it into the air, and twisted the knife deeper into his gut.

Styles's shoulders fell forward, his jaw loosened, saliva trickled from the corners of his mouth. He grasped weakly at my blood-slicked hands. I pushed harder, until my knuckles entered his gaping, wounded flesh. "You. Killed. My. Mother. And. Father."

He crumpled to his knees. I kept my grip on the knife and sank to the ground with him, my fist now hot with his bloody flesh. The color drained from his face; red spider-like lines erupted over the whites of his eyes. We knelt there, our faces just inches apart as I watched the life drain from his body.

"No, not your father," he rasped. "You're doing that." His blood-drenched lips curled back. "Right now."

My mind erupted in fury. "You lie!" I gripped the knife with both hands, ripped upward through his rib cage, and yanked it back. Blood gurgled from his lips just before he fell face-first to the ground.

Shock permeated my muscles. I swayed, struggling to stay upright. The knife fell from my hands. I swiped at my tears with blood-covered fingers before my focus snapped toward the shack.

Meg! I've got to get to Meg.

I tottered forward and collapsed, pushed back up on my knees, and glanced back at Styles's lifeless body. The bloody knife. My bloodied hands. So much blood. My father's blood?

Do you hear me, Marine?

Aye, ma'am.

Say it again.

Kill, kill without mercy.

Marines! What makes the green grass grow?

Blood, blood makes the green grass grow.

Louder.

Blood, blood makes the green grass grow!

War. War was nothing but brown sand and red blood. A putrid mixture that crept and oozed into every crevice of our bodies, our minds . . . our souls.

I gasped for air, swallowed against the bile rising in my throat, clutched my stomach, and lurched forward and heaved and heaved until I was emptied. I swiped at my face, only to shudder in pain. My nose was swollen. It oozed snot and blood.

Blood, blood, makes the green grass grow.

I stared at the ground under me. Tried to make sense of it all. *My father?* It couldn't be. Billy Drake was my father. Wasn't he? Not Styles . . . It all came rushing back: *She had a lot of boyfriends . . . I knew your mother well . . . what she did with that body . . . gypsy whore, gypsy whore!*

Blood dripped from my nose and pooled on the ground around my hands.

Blood, blood makes the green grass grow.

Marines! Let me hear your battle cry.

I tipped my head skyward. A cry escaped from somewhere deep inside me and rose into the air, low and menacing, like a frightful monster. *Ahhh . . . !* It echoed upward through the bare tree branches, spurring a massive release of birds, their dark wings frantically batting at the gray-white sky.

Then came another cry—woeful and distant, high-pitched and laced with hope. *Wilco!*

"Wilco," I whispered.

My eyes strained against the impending darkness. A familiar outline bounded my way. *Wilco!*

Pusser trudged behind him. "Meg," I called out. "She's hurt. Call for medical assistance." Pusser got on his radio.

I raised up and held out my blood-stained hands. Wilco ran full speed, body stretched out like an arrow. About ten yards out, he went airborne, flying into my chest and knocking me backward. We landed in a muddled mess of human and dog; his wet nose, cold and comforting, wormed its way over my wounded face.

Laughter rang through the air. Mine.

I pulled my dog closer and held on tight.

It was over.

CHAPTER 18

Pusser handed me a foam cup full of coffee and sat in the waiting room chair across from me. A television, mounted to the wall, was tuned into the early-morning news. The press had already broken the story about Styles's death.

Broken was the operative word. The same reporter who had sprinted after me the day after my mother's remains were found used his baritone voice and dramatically scowled into the camera. He informed viewers that a beloved local veterinarian had been brutally killed when he uncovered a drug operation in the same woods where the bodies of two Traveller women had been recently discovered. "It appears an officer may have also been involved and injured trying to valiantly save Doctor Styles."

Deputy Parks had driven me in her patrol car to the hospital while the ambulance crews tended to Meg and Eamon. From behind the cold pack the paramedics had given me for my face, I'd spied the news insignia on a car scurrying to the scene. They must have just assumed the deputy had rushed one of their own back for care.

Pusser groaned. "No one said—"

"Don't worry," I offered. "Once they figure out it was only me, another Traveller, that Parks carted off, they'll drop that part like it was never said." Pusser didn't respond. He knew I was right. By noon, they'd probably have enough information to broadcast a full, maybe even close to factual, report. I wondered if once McCreary folks heard one of their own, a beloved veterinarian no less, was a killer, plus a drug dealer, they'd back off the eviction process for the Travellers. Only time would tell.

"You worry me, Callahan."

"I worry you? Why's that?"

"What you did to Styles. That's why."

"He pointed a gun at my face. A big gun."

"Don't give me that crap. This went way beyond self-defense. You practically gutted the guy. The coroner needed a separate bag for his innards."

"You going to make a big deal out of it? Bring charges against me or something?"

"No."

"Then why bring it up?" I watched him take a gulp of coffee, amazed at how he could drink with a toothpick in his mouth.

He met my gaze and narrowed his eyes. "You got them, don't you?"

I groaned. My head was throbbing, my eyes halfway swollen shut, and my busted nose looked like someone had shoved a golf ball up my right nostril. My jaw was an ugly color of purple and my tongue a puffy mess of raw flesh where I'd bitten. Just sipping coffee hurt like hell. I was in no mood to play twenty questions. "Got what? What are you talking about, Pusser?"

"Yips. Flashbacks. Whatever you want to call 'em. The war's still with you, isn't it?"

Not this. I don't need this from Pusser.

He continued. "You getting help?"

I chuckled. "Sure. I got help. They ran me through a bunch of VA docs, shrinks, group therapy, you name it. Only the best from Uncle Sam." And there was a reason it was *Uncle* Sam and not *Aunt* Samantha. The VA did their best, but despite the insurgence of female soldiers, it'd been a male-oriented system for decades. Vaginas threw them for a loop. That, and the piles of disability paperwork . . . well, I guess somewhere down the line I'd found that the best cure, the easiest anyway, came from Dr. Jack Daniels. *I really must set up an appointment soon.* I chuckled to myself, took a sip of coffee, and missed the brim. It dribbled down my chin.

He handed me a napkin. "Is it bad?"

I dabbed at my mouth and looked away. Bad? I almost laughed out loud. Guess it depended on what he meant by bad. I was here, wasn't I? A lot of my buddies weren't. They couldn't handle civie life. One by one, they succumbed, checked out, jumped, ate their guns . . . whatever. Just another sister who chose to end it rather than deal with the constant mental shit. I shifted in my seat. Pusser didn't get it. How could he?

It ticked me off that he'd even brought it up. I ignored him and changed the subject. "Thanks for seeing to my dog."

Pusser opened his mouth as if to say something, but let it drop. "Sure. Your grandmother was happy to see him." Parks had taken me straight to the hospital. They wouldn't let my dog in, so Pusser took him to Gran's.

"Yeah. They've bonded."

He smiled. "Glad your cousin's okay."

She was still unconscious, but the doctor had her on an IV drip to slowly get the drug out of her system. He said by tomorrow she'd come around. Everything that had happened would hit her then. I was almost glad she could avoid it for a few more hours. "Depends on how you define okay."

Pusser raised his brows.

"She was naked in the shower when that SOB ripped open the curtain and stabbed her with a needle."

He drained the last of his coffee. "She's traumatized. I get it, believe me. But she'll get over it." He spit his chewed toothpick into his empty cup. "Least she's alive."

Spoken like someone who's never experienced real trauma.

Pusser cleared his throat. *What now?* I wondered.

"You were right."

"Great." I didn't know what I was right about and didn't much care. He didn't say anything else, waited me out. Okay, maybe I did care. "About what?"

"That I needed to look just as hard at, ah . . ."

"Settled people?"

He smirked. "Yeah. Settled."

"So Al was involved too?"

"No, not him. But when you called from Doc Styles's place, told me about the drugs, it got me to thinking. Sure, we had Eamon pegged in some way for drugs. But no way would a small solo businessman like Styles have anyone else order his controlled substances for him. And even if he did have someone else ordering, the cost would be really obvious for that much ketamine."

"So that's why you came to the clinic?"

"Yup. You've got good instincts, Callahan."

But not good enough, fast enough, or I wouldn't have ended up doped and nearly blown to bits.

He continued. "Case you're wondering, Al talked."

"Oh yeah?"

"We recovered insulated gloves and a baseball bat in the vicinity of the substation transformer, all with his prints."

"He was going to take down our power supply."

"That's right. Once we confronted him with the evidence, he talked. Said he was planning to take out the transformer fuse on the main power supply. It was just the first step in several attacks he and his cronies planned to carry out against you folks."

"In an effort to get us to leave the area. So it had nothing to do with Meg personally."

"Seems that way. Those lines belong to Tennessee Valley Authority Electric. It's a federal offense to mess with power grids. He'll be tried in a federal court. He's facing substantial prison time."

Good. I didn't care if I ever saw his sorry ass again. I didn't have to worry about mentioning the prostitution ring he'd run. No need to get more people in trouble for Al's mischief when Al was already being put away.

I gave up on drinking the coffee and set my cup aside. "I got to thinking about how Styles took the ring off Meg's finger when she was unconscious."

"Yeah?"

"He was at the diner yesterday when Meg showed it to me. He must have known it was Sheila Costello's."

"A dead girl's ring. Sick."

"You're thinking Eamon killed Sheila?"

"How else would he have gotten the ring?"

I shook my head and instantly regretted the movement in my throbbing skull. "It doesn't make sense that he'd kill Sheila, then give her ring to Meg. Talk about implicating himself."

"No one said the guy was smart." Pusser lifted his chin. "Anyway, Meg and Eamon were a liability. Styles figured they knew too much."

"Yeah, but I can't believe Meg knew anything about the drugs."

Pusser didn't respond. He was a hard one to read, but I was sure he'd grill Meg later. That was his job. But I knew her—no way was she involved except by association with Eamon.

He continued, "Styles was cleaning house. Meg. Eamon. Sheila. They were all liabilities for one reason or another. Maybe

Dublin Costello too. Suppose we should run your dog through the woods for his body."

"You think Styles killed Dub Costello?"

"Probably."

"And what? Burned the trailer to hide evidence?"

Pusser shrugged again.

"So Kevin Doogan's no longer under suspicion?"

"I didn't say that. Maybe the whole damn clan's involved. With Styles as the ring leader. Won't know how deep this thing runs until we talk to Eamon. If we can get anything out of him."

There was a flash of movement over Pusser's shoulder. A nurse came our way.

"Sheriff Pusser." Her voice was flat.

Pusser turned around. "Yes."

"You wanted to know when the patient was available."

Pusser rose from his chair. "Thank you." He looked at me. "Coming?"

"You want me in there?" The clock on the wall said it was after ten already. It was Wednesday. I needed to get to work. "Not sure I have time. I gotta be to work in a couple hours." I was on Drake's bad side already. If I was late today, I could pretty much kiss my job good-bye.

"It won't take that long."

"Why would you want me in there?"

"He's one of you. That could be an advantage. He'll trust you."

"Not me. Eamon and I aren't friends." For all I knew, Eamon had taken part in Styles's killing spree before becoming a victim himself.

Pusser reached into his pocket for his toothpick cylinder. "Well, he sure as hell doesn't like me." He slid a fresh toothpick between his teeth and tipped his head toward the hall. "Come on."

"You don't want me in there, Pusser. I . . . I . . ." What if I found out Eamon had killed Sheila? Was involved is getting Meg nearly killed? What was it Pusser had said? I'd gutted Styles. The coroner needed an extra bag to transport his guts. "I might lose it in there."

He leaned down, his toothpick bobbing just inches from my eyeballs. "I think you underestimate yourself, Callahan. Let's go."

Pusser was right. Eamon didn't even acknowledge the sheriff; instead, he focused his wary eyes on me. "Meg. Is she . . . ?"

"She's okay. No thanks to you. You could have gotten my cousin killed."

Pusser had stepped back, faded into the background. It was just Eamon and me talking.

I continued. "She loved you."

"Still does love me. We're getting married."

"Doubtful. She never would have been with you if she'd known what you were doing. You're a drug dealer."

He pressed his lips together and looked away. I could feel Pusser staring at me from behind.

"You're nothing but scum, Eamon."

He didn't respond.

Pusser spoke up from across the room. "The feds tracked down the other drug runner, and he's cutting a deal. He's already talking. Claims you and Styles were in on it together. You did the cooking. Styles made the connection with the Mexican gang. They were piping your stuff all the way down to Texas."

Eamon kept his mouth shut. He looked pale and pathetic, lying uncovered in the flimsy gown and socks the hospital provided. A white bandage covered his shoulder and part of his chest. The doctors said the wound wasn't serious. The bullet had lodged just under his left clavicle. Still, it must've hurt like hell, and he'd lost a lot of blood.

Pusser shifted his weight and stepped forward. "We've got

the Mexican's testimony, and I'm betting your prints and DNA are all over that drug shack. You'll get prison time for the drugs. But if you cooperate . . ."

"You lie, *musker*. You cops never give us a break."

Pusser backed off again. I stepped up and tried another angle. "Why did Styles kill my mother?"

Eamon looked my way. "I don't know that he did." I believed him. I doubted he knew anything about the first murder—it was more personal than business. I thought he knew something about Sheila's death, though.

"She was killed with the same gun as Sheila Costello. The same gun that was at the shack. I saw Styles put it in your hand when you were passed out on the floor of the shack. He was framing you."

Eamon blinked but didn't look my way.

"Did he kill Sheila too? Or was that you?"

His head snapped my way. "I didn't kill nobody."

Maybe, maybe not. Styles was dead. There was no one left to refute whatever story he came up with.

"How'd you get the ring?"

"Found it at the vet clinic. On the floor. I figured one of those rich McCreary ladies lost it. They're out at the clinic all the time with their yappy purse dogs. Didn't know it belonged to Sheila 'til the cops told me about it."

"Sheila, huh?" Pusser spoke up. "Were you and Sheila sleeping together?"

Eamon shifted and looked at Pusser. His eyes were filled with hate. "I'm with Meg. We Pavees aren't like that. We're loyal." He looked my way. "Except you. You working with the cops now?"

I ignored the question. Pusser eyed him closely. "Dublin Costello thinks you were banging his wife."

"Dub Costello's a crazy son of a bitch."

I glanced at Pusser, but we both stayed quiet. Eamon went

on. "He made her do all sorts of sick things. When she refused, he beat her. Enjoyed it too. Sick bastard. You know what he did?"

Eamon looked at me. I lifted my shoulders, inviting him to continue.

"He killed her cat. The one I gave her. Right in front of her. Slit its throat." I squeezed my eyes shut. The bloodstain Doogan found on the carpet. The image of Dublin killing a small kitten in front of his terrified wife turned my stomach.

Eamon was still talking. "He did it to scare her. Told her that's what he'd do to her if she didn't do the things he wanted. She was terrified out of her mind."

Pusser spoke up. "And what were you? Her hero?"

"What do you mean?"

"Did you come to her rescue?"

"No."

"Maybe you tried, but she didn't want you. Is that what happened? She was scared and you knew just how to make her feel better. How to comfort her. What? Was she not into you? Is that how it went down, Eamon? She didn't want your comfort? Maybe you tried to force her? Things got out of hand?"

Eamon recoiled. "What? No! That's not what happened."

Pusser kept up. "Maybe you didn't mean it. It just happened."

"No!"

"Bet you hated the guy." Pusser leaned in closer. "He hurt your girlfriend and killed her cat. That'd be enough to push any guy over the edge."

Eamon's eyes rounded. "What?"

Pusser went on. "Dub Costello's missing. Maybe you had something to do with that."

Eamon clamped his lips together. He wouldn't look at me. He was shutting down. I shot Pusser a look, but he kept pushing.

"We've got you for the drugs already," he said. "You're going to prison. For how long, I don't know. But if you cooperate with us, it might work in your favor."

"All you coppers are liars. You're not going to do jack for me. I want a lawyer."

Pusser took that as his cue. "Sure, if that's what you want. You have the right to remain silent, anything you say . . ."

The words were lost to the roar of rage in my head. My jaw tightened. Maybe Eamon didn't know anything about my mother, or Dublin, but he knew something about Sheila's murder. I wanted answers. Doogan *deserved* answers. And I knew how to get the truth out of him. And I would. That's why Pusser had wanted me in here. I could do things he couldn't and get by with it.

I was one of them. A *gypsy*.

He was a cop. The law.

"Why did Styles kill Sheila?" I bit the words out through clenched teeth. Pusser turned away and let me take the lead again. He faded even further into the background this time. I heard the faint clicking noise and turned to see him leaning against the hospital door, his arms crossed over his chest. No one was coming into this room. Or going out.

Eamon's eyes darted between Pusser at the locked door and me. Sweat broke out on his top lip, but he didn't talk.

My mind snapped. *Enough!* I ripped Eamon's sock from his foot and crammed it halfway down his throat. He gagged. His eyes bulged. He thrashed from side to side, unable to raise his bandaged arm at all, grabbing me with his other hand, but I held it there. "You don't get a lawyer, Eamon. That's not how this is going to work." I was just inches from his face. Spit spewed from my lips as I spoke. "We're settling this by clan rules." I raised my other fist and brought it down hard on his shoulder. Muffled cries of agony filled the room. I raised my fist again.

He held up his hand. His eyes pleaded for mercy.

I unclenched my fist and removed the sock. "Tell me what happed to Sheila Doogan."

Pusser was back next to the bed, listening as the words tumbled from Eamon's mouth. "Styles shot her. I was there. I saw it." He clenched his stomach and rolled to the side. I grabbed a pink, kidney-shaped bowl from the side table and held it under his mouth while he puked.

After he'd emptied his stomach, he sat back, gulped air, and talked again. "We were friends. Sheila and me. That's all. I found her one night, badly beaten by that asshole husband. She was in pain. I gave her some K, just enough to get her through the night. But she liked it. She came back for more. I didn't know how to say no." He licked his lips and pointed to his water bottle.

I shook my head. "Keep talking."

"She came by one night when Styles was there. We'd just gotten a shipment of ketamine. We were loading it to take out to the cabin."

"In the ATV?" I asked.

"Yeah. Styles had a rule. No local sales. I carried the stuff during travel season to contacts down south. Then he cut a deal with the Mexicans. They'd been having trouble meeting their supply demands, with stricter border security . . ." He coughed again. "He was making good money. Enough that he was going to leave and go to some island in the tropics."

I filled in the blank. "But Sheila threatened his plan."

"Yeah. So he shot her. And buried her body out in the woods."

"And he transported her there in the ATV." I already knew the answer. Wilco had picked up on human remains inside that ATV. But Eamon didn't respond. "Or you did." He shifted his eyes away.

My fists clenched. Eamon was just as guilty as Styles. "Maybe you didn't kill my mother, or Dublin, but you helped kill Sheila Costello. First with the drugs you gave her. Then by standing by while Styles killed her. And then helping to hide her body." My body quivered with rage. I raised my fist again, but Pusser caught my wrist. I looked back at him.

A slight smile hinted at the corners of his mouth. "We got everything we need."

I looked at my fist, back at Eamon's face, at my fist again. My head swam. The vomit smell. My exhaustion. It was all too much. I bolted.

Pusser caught up to me out in the hall. "Hey. Good job in there."

I wheeled. "Good job? I coerced his confession."

"Yeah. So? He needed a little persuasion. It's not like he's going to rat you out. Gypsy loyalty, right?"

I hated how, once more, he'd thrown the clan's principles in my face. He was right. Eamon wouldn't tell anyone what I'd just done to him. Clan justice wasn't something you talked about—it just happened. And once the clan knew he'd had anything to do with drugs, let alone with a clan woman's death, my sucker punch to his shoulder would look like a love kiss. Yet even with that depth of retribution for our own wrongdoers, the clan would never help law enforcement even when it was on their side. Where did loyalty and truth intersect?

I stared hard at Pusser's face. His eyes were dark, deep set, almost hidden under his fat, pockmarked cheeks. They regarded me with respect. Not disdain. Not prejudice. Just respect. I realized that all Pusser had cared about this whole time was the truth. And he was maybe the one person who had been completely honest with me throughout this whole ordeal.

Tears stung my eyes. "You used me."

"You could look at it that way. Or you could say that we make a damn fine team." He reached into his pocket and took out a hanky. A cloth one.

"Here." He handed it to me. "You'd best get to the motel for work, if you can call it that. Still think you're wasting your talents. You're a cop, Callahan. You've got the training. More important, you've got the instincts too. You should come work for me. I could use you on my team."

I didn't answer. Couldn't. Instead, I brought the handkerchief to my face and turned toward the exit. It smelled like cinnamon.

I found the smell comforting.

CHAPTER 19

I pulled in front of Gran's trailer, expecting to see a crowd of people or at least family lingering to take advantage of leftover food and liquor from my mother's wake. Instead, the front curtains were drawn, and the only one other vehicle parked outside besides Gran's Buick was Colm's pickup truck.

Something was wrong.

I'd called to check on Gran a few hours earlier, when I'd arrived at my job. She seemed tired. The funeral, my brush with death, Meg's hospitalization, and the news of Eamon—it'd all taken a toll on her, but she was healthy. Perhaps it'd been too much for Gramps? That must've been it. He'd taken a sudden turn for the worse. So much that they'd called for the priest?

I stepped out of my car, tipped my head back, and whispered skyward, "How much more can we take?"

Wilco greeted me just inside the door. I paused to give him a quick pat before heading back toward the kitchen. The place was nice and tidy. The smell of spicy fried cabbage and sausage, one of my favorite meals, hit my nose and got my stomach juices flowing. I was starving. But Gran wasn't in the kitchen. I backtracked and headed toward Gramps' room, stopping short when I heard Gran's voice coming from her bedroom.

I headed that way, then, through the crack in the door, I saw Colm. He was sitting in the green upholstered chair that Gran usually kept in the corner, stacked with mending and clothes that needed ironing. He'd pulled the chair close to the bed and was leaning forward, a beautiful gold-trimmed purple stole hanging from his neck as he whispered something. Across from him, I saw Gran sitting on the edge of the bed, her feet planted firmly on the floor and her hands folded in prayer. My heart sank. What happened? Gramps? Was I too late?

I reached out, ready to push the door open the rest of the way, when I heard her say, "Father, forgive me, I've sinned against you."

I jerked back. Confession. Colm was hearing Gran's confession. I turned and tiptoed from the doorway. But her next words permeated the air like a sword through flesh. "I killed him." Her voice, blunt and hard at first, turned to gasping, then a flood of cries, her heart-wrenching sobs interspersed with pleas for mercy.

I kept walking, faster, fleeing back down the hallway. No! I turned toward Gramps' door. Gran? Murder? Had it been too much for her? Gramps' illness, my mother's death, the financial stress, the press . . . what did she do? Those scratches! She'd tried to cover them, explain them away, but I knew. Gramps had done that. He'd become more agitated, abusive even. Self-defense. That's what it was. Self-defense. No one could blame Gran for defending herself. Just like I'd defended myself against Styles . . .

The odor hit me as soon as I stepped inside his room. The stench of death. My hand flew to my face, covered my nose and mouth. Oh Gran! We should have called in hospice. Or paid for a nurse. I should have helped more. *My fault. My fault.*

The sound of Gramps' oxygen converter hissed in the air. He turned his head. "Anne?" His features darkened. "Oh, it's you."

"Gramps?"

"What do you want? Where's your grandmother?"

I stepped closer. "You're okay."

"Okay? Like hell. I'm hungry."

His chin worked back and forth, gray whiskers protruding like quills on a porcupine. He needed a shave. A bath. I caught another whiff of something foul, stepped back, and gagged a little. I cleared my throat. "Gramps, you need to change your clothes. Can I help you?"

"Your grandmother takes care of that. Don't touch me."

"Okay. Do you want me to bring you some supper?"

"You'll spit in it."

"Gramps, I would never—"

"Where's Anne? Where is she?" His fist clenched at his side. "Is she with that man again?"

"Father Colm?"

He continued. Louder now. He was getting worked up. "Not the priest. Him. The outsider. I heard them talking, making plans to go away—"

"Fergus." It was Gran. She walked in and placed her hand on his. "I'm right here, Fergus. Right here." She turned red, swollen eyes my way. She startled for an instant at the sight of my battered face, then went on, "It's been a difficult day. I'm afraid he's very confused."

I swallowed. "He's hungry," I told her. "But he doesn't want me to get him a plate."

"I'll heat him some leftovers."

"No. Stay here, Gran. I'll get it."

She held up her hand. "I'll tend to it. Father Colm's come to see you. He's in the front room."

I reached out. Touched her cheek. "Gran. Is there something going on? Something I should know about?" She eyed me sharply, wary. I withered. "I'm just worried about you."

Her posture relaxed. She clasped her hand around mine, pulling me toward the door and out into the hallway. "There's no reason to worry, child. Not anymore. I've seen to everything."

The hairs on the back of my neck stood up. Her words rang with so much finality. So much earnest emotion.

I killed him. I killed him.

And other things she'd said. All just words, none of them meaning much at the time they were spoken. But now, now they flew back through my mind: *I went looking for you last night . . . I wasn't strong for you back then . . . I've seen to everything.*

"Gran," I could hardly get the words out. "The other night. When Dub Costello's place burned down . . ."

"I don't want to discuss it."

"But Gran. I have to know what happened."

"Why? Why do you have to know everything, Brynn? Can't you just let some things go?"

"No. No, Gran. I can't." My lip trembled. "Dub Costello. Is he dead?"

She folded her arms across her chest.

"Gran?"

Something seemed to flicker in her eyes, a thought, a resolution, and then it came out. "The other night, the night of the fire . . . your grandfather. Well, you know how he'd been so agitated that day. Remember? We had to give him the pills."

The pills. I'd seen their instant calm descend on Gramps. How the tension drained from his body. My body ached with tension now, begging for a release . . . I squeezed my eyes shut, opened them again, and stared into Gran's pale face. "Go on."

"He was so upset about Mary. He got confused. He thought you were Mary. Then he told me something, something I'd never known. Something you'd kept from me."

I looked in her eyes, and she held my stare. "I haven't kept anything from you, Gran. Never."

She reached out, clasped my arms. "Yes, you have. And you

could have told me. You *should* have told me." Her voice thinned, her eyes bored into mine. "What he did to you. You should have told me what he did to you."

What? "I don't understand . . . told you . . . ?"

She leaned in closer. "The rape." Tears pooled in her eyes. "All these years and I—"

"But you knew."

She shrunk back. "No." Her eyes rounded. "No, child. I didn't know."

"But I told Gramps." I clutched my stomach. "I told Gramps! And he said you . . ." As her bewildered eyes searched mine, I realized, no, she never knew.

"I said what?"

"He said you . . ." I clenched my stomach. "You weren't home. Remember? You were at Aunt Tinnie's that month. It was right after Uncle Donal died. You were gone." She nodded. "Gramps said he called you the next morning. Said you were upset that . . . that I was disrespecting the clan's ways. That whatever Dub did was . . ." I couldn't finish.

She raised her chin, her gaze settling on the door behind me. Her eyes narrowed. "Yes, he called me. Only said you wouldn't marry Costello. I asked to talk to you, but he said you didn't want to talk. I didn't push it, figured we could talk when I got back, we'd sort it out." She looked back at me, her eyes glistening with emotion. "But you left before I got back. Enlisted. Gone off to the settled world, just like your mother. It 'bout broke my heart." Tears now traced the lines in her cheeks. "But all I knew was that you didn't want to marry Dublin. Were sick of our clan ways. I never knew what he'd done to my baby. If only you'd called me when it happened."

"I'd come home bloody and crying, told Gramps. He'd been angry, but angry at me, said it was my fault. That I'd led Dub on. That I was like my mother." I looked down. "I was . . . confused. Ashamed. It was true I wanted out. Maybe if I hadn't gone to his place that night. Or worn those jeans or—"

"No!" Gran gripped my shoulders. "None of it was your fault. You've got to believe that." She gave me a little shake. "Listen to me, child. I would have never blamed you. I just didn't know what he'd done to you. If only you'd still been here when I got back, we could have talked."

If only. But I'd gone away right after it happened. So confused, so angry and full of . . . what? Spite? Fear? Determination not to be like my mother? Or to be like the woman I envisioned her to be? All I knew for certain was that I wanted to get out of here. As far away as I could. And the Marines offered that.

I'd practically lived on the streets until I got through MEPS and shipped to Basic. "I tried to call you. Gramps said . . ."— my lip quivered—"you didn't want to talk to me. That you agreed it was my fault."

Her face crumpled. "I didn't know you called. And I was so hurt that you'd abandoned me. Just like your mother did all those years ago."

A year passed. I deployed, got my first combat patch, saw things, felt things that made that rape seem like child's play. I became edgy, almost non-functional. Eventually, a chaplain set me up with a morale call home, and I reached Gran. We talked. And talked. But never about the reason I'd left, my abandoning the clan's ways, and never about Costello. Or the rape. By then I'd just wanted to forget it'd ever happened. Gran had cried on the phone, told me she loved me, and I'd cried too. We'd buried the past, a past neither of us wanted to face.

And now here we were.

The hiss of Gramps' oxygen machine pierced the silence. I listened to his steady, rhythmic drag punctuated with coughing spurts and glared at the shut door. "He did this." An angry flush washed over me. "Damn him. Why . . . why?"

She wiped off the tears from her cheeks. "I don't know. Maybe to protect me. I just don't know. We'll never know. His mind is too far gone now."

My muscles tensed. "I hate him."

"No!" Her stern look, the look of the woman who'd scolded me as a child, glared at me. "Hate's going to destroy you. I already watched my Mary destroy herself with booze and drugs . . . and I can't have that for you."

I opened my mouth to object but couldn't bring myself to lie. Not anymore. "I'm just like her. I am." Anguish racked at my chest, pulled the air and words from my lungs.

"No. No, you're not. Listen to me. It's not your fault. All these years, all the things left unsaid, all the lies. Lies have a way of twisting people's lives. I know that now. There's been too many lies in this family. The lying stops. It stops now." That flicker in her eye returned, and I understood—the lies had to be finished between us. Here and now. "Do you hear me?" She paused, then began again, as the whole story came forward. "After your grandfather told me about the rape the other night, I became infuriated. I went outside, looking for you. You weren't in your car. I didn't know where you were."

Because I was in Doogan's bed.

"I wanted to talk to you. Get the story. When I couldn't find you, I went looking for Dublin instead. I confronted him. Things turned ugly. He laughed at me, laughed about what he'd done to you, and then he got violent." She shivered. "Oh God. I was so scared. I imagined how scared you must have been that night. The night he raped you."

A childlike trembling threatened to overtake me even now as the scene came back. I could only nod.

"He came after me. But I found courage, Brynn. Courage for both of us. I had my pistol with me, like always. And when he came for me, I shot him. But he kept coming, and I shot him again. Over and over. I couldn't stop. I was so frightened, but

angry too. It's like the years of hate came out of me . . . I kept
thinking, an eye for an eye, a life for a life. He robbed you of
your life, Brynn. Of our life together as a family. I wanted him
dead."

"No! Don't say that, Gran. It was self-defense. Self-defense.
No one could blame you. It was you or him."

Her face fell. "I don't know, child. Maybe only God knows.
I'll wait for my judgment."

"Gran. God knows you. You're innocent. Go to the police.
Tell them what happened. I know Pusser. He's a good man.
He'll stand by you."

"We're Pavees."

"No. Pusser's a fair man. Deep down. I know he is. He'll
help us."

"But he won't help Kevin. He's got a record."

"Doogan? What do you mean?"

"Kevin was outside his trailer, smoking. You know how he
did from time to time. He heard the shots. I was so upset. So
scared. And shaken."

I understood. "The voices Gramps heard outside the window. It was you and Doogan. Where is he? Where's Doogan?"

"I don't know. He helped me get cleaned up. Then he said he
was going to put the body somewhere that it'd never be
found."

"Then he burned the place."

She shrugged. "I never saw him after that."

I let it all sink in.

She continued. "So you see, while the settled law might understand why I killed a man like Dublin Costello, they'd never
forgive Kevin's part in the crime."

She was right.

"Listen, child, we Pavees have always taken care of these
things ourselves. It's always just between us and God. The settled law doesn't really matter. Not for us." I saw the look of

desperate appeal in her face, the desire—no, the need—to break through so that I understood.

Law: retribution, punishment, and justice. Where did they fit and make any sense for us Pavees? It was a kindness that Doogan helped Gran, to keep this elderly woman from enduring the world of settled justice, even if it would have likely gone in her favor. And for his kindness? Settled law would mete out his punishment. Yet . . . I'd been the settled law. "But it does, Gran. It does matter."

Her hands dropped from my arms. Her lips pursed; then a look of resignation crossed over her expression, and bits of sadness clung to the edges of her eyes. "Then you'll have to figure it out for yourself, Brynn. You'll have to decide where your loyalties lie. Who you are: Pavee or settled. As for me, I'm right with God. Father Colm just saw to that."

CHAPTER 20

Colm stood as I approached. "Brynn."

I looked at the floor and rubbed my fingers over my scar. "Gran said you came to see me."

"I did." He stepped closer, and as I raised my face, his eyes filled with concern as he took in my swollen nose, bruises, and blackened eyes. He gasped. "Are you okay?"

I brushed my hair forward, hating that he was seeing me this way. "It looks worse than it is."

He pulled a piece of paper from his pocket and unfolded it. "Can we go somewhere private?"

I motioned him through the front room and kitchen and out to the back steps. Wilco followed. "We can sit here."

He yanked up his coat collar and sat down on the steps. I sat on the same step. Wilco inserted himself between us. The yellow porch light cast shadows of our three hunkered forms.

We sat in awkward silence for a few seconds, until I blurted, "If this is about the other day . . . I'm sorry. It won't happen again."

His eyes met mine. "No, you're right. It won't happen again."

I swallowed hard and looked away. Wilco leaned into me. I wrapped my arm around his back and dug my fingers into his fur. Down a ways, a neighbor revved his bike's engine, eliciting a full-out bark fest from all the neighbors' dogs. Wilco didn't even flinch.

"This isn't about us, Brynn. It has to do with your mother." Colm hesitated. I waited. "I told you that Father Don had become agitated when that letter arrived from your mother."

"Yes. But you said that he's not well. My grandfather's the same way. He's confused all the time. And has a temper. Sometimes he's uncontrollable." Again, I thought about those scratches on Gran's arm. I'd assumed they'd been inflicted by Gramps. Now I knew otherwise.

"Watching our loved ones suffer is a difficult cross to bear." He looked out over the backyard. He still held the folded paper between his fingers. "Father Don remembered something today. A package that your mother left in his care a long time ago. I wanted to talk to you about it before the police tell you."

"The police?"

"Yes. I called them right away." He handed me the paper. I held it up to the porch light. The handwriting was large and loopy, feminine. I looked at the signature. "My mother wrote this."

"It's a photocopy of the one included in the package Father Donavan was holding in his room. The box contained the video surveillance tapes from a robbery that took place years ago."

I looked up from the paper. "The drugstore owner was killed in that robbery."

"That's right. It's a confession. Your mother and her boyfriend, Billy Drake, and another man—"

"Hank Styles."

Colm squinted. "You already knew?"

I looked back at the papers. Two long pages, front and back, and the photocopy quality was poor. I couldn't read it fast enough. "No. Not all of it. Tell me. What do these say?"

"According to your mother, Styles worked at the drugstore. He had a key and would go in at night, take some pills, and change the numbers in the books. Then they'd sell the pills to local kids."

Even back then, he was a drug dealer. Then again, so was my mother.

Colm was still talking. "In the letter, your mother admits that she and Billy Drake were in on the drug dealing."

"I'm sure she was desperate for money. Her situation was impossible. A single mother, no support from home, no education, no way out." *Excuses, Brynn. Excuses.*

"Styles had taken to carrying a gun. He thought it made him look tough and came in handy when kids tried to stiff him for money. He was carrying it that night when the three of them keyed into the drugstore for more pills to sell. They didn't realize the owner was in the backroom. He caught them in the act. Threatened to call the cops. Styles panicked and shot him. They tossed the place and cleaned out the cash to make it look like a robbery."

"The surveillance tapes?"

"Styles knew about the security cameras. He took the tapes and told Billy to destroy them."

"I don't understand. Why'd Billy keep them?"

"I think that was your mother's doing." Colm leaned forward. "Prior to this crime, when she first got pregnant, your mother was scared. I mean, a Pavee girl, pregnant out of wedlock. And by a boy outside the clan."

"I can imagine she was terrified." A shiver hit me. *That could have been me—pregnant with Colm's child, abandoned and alone. What would I have done?*

I saw Colm swallow. Hard. Were the same thoughts in his mind as well?

He continued. "Father Donavan seemed to remember your mother quite well. I think she'd been coming by the church to visit with him for some time. Confiding in him. The details are mixed up in his mind, but he did mention a baby. I think he was trying to help her, counsel her." He adjusted his collar again. "I'm just assuming that last part, of course. I don't think we'll ever know for sure. But he remembers that she was concerned about you."

I blinked back the tears forming along the edges of my eyes.

Colm continued, "She explains in the letter that Styles went after Billy, and she was worried that he'd come after her too. And her family. She couldn't confide in your grandparents because she knew it would endanger them."

"And she couldn't trust the law."

"No. The letter talks about how afraid she was of the law. The prejudices the Pavees faced at that time from the settled folks."

"Still do."

Colm frowned. "She feared what she'd done would affect the whole clan. Especially your grandparents."

"She must have felt desperate."

"Yes. Disappearing must have seemed like her only choice. She left the tapes and the letter with Father Donavan as a safeguard, in case anything ever happened to her. So someone would know the truth." He looked my way. "So you would know the truth. The truth about her. What she'd done."

We sat in silence as I put the pieces together in my mind. My grandfather's pending death prompted my mother to come home. She must have checked into the motel where I now worked and left behind the article I found in the laundry. Styles said she'd confronted him, wanted him to repent, wanted the truth out. But there was no statute of limitations on murder. And she had been the one person left who could point the finger at him. "And in the end, it was the truth that got her killed."

"I believe so."

"She wasn't all bad."

"No, Brynn. She wasn't. She made a lot of mistakes, mistakes that she regretted, but she loved you. So much so that she left Bone Gap and everything she'd ever known to protect you. It must have been the hardest thing she'd ever done." He reached out and ran his hand along Wilco's back, his fingers briefly brushing against mine, then retreating.

Colm started, "If you'd like me to—"

"No." The answer came fast, harsh. I wasn't even sure what he offered—a blessing, prayer, confession, whatever—but it didn't matter. "I mean, thank you for telling me, but . . . I just need some time." He hesitated, then nodded, rose and stepped softly back up the porch, the screen door squeaking as he went inside.

Gran had made her peace with her sins: *As for me, I'm right with God. Father Colm saw to that.*

A confession away from peace? Not for me. Questions skittered like searing shrapnel across my tired life. And somewhere in the midst of all the pain and death and regrets and mistakes, the biggest questions lodged in my war-torn mind:

Had I misjudged my mother all these years? Or killed my own father? Alienated myself from everyone who mattered in my life . . . and all for what? What was *my* truth?

You'll have to figure it out for yourself, Brynn.

My feet belonged to the settled world, even if at times prejudice tainted my path. Yet I lived in my mother's world, the Travellers' world, even when its loyalties battered our lives.

Wilco and I sat with our silhouettes outlined in the golden glow of the porch light. Wilco shifted, looked up at me with that quirked eyebrow he used as if questioning me or maybe trying to tell me something. I could never be sure. In the distance, a dog howled, but Wilco held me in his stare. He heard nothing, saw nothing but me.

"It's okay, boy."

I felt tears in my heart, but I couldn't cry. My family loved me—my mother enough to leave me behind, my Gran enough to—

Wilco's wet nose nudged my face. I leaned in, wrapped my arms around my dog, and buried my face in his fur. I knew where I belonged.

Right here.

Acknowledgments

The making of a book is a collaborative effort, and I have the following people to thank for being part of the team. My agent, Jessica Faust. My editor, Michaela Hamilton. My publicist, Morgan Elwell, and all the hardworking people behind the scenes at Kensington Publishing. I'd also like to extend a special thank-you to Sandra Haven, freelance editor, friend, and the best pair of second eyes around. I am grateful to the following people who have provided me with the expertise needed to write this story: Sergeant Matt Eberhart, USMC; Sergeant Leanna Miller-Ferguson, USMC Disabled Veteran; First Sergeant David Scott, U.S. Army; Kathy Chiodo Holbert, owner of Chiodo Kennels and former civilian HRD canine handler, Iraq and Afghanistan; and Amanda Bourg, PhD, psychologist. And thank you also to Mike Wilson, Eastern Illini Electric Cooperative, for his valuable insight on electrical grids. All these people are experts in their fields. Any mistakes made within these pages are mine and mine alone.

As always, my most heartfelt gratitude to my husband and our children for their continuous support and encouragement.

SPLINTERED SILENCE

Susan Furlong

ABOUT THIS GUIDE

The suggested questions are included to enhance your group's reading of Susan Furlong's *Splintered Silence*!

DISCUSSION QUESTIONS

1. The Irish Travellers are looked down upon by the local people, despite the fact that many of them have been settled in America for generations. Why do you believe they are discriminated against? What makes the Irish Travellers different from the settled people?

2. Brynn is torn between two worlds: that of the settled people and her Irish Traveller clan. Her investigative training fits the needs of law enforcement, but she is home to care for her family. Have you ever struggled with a division like this? Is Brynn doing the right thing by working with people who are not of her own background? What do you think is more important—fulfilling your family's expectations or society's?

3. The Irish Travellers are dedicated to clan loyalty. What is your opinion of this? Do you sympathize with the clan's need to look out for their own? How does this sort of loyalty allow issues to fester within the community?

4. When Doogan expresses his prejudice against Mexicans, Brynn thinks, *No matter where a group of people stood in society, they could always find someone else they believed were beneath them.* What similarities do you see between the prejudices the settled community has against the Travellers and how the Travellers feel about the settled people? How much is unfounded prejudice, and how much is legitimate distrust? Was Doogan's prejudice toward Mexicans any different, and why?

5. Wilco was trained as a military dog and severely maimed while performing his duties. Should animals be used in this way?

6. What is the significance of Wilco in Brynn's life? How does he help Brynn deal with both her emotional and practical issues? In turn, how does Brynn help Wilco?

7. Brynn struggles with PTSD throughout the novel. How does it affect her? How do others react to it? Is there a significant change in her condition by the conclusion? What about Wilco's struggle? Discuss potential ways Brynn and Wilco can tackle their PTSD in future books.

8. Why is Brynn hesitant to help Doogan find his sister at first? Why does she change her mind? Ultimately, do you think she made the right decision to assist Doogan? Did this help or harm her healing process?

9. Drugs are at the heart of this book: the drug trade that destroys lives and the drugs that allow Brynn to survive her past and her injuries. Where do you draw the line between drug therapy and drug abuse? What do you think is the best course of action for returning veterans with chemical dependencies due to PTSD? How did your perception of chemical dependency change throughout the novel?

10. How does the quote at the beginning of the book apply to Brynn and her inner turmoil? What are some of the excuses Brynn uses to remain in denial about her drug and alcohol use?

11. Brynn and her Gran have a complicated relationship. Is it ultimately a positive relationship or a negative one? Do you understand why Gran lied to Brynn about her mother? What would you have done in her situation?

12. When Gran describes Mary being in trouble and drinking too much, Brynn thinks, *Like mother, like daughter.*

How much of Brynn's troubles do you think are hereditary and how much circumstantial? Do you think Brynn's knowledge of her mother's troubles will help or complicate her own healing?

13. When Brynn learns about the letter from her mother, she excuses Mary's participation in drug dealing by saying, *"Her situation was impossible. A single mother, no support from home, no education, no way out."* Then she thinks, *Excuses, Brynn. Excuses.* What other ways out were there for Mary? Instead of joining the Marines, was there a different way out for Brynn?

14. Gran says, *"I never wanted to hurt you, child. Never. Everything I did, right or wrong, I did out of love for you."* Do you believe it was really love that made Gran lie to Brynn about her mother? Or fear that Brynn might turn out the same way? Or embarrassment she didn't want to face? Have you faced lying to a loved one for a reason you felt was justified?

15. Lies have destroyed Brynn's relationship with her family. How do you think she and Gran can go forward after the lies are revealed? Do you think they can avoid lying to each other in the future?

16. As a young man, Colm turned to the priesthood without explaining to Brynn why he didn't return for her. How do you think it would have changed Brynn's life if she'd known why he abandoned her?

17. Brynn's feelings for Colm (and his feelings for her) are tested as they reunite after all these years. What triggers their feelings to escape into a kiss? How do two people repress their emotions once their lives have taken separate, irreconcilable paths?

18. In reference to her grandfather's callousness about her rape, Father Colm asks Brynn, *"Have you forgiven him?"* Do you think Brynn should forgive her grandfather, or was what he did unforgiveable? What would she gain—or what would her grandfather gain—by her forgiveness?

19. How does the relationship between Brynn and Sheriff Pusser change throughout the book? What are some defining events that led each to see the other in a new way? Do you feel they use each other in fair or unfair ways?